Casting Off

P. J. Paris

To Ishbel

Best Wishes

Philip Paris

BLACK & WHITE PUBLISHING

First published 2016
by Black & White Publishing Ltd
29 Ocean Drive, Edinburgh EH6 6JL

1 3 5 7 9 10 8 6 4 2   15 16 17 18

ISBN: 978 1 78530 057 8

A CIP catalogue record for this book is available from the British
Library.

Typeset by Iolaire, Newtonmore
Printed and bound by Nørhaven, Denmark

Casting Off

By the same author

The Italian Chapel
Orkney's Italian Chapel: The True Story of an Icon
Men Cry Alone
Nylon Kid of the North
Trouble Shooting For Printers

Foreword

At the beginning of 2015, I began writing a stage play that told the story of three elderly women in a Highland care home who have to devise a way to raise money when new owners increase the residential fees. The result, *Casting Off*, is a comedy which also examines several serious issues such as loneliness, friendship and sacrifice as well as how reaching out to strangers can completely change our lives.

The seventy-minute play toured during the autumn and the response took everyone by surprise, particularly me! Even on the first night, innocent Dorothy, prim Miss Ross and worldly-wise Joan performed to a sell-out audience. The following novel is based on the same storyline although there are, of course, many more characters, subplots, secrets and surprises.

www.philipparis.co.uk

One

Mr Ferguson was dead. Miss Ross could tell by the feet. They were sticking out of his bedroom door into the corridor along which she had been walking. One foot, partly covered by a thin, brown sock, was only slightly less repulsive than the other, which was bare and purple, with badly trimmed and not very clean toenails.

She acknowledged her diagnosis was hardly scientific. Even the pathologist in *Lewis* would have made a brief examination of the body before announcing the victim had been dead for so many hours and minutes. However, the feet looked so lifeless that, well, one reaches an age when you simply know these things.

With no desire to risk seeing other naked, potentially purple bits of the old man, Miss Ross turned around and set off to find a member of staff.

This was the second resident to die in the last few weeks. Soon there would be two new faces in the dining room, staring around in surprise. (Wasn't it only the other month that they were young?)

The deceased was removed discreetly by Mr Dunn, the local undertaker. It was a sad reflection of their lives that he visited more often than many families, a point not lost on Dorothy, who hadn't seen her son for ever such a long time. The thing was, she never wanted to appear interfering and increasingly waited for Andrew to make contact, while he, in turn, increasingly did not. Everyone seemed so busy these days. Everyone, that is, except those living at We Care For You.

Dorothy felt they shouldn't complain. You got on with the task ahead, regardless of what fate put in the way. They had had their lives. One had to make room for new generations and as people got older they needed less and less room until . . . there was Mr Dunn.

Of course, this latest departure was the main topic of conversation over lunch. Being the third Tuesday in the month, this was boeuf bourguignon, a description that initially put off several people until they realised it meant meat stew. The cook, brought in recently by the new owners, knew a great deal more about food than she did about elderly folk.

'Poor Mr Ferguson,' said Dorothy. 'Coming upon his body like that must have been a terrible shock, Miss Ross.'

'I knew he was dead as soon as I saw his sole.'

'My goodness, you saw his soul! What did it look like?'

'Not very pleasant . . . purple and a bit fluffy.'

'Purple?'

'Yes.'

'Well, I never. And a bit . . . fluffy?'

'Someone needs to show that new cleaner how to use a Hoover properly.'

'The cleaner . . .?'

'She's from Poland.'

'Oh . . . don't they have Hoovers?'

'You would hope so, but she needs to be shown how we use one in Great Britain.'

'Mmm . . . I see.'

It was obvious that Dorothy didn't see. She could be exasperatingly slow on the uptake on occasions. There was no hint of dementia or that sort of thing, not like some in the care home who displayed significantly more than a hint. No, what lay behind those large NHS glasses with their red-tinged frames was more of an . . . *innocence*.

She could have been an exhibit, plucked straight out of one of the museums of 'bygone days' that seem to have sprung up in even the smallest towns. Magically brought to life in her long A-line skirt, blouse and hand-knitted cardigan, Dorothy was a living reminder of an era long gone when things were so much simpler and wholesome. It was partly why there was something so very appealing about her.

'It's a sign of the times,' said Joyce, tucking into a second helping. She was an enigma as regards eating. Without exception the others gradually ate smaller meals, becoming thinner and more frail as the years passed, but Joyce was, to put it bluntly, rather the opposite. 'I think it's all part of this dumbing down people keep talking about. Nothing's the same as it used to be . . . portions in restaurants . . . standards of behaviour . . . Hoovering.'

Miss Ross groaned inwardly, sensing the start of yet another conversation about how the good old days were so much better. She was saved by the appearance of Walter, a pleasant man, someone who would have at one time been referred to as 'dapper'. He was a completely changed person from the sad figure who had arrived eighteen months earlier, broken by the death of his wife of more than forty years.

3

His lovely niece had made such a huge difference to him over the last three months, visiting every Thursday without fail. She always had time to blether, helping out with little tasks if she could and often staying for most of the day. Yes, an altogether thoroughly nice young woman.

'Mind if I join you?' asked Walter.

The women around the table smiled and nodded. In reality he didn't need their permission at all, but it was polite of him to ask and it made them feel as though they could still make decisions.

'We were discussing poor Mr Ferguson,' said Dorothy.

'I wonder who we'll get to replace him,' said Deirdre. 'I hear there's someone called Joan taking the other empty room.'

Miss Ross didn't bother asking how she knew, suspecting that the information had been obtained during one of her many spying sessions. Deirdre had a habit of stopping to catch her breath in strategic doorways. She was the home's official source of gossip and its unofficial authority on morals, particularly other people's.

'I wish they would do something about that man,' said Deirdre, her eyes resting on Mr Forsyth, naked as the day he was born eighty-four years earlier. It was not an uncommon sight and the majority of those present simply carried on with their meal. Ben, one of the young male carers, appeared only seconds later with a dressing gown, which he deftly got him into.

'Here you are, Mr Forsyth. You'll catch cold without this and that wouldn't be any good, would it?'

The old man seemed as happy to be with clothes as without and once suitably attired he sat at a table and Ben fetched him something to eat.

There were activities in the home most days, as well as visits by a variety of professionals, from the local hairdresser to the optician, both of whom brought with them an array of portable equipment. That afternoon was the turn of the dentist and the gentleman with his accordion. The former was often known to sing during his sessions and although he didn't have a great voice he certainly knew more tunes than the latter.

Walter usually retired to his bedroom when this particular musician came. He would pursue one of his favourite hobbies of choosing a famous game of chess between grandmasters of the past and then playing out the moves on his beautiful handmade board. He had lacked an opponent when he'd first rekindled his interest six months earlier. That was before Julie started visiting. Everything in his life had changed dramatically since then. Having a chess partner was only a tiny part of it.

Two

Tuesday, 23rd February

Where have the years gone? Where has the love come from? The losing of one and the gaining of the other have crept upon me with equal astonishment. It is only at this point in my life that I truly understand the point of life. What can I do, so near the end? I feel it. The light is dimming in this ageing body, even as that other light shines so brightly. I must keep both for as long as possible.

Three

For two residents, each day began shortly after five o'clock. Both had been farmers and were so conditioned to rising early that they couldn't get out of the habit. Mr Forsyth, at least dressed for the time being, would go off to milk his cows or check on his sow, which always appeared to 'need servicing'. This resulted in the regular scenario of staff trying to convince him that the animals had already been seen to and preventing him from leaving the building and setting off one of the alarmed doors.

Many people could get themselves out of bed unaided and by the time the day staff started at eight o'clock there were usually several folk milling around. The home had thirty bedrooms and these were generally only empty during the period between the departure of the previous occupant (normally in the company of Mr Dunn) and the arrival of the next one.

Like most similar establishments females greatly out-numbered males and, just as in the outside world, little groups and friendships were formed which invariably led to jealousies, upsets and fallings out, not entirely unlike those encountered during Primary Four break times at school.

Dorothy and Miss Ross sat together in the dining room for breakfast, as they did for most meals. There could hardly have been a greater contrast in terms of their personality and background, or even their clothing. Whereas Dorothy conveyed a sense of being 'soft and cuddly', the retired headmistress was – it would be unfair to say 'hard' – rather 'precise'. Indeed, she would not have been offended to be considered prim. Despite the consistently warm surroundings, a tweed skirt and stiff white blouse were almost trademarks, along with her large pearl necklace.

These differences didn't bother them and since the arrival of Miss Ross three years earlier the two had been firm friends. They shared several interests and could often be found in Dorothy's bedroom, knitting and chatting as if they had known each other all their lives.

Miss Ross studied the other residents, a habit she couldn't stop herself from doing, although she always tried to hide it. Some of the least physically able had the sharpest minds, while those who appeared in extremely good repair were off chasing cattle every morning. In between, there was every variation and combination.

At the next table old Mrs Campbell, frail but still independently mobile with her Zimmer and in full charge of her mental faculties, was helping old Albert with his cereal. He seemed to be puzzled by the idea that his flakes needed to have milk added before he ate them. However, there were still times when Albert was quite lucid and really good company.

This was obviously a bad morning. On these occasions it was particularly difficult to imagine him as a sergeant in the army, a career which had taken him around the world and in which he had served with distinction. Yes . . . frailty, illness and care homes were great levellers. Whatever someone might have achieved in life, one of the three would probably get them in the end.

'I do miss not being able to dip little soldiers into my egg,' said Dorothy, forcing her friend away from her analysis of humanity and back to more mundane affairs. 'I don't know why they have to be so hard boiled that they resist all attempts of penetration. My soldiers bend at the waist as if they're bowing to the queen.'

'Maybe it's the toast.'

'What's wrong with it?'

'Well, perhaps these days it's not as strong as it used to be. The problem might not be the egg, but the bread.'

Dorothy thought carefully about this for a few moments. Miss Ross was a highly educated person and whenever she said something it was generally profound and worth listening to. On the other hand, she did have a habit of teasing her.

'Oh! You're having me on.'

'They're the regulations,' said Miss Ross smiling. 'The kitchen staff are not allowed to serve us eggs that are in any way runny. It's a health and safety matter.'

'Health and safety! I wish the powers-that-be would stop interfering with our treats. When I was a child I used to love cutting up my toast and dipping the pieces into my egg. It never did me any harm.'

'You have to dig it out with your spoon, place it on your toast and eat it that way.'

'I know. That's what I do. But it's not the same, is it?'

Dorothy was such a sweet, gentle person that on the rare occasions when she did complain her comments always came out in such a way that Miss Ross could never prevent herself from laughing.

'I don't see why my predicament is so funny,' said

Dorothy, although she then burst into giggles. 'I mean, look at that. My little soldiers have no chance. It would repel the SAS!'

'If you don't get the yoke . . . you'll never see the runny side of it.'

Some of the others watched on with amusement at the two women, now helpless with laughter at their table. What on earth could they find so entertaining at this time of the morning? They had only spoken to each other the night before.

★ ★ ★

'Everything's changed around,' said Joyce, joining some of the others at a table. They were in the café at the nearby garden centre. It often hosted a group from We Care For You and, indeed, felt so much like a second home that Joyce had brought some slippers in her bag. She slipped off her shoes, put them on and sighed contentedly.

'Do you mean where things are on the shelves?' asked Walter, a total contrast in appearance in his blue blazer and matching tie. He had three such outfits, in blue, a sort of mauve-red and dark green. They were all very smart, although, if one were completely honest, he did look a little overdressed in the present surroundings.

'No, I mean what they sell. At one time you came to a place like this to purchase something you could stick in the ground. Now it's bedroom furniture, books, kitchenware and scented candles. Don't try to actually find a plant. It'll probably turn out to be plastic!'

'You couldn't even get a cup of tea and now many of them have proper restaurants,' said Deirdre. 'If you can't get a three-course meal, you almost feel disappointed.'

10

'Yes, well, I didn't say all of the changes were bad,' said Joyce, beginning scone number two.

'You can actually buy quite a good selection of wool here,' said Dorothy, 'in the craft section. The last time I went into a wool shop they didn't have any.'

'No wool?' queried Walter in disbelief.

'Their balls had only twenty per cent content at most. I was quite cross.'

'Steady on, Dorothy,' he said. 'I hope it didn't lead to violence.'

'I went up to the desk. "You tell me, young man," I said, "how you can look me in the eye and say that your balls have come from a sheep."'

'You didn't!' said Miss Ross.

Walter bent over in his chair and started making a strange gurgling noise. Mrs MacDonald, a small, rather non-descript woman, patted him on the back.

'What did the salesman say?' asked Miss Ross, on the verge of losing control.

'Nothing. I think he must have dropped something because he disappeared down behind the counter and I didn't see him again.'

'It's all this dumbing down,' stressed Joyce, using one of her favourite phrases. 'Where have all the people with expert knowledge gone?'

'Most of them are probably in care homes,' said Deirdre.

Eight of the residents had gone on the outing, as well as Anna, one of the carers, and Hamish, the handyman/gardener/minibus driver. The others in the group were Albert and Mrs Butterworth. Although the latter was rather accident-prone, it was only Albert who was likely to wander off and get lost. During the previous visit he had locked himself in the toilet and had had to be let out by a

11

member of staff. This visit was pleasant and uneventful . . . the interesting incidents occurring when they returned.

* * *

As the group entered the reception area they saw Matron listening to a woman with unnaturally blonde hair, a low-cut top and a rather loud voice. The two were standing beside the large display board that contained photographs of all the staff, clearly identified with their names and titles, along with details of who was working that day.

The stranger stopped talking and eyed the arrivals with bright, inquisitive and rather mischievous eyes. People mingled nearby, waiting for the slower ones to come in. It was an unspoken little courtesy observed by everyone whenever they got back from a trip.

As soon as she realised who this woman was, Deirdre made straight for her, determined to be the first to say 'hello' in the hope that this might give her some leverage in terms of future domination.

'You must be Joan. I'm Deirdre,' she said, holding out her hand. 'If you ever need anything explained, just ask me. Everyone will confirm I'm the one to know!'

If the new resident was surprised at being identified this way, she didn't show it and pumped Deirdre's hand up and down until the latter began to look quite flustered.

'Pleased to meet you,' said Joan, her voice carrying clearly.

'Oh . . . yes . . . indeed . . . thank you,' said Deirdre, looking around for her accomplice and full-time support. Spotting Mrs MacDonald close by but hesitating to join in, she beckoned her over. 'And this is Mrs MacDonald, a very dear friend.'

The 'very dear friend' was taken aback. A compliment from that direction was about as common as pork at a bar mitzvah. Joan greeted her pleasantly, without any excessive arm action.

Miss Ross, like most of the others present, was watching the scene being played out before them and suspected that the latest arrival was going to provide some lively entertainment over the coming months. She certainly seemed to have quickly sussed out the home's gossip. Yes, this was a woman who had seen a few things in life, someone perhaps to be wary of?

Matron started to make introductions to the group, which was fairly uneventful until she reached Albert, who took out a mouth organ from his pocket and began to play. In reality there were only two notes, as all he did was suck and blow without moving the instrument. However, Joan paid attention as if it was a great performance, and he beamed with pleasure at her applause and praise.

'And finally, this is Miss Ross and Dorothy,' said Matron when she reached the remaining two in the group.

Close up, Joan was older than she appeared from a distance, the heavy make-up less successfully hiding the ravages of time. She would have been a handsome woman in her prime and her features still had firmness.

'I'm very pleased to meet you, Miss Ross,' she said, then noticing the bag Dorothy was carrying added, 'and I see you are a knitter.'

'Oh, I've done it since I was a child.'

'I'm a keen knitter myself. The current project is an Arran cardigan. We could swap patterns.'

'Yes, well, that would be nice.'

'All my bits and pieces have been delivered to my room, but I haven't seen it yet. Too busy chatting to Matron! I'm sure she's got better things to do. Perhaps you could take me there and then afterwards we could have tea?'

Joan slipped an arm through one of Dorothy's and the two women walked away down the corridor, chatting like old friends. Matron, seeing that she was no longer needed, went to her office. Deirdre, who had been hovering around in the background, decided there was no benefit in her staying either. Everyone else had dispersed about the building once they had been introduced.

Miss Ross stood by herself as if she had somehow been left behind. An image forced its way into her mind. When she was a child, she had come across a doll that used to be a favourite toy but which hadn't been played with in ages because she had forgotten about it. The doll had lost its appeal and had been thrown back into a box.

Miss Ross suddenly felt terribly alone.

Four

Monday, 29th February

Education has been the rock to which I have steered the course of my life. It has given me a purpose and sense of worth that has seen me safely and successfully through these many years. Now I feel rudderless, adrift on a hostile ocean that threatens to swallow me in loneliness, to devour me whole and not leave even memories. Why do I feel so threatened? Why am I so afraid of this new woman?

Five

The next morning began rather unfortunately when Albert and Mr Forsyth met in the corridor. It was purely chance that no one else was around. The night staff were busy handing over to the next shift, a process that had the potential to be more than a little fraught at times.

For some reason, from the moment the old farmer had arrived two years earlier, the two men had taken a strong dislike to each other and ever since everyone had done their best not to leave them alone together. They glowered with growing agitation before charging as fast as their frail legs would propel them. With fists feebly lashing out and hands weakly grabbing at throats, they both lost their balance and fell to the floor, their shouts bringing several people rushing from the meeting.

The men were helped to their feet and sat in chairs away from each other, by which time they had forgotten that anything had occurred and appeared to be in their usual state. However, Albert had a tiny cut on his lip. The 'fight', if it could even be called that, would have to be reported and a GP from the local surgery asked to call and check them out.

Matron sat in her office and sighed deeply. Strictly speaking she wasn't a 'Matron' but the manager of the care home. Her name was Maureen and new arrivals were always invited to call her that. However, she bore an uncanny resemblance to Hattie Jacques, famous for playing the role of Matron in the 1960s *Carry On* films, and many of the older residents felt comfortable with the term because it helped to make them feel safe. The title had stuck.

Maureen didn't mind. What she did mind was that this brief encounter would reflect badly on the staff, who all worked so hard. They had done their utmost to prevent such an event occurring . . . and now?

Now their dedication and professionalism would be called into question. Everything else they had achieved would be overshadowed. It was so unfair and in no way reflected the real situation. Maureen sighed again, then opened the incident book in which she would have to write a detailed report before entering the facts into each resident's case notes.

* * *

Joan quickly established herself as a highly popular addition. She played an audience well and seemed to have a never-ending supply of funny and often slightly naughty stories about her three husbands, all of whom she had outlived.

On the Wednesday lunchtime of her second week she was entertaining people at her table with yet more tales. There weren't any trips that day, which meant the dining room was busy.

Miss Ross, sitting next to Walter at another table, was

thinking about Monday evening, when she had walked into Dorothy's bedroom to find her friend knitting in her usual armchair, with Joan in a seat just along from the one that Miss Ross always sat in. They were in a little semicircle.

She had looked on in horror, yet made no comment. She had simply sat down, innocence on one side, and on the other an overly exposed bust that required a bra made by Balfour Beatty. However, this was Dorothy's bedroom and it was up to her if she wanted to squeeze in another chair and invite someone else. But everything had changed.

'Penny for them,' said Walter.

'Sorry,' she said, rousing herself. 'I was just thinking how nothing remains the same, no matter how much you want it to.'

Although she made no reference to anything in particular, Walter was aware that the dynamics of her friendship had changed. For a moment, he wasn't sure how to tread these potentially stormy waters.

'Our new arrival does seem to be making a few waves,' he said quietly. 'Although I have to admit to finding her very amusing, and she's extremely kind and patient with those residents who are confused.'

What he said was true and, in fairness, Miss Ross couldn't say that she actually disliked Joan. She was perhaps a bit brash and loud for her tastes, but those traits could also be levelled at Joyce, who was always good company. No, it was the intrusion.

Her thoughts were interrupted by Walter giving a small cry of surprise. The reason for this was obvious immediately. A white bap had just hit him on the forehead, dropped into his bowl and splashed leek and potato soup onto his dark-green blazer and the surrounding

18

tablecloth. As he was taking in this unexpected development, a piece of baguette hit him in the chest and fell into his lap.

Walter looked for the source of the flying food and his face took on an expression that even Miss Ross's extensive vocabulary would have been hard pushed to describe: shock, fear, longing.

'Angus!' he whispered, looking at a man who had been brought into the dining room by Anna.

The carer looked totally flabbergasted. There had been no reference to dementia or emotional problems in the notes and briefing for this new resident, who was moving into Mr Ferguson's old room. During the previous ten minutes he had appeared a perfect gentleman. Now here he was, standing near a bread basket and about to hurl another missile.

'No, that's not how we do things here,' said Anna. 'Please put that down!'

'It's him!' cried Angus. 'Him! Here! After all these years.'

A crusty brown roll flew through the air, but the aim was wild and it knocked over a water glass further along the table. He picked up a white sesame seed bun, but Ben stepped up to him and gently took it from his hand. In his youth Angus had been a strong man but his tall frame was a shadow of what it had once been. Totally defeated, he bowed his head, making his stoop appear worse, and muttered 'Sorry' over and over again. With great tenderness, Anna took his arm.

'Come on, love, let's go to your room. You can have lunch in there, if you want. I'll bring something once you've settled in.'

With that, she led him away. Everyone had fallen silent at the extraordinary scene and when the man left no one knew what to say. They all stared at Walter, who looked ashen.

'Here, I'll take that and bring you another,' said Ben, removing the bowl with its unwanted addition bobbing on the surface.

Walter gave no sign of having heard and after a few moments he stood up slowly.

'I'm going upstairs,' he said quietly to no one in particular, then left, not even bothering to wipe the soup from his sleeve.

Six

Tiddles, like everyone else, was particularly fond of Dorothy. The cat, however, unlike the others, loved to sit on her lap, buried underneath the current part-finished woollen garment whilst the needles clicked comfortingly above. He was already sitting on the armchair in Dorothy's bedroom when she came into the room, carrying that morning's post.

'Ah, there you are. Isn't it lovely when the sun streams in through the windows and the birds are singing their little hearts out?'

Dorothy put down the items next to the framed photograph of her late husband, which was always on the little table nearby. She picked up the cat, sat down, laid him on her lap and sighed contentedly.

'Aren't we lucky, Tiddles? Yes, we are. I wonder what we have today,' she said, picking up the small pile again. 'Look! A postcard from Andrew. *Dear Mum. Hope all is well. Having a great time. Love Andrew, Susan and Olivia.* Oh . . . Malta. Well, I'm sure it's nice. It sounds very far away. Still, they must have a postal service . . .

'Mmm, this looks very colourful,' she continued,

examining a circular. '*See the world in a fortnight. Luxury cruises from only four thousand pounds.* What do you make of that, Tiddles?'

If the cat made anything of the optimistic offer, he gave no indication.

'Yes, me too. I remember when our holiday budget was forty pounds and I bet we had a lot more fun.'

Dorothy dropped the circular into the wastepaper basket and stared at the remaining official-looking envelope without making a move to open it. She remembered as a child her parents had always regarded such items with dread. They never heralded anything good. Dorothy recalled that nightmare morning when the telegram arrived with news about her older brother, Edward. The war was so near the end it somehow made the tragedy even more difficult to reconcile.

But that was a very long time ago and this was probably no more than a reminder about an appointment. It couldn't be anything much more than that. She took a big breath, told herself not to be so silly and opened it. As she read the letter inside, her expression changed from one of curiosity to confusion and then horror.

Always bad news.

'No! This can't be right.'

Turning to the black-and-white photograph next to her, which she did many times each day, she held up the letter to the image of the man.

'Willie! What am I going to do?' she said, putting a hand to her mouth and fighting back tears. Before the spirit of her husband could offer a response, the door opened and Joan entered, likewise clutching a similar letter.

'Oh, love,' said her friend, sitting down in 'her' chair. 'The new owners want to increase my fees by a hundred and fifty pounds a week and I've only just arrived. I can hardly believe it.'

'They want even more from me.'

'That's because of your lovely bedroom. We've all been revalued.'

'What am I going to do? I can't afford such a rise. I'll be turned out onto the streets! Who would have thought it would come to this?'

'It hasn't reached that stage yet. I'm sure Miss Ross will have some advice. You mustn't despair.'

Miss Ross, as if hearing her name, walked into the room, appearing equally as shaken as the other two women.

'I had to check on Mrs Campbell. Poor soul. Ninety-three next week. She was in an awful state. I couldn't leave her until someone had brought Matron, although Matron was on the verge of tears herself. I had to stress that we all understand none of this has anything to do with her.'

'Fancy sending a letter like that out of the blue,' said Joan angrily. 'What a way to treat elderly folk.'

'It's a sign of the times,' said Miss Ross, sitting in the remaining chair and fearing for a moment that she was beginning to sound like Joyce. 'We're not considered people any longer, only square footage. Numbers on a stranger's balance sheet.'

'Will you be able to manage, Miss Ross?' asked Dorothy, always more concerned about others than herself.

'I was a teacher for almost thirty years and a headmistress for ten, so, yes, I can manage, but what about both of you?'

'I'll be all right,' said Joan. 'But not Dorothy.'

'Do you think it would help if I said I would eat less and cut down the heating in my room?'

Miss Ross felt such a chill in her heart that she couldn't

reply and sat running the string of pearls through her fingers, a habit that always betrayed any inner turmoil.

'I thought I would see out my last years quietly with my dear friends for company. I didn't think I would have to face such a terrible situation.'

'You're not alone in this,' said Joan. 'Although I've no idea what to suggest.'

The three women sat in silence, each holding a simple, innocent-looking A4 sheet of paper that threatened to destroy so many lives.

'We're not taking this lying down,' announced Miss Ross, leaving her pearls for a moment to tap the sheet forcefully with her hand, as if she was poking the sender in the chest.

'But what can we do against a big organisation?' said Dorothy, appearing more crestfallen and shrunken by the minute. 'Three forgotten elderly women in a care home . . . not much use to anyone any more.'

'We're not forgotten,' said Joan.

'Maybe you're not.'

'And we're still useful . . . we just have to find out what for,' said Joan, glancing around the room as if searching for a clue as to their worth to society. Her gaze came to rest on a couple of items nearby. She picked one of them up. 'Apart from knitting egg cosies.'

'What am I going to do?'

The room fell silent, as Dorothy's question went unanswered. They became aware of sounds around the building, someone crying softly nearby, a man's voice downstairs shouting angrily, hurried footsteps in the corridor outside. All the residents faced the same dilemma and despair hung in the atmosphere as if Ben had gone around spraying it into every nook and cranny, as he did on occasions with the spray for fleas.

'What am I going to do?'

'We need a plan,' said Miss Ross.

'What sort of plan?' asked Joan.

'A way to make money so that Dorothy can stay. What do the new owners want?'

'An extra two hundred pounds a week.'

'So you have to raise eight hundred pounds a month.'

'It's a tremendous amount. When I was a girl, it would have taken my father more than a year to earn that much.'

'Can you survive for a while?' asked Miss Ross.

'A short time, then I'll have nothing.'

'Dry your eyes. We haven't got this far in our lives to be cast aside by some money-grabbing bureaucrat who has never even met us. Come on. There's nothing like knitting to aid the mental process. Let's get our thinking hats on.'

Miss Ross, not generally one for dramatic actions, crumpled her letter and threw it into the bin, where it landed on top of the image of a cruise ship. She picked up a part-finished sock and set to work with a furious concentration. Her example inspired the others and after a few moments the room was filled with the clicking of needles.

Joan was the first to suggest something.

'How about selling the items we knit, instead of giving them to charity?'

'But we've always given them to charity,' said Dorothy.

'No, Joan's right,' replied Miss Ross. 'You're the priority now. But we simply couldn't knit fast enough and people today aren't willing to pay for the time involved in ordinary craft work.'

They fell silent and gradually resumed knitting. The cat, unaware of the tension and despair surrounding him, slumbered on contentedly in his favourite spot.

'I could sell my possessions!'

The others stopped and tried to appear optimistic while glancing around the room, as if seeing it for the first time. But they knew what was there: old furniture, a few knick-knacks, a couple of photographs . . . Joan picked up a small glass vase that stood on the table next to her chair. Sticking out of the top were three pink plastic flowers, which were embedded at the bottom into a solid, yellowish material that was meant to represent water.

Joan thought it looked like wee and was often beset by a strong urge to have a quick sniff to check that indeed it wasn't. She tipped the vase on its side but nothing moved, apart from a little dust, so she replaced it. The truth was, the possessions were worthless, but neither of them would dream of implying such a thing.

'What we need,' said Miss Ross tactfully, 'is a regular income, something that brings in money every month.'

They fell silent, apart from the clickety-click of needles. Dorothy had made thousands of items over the decades, clothes for the family, gifts for friends, eye-catching objects for the church bazaars. Now Willie was gone and Andrew, well, where was he? Grown up and living his life with his own family. His wife Susan wasn't really into handmade craft clothes, so these days Dorothy usually gave away what she made to the local charity that raised money for the homeless.

'I suppose I could move into one of the small bedrooms downstairs, at the back of the building. They must be cheaper.'

'Oh no,' cried Joan. 'They don't have any views and never get the sun.'

'And they wouldn't be big enough for us to meet in,' pointed out Miss Ross. Since Joan had joined them it was quite cramped enough and any less space would make it impossible. 'And even they have a waiting list.'

'If I have to wait long, my money will run out before there's anything available. Even a cheaper room here doesn't seem to be an option.'

'This rise in fees affects all of the residents,' said Miss Ross. 'We can be much more effective with a larger number, rather than just the three of us. Let me chat quietly to a few people and see if we can get together and come up with some ideas.'

In response, Dorothy burst into tears.

* * *

The atmosphere in the lounge that evening was subdued. Even the television was turned off. People gathered in little groups, discussing the unpleasant news. Mrs Campbell was particularly upset and Matron did her best to comfort her and some of the others. A few residents complained to Matron, but she had no more information than what was in the letters. All the fees would go up in three weeks' time, on 1st April, as though the whole thing was a cruel April Fool's joke.

Walter was subdued for other reasons: memories of terrible guilt and shame. He had set up the communal chessboard at a table that allowed him to sit by himself and reduce the risk of being drawn into any conversations he didn't want to have, such as why had the new resident hurled bread rolls at him.

Angus had stayed in his bedroom since arriving the previous day and the lounge fell silent when he appeared in the doorway later on. Everyone was curious about the home's new male resident and they stared at him as he stood, unsure what to do, the over-large jumper hanging on his slender frame and making him appear somehow . . . abandoned.

He saw Walter watching him, indicating with his head the chair opposite. The invitation to play chess was unspoken, though obvious. Angus glared back for a few moments, then walked over to sit as far away from him as possible.

Seven

Age is a relative thing. People often referred to 'old' Mrs Campbell, who shuffled around with difficulty and determination in equal measure, yet she in turn would refer to 'old' Mrs O'Reilly who, at ninety-nine, was certainly the person in the home who had lived the longest. However, the almost centenarian called many folk 'old' even when they were significantly younger. The definition was perhaps as much to do with attitude as physical or mental ability.

Joyce went to chat with their one Irish resident, who had arrived almost a year earlier, having survived independently for a commendable length of time.

They had become quite close, their natural wit and desire to entertain those around them proving in the early days to be both an attraction and a hindrance to friendship.

However, they enjoyed each other's company so much that, as well as having a wee dram, companionship became inevitable. They sat by the window in Mrs O'Reilly's bedroom, the first-floor position providing a good view over the extensive garden. Outside, Hamish was building a new chicken coop. The hens were extremely popular with residents, although they were not allowed to eat the eggs, no matter how well cooked.

'It's always a pleasure to see a strong, handsome young man working physically hard,' said Joyce. 'There's something very appealing about it.'

'Whenever he helps me into the minibus, my hand always seems to land on his thigh . . . just for extra support, you understand. I do like a shapely leg. I had a fine pair myself when I was younger.'

'Oh, I could well imagine.'

'Christ, you must have a good imagination!'

'Was a pair of attractive legs important in the job you did, Mrs O'Reilly?'

'Well, you could say that. It's not something I usually talk about. I used to be a Windmill Girl.'

Joyce had never been to the well-known London theatre, but she knew of its reputation for beautiful nude dancers.

'I think you need to tell me more,' she said with delight.

'We had such fun,' said Mrs O'Reilly, reminiscing. 'When I was involved during the thirties, we performed to a packed hall every night and there were often famous people in the audience, including nobility. We also played alongside some top acts and I got to know many performers who became household names years later. It was all new and exciting.'

'From what I understand, it was all nude and exciting!'

'We were pioneering. The first live nudity on stage. But we weren't allowed to move.'

'Not move? What did you do, stand like statues?'

'Legally, that's exactly what we were meant to do. As long as we didn't move, no one was breaking the law. That was very important. Of course, we started to find ways around it, such as standing or sitting on props that revolved or went up and down. Technically our bodies were perfectly still, so the authorities couldn't complain. The audiences loved the extra thrill of bits of flesh bobbing and bouncing about. Now you see it, now you don't.'

'Mrs O'Reilly! What would Father Connelly say?' said Joyce, which set them both off laughing.

'I like him immensely, but I've never felt the need to confess anything about those days. None of us considered we were doing anything wrong, not really. It was a completely different era.'

'Well, your secret is safe with me . . . Speaking of posing, I hope everyone keeps their clothes on this evening. I gather Mr Dunn is going to be one of the models and the sight of the undertaker displaying his wares might result in a sudden rush of unexpected business!'

Once a year the nearby dress shop organised a fashion show, during which staff and a few invited guests walked up and down the lounge wearing a selection of generally outrageous outfits. The event always caused a great deal of anticipation and good humour, and with non-residents allowed to join the audience it also raised money for several charities.

Being the second Wednesday in the month, lunch was smoked haddock florentine with dauphinoise potatoes. However, the cook, having learnt more about the 'service users' she was providing for, described this on the menu as *Fish Pie with Potatoes* and as such it was very popular. All the talk around the tables concerned that evening and there was a great deal of speculation about what might be worn.

In the afternoon someone from the nearby supermarket arrived with bunches of flowers that had reached their sell-by-date and which would otherwise have been thrown out. Although it didn't cost the retailer anything, the gesture was much appreciated and it helped to ensure that those who wouldn't otherwise receive flowers at least had them regularly in their rooms.

A couple belonging to the Friends of We Care For You also turned up. A small group connected to the local church visited on a rota basis. They would talk to residents, read to them if their eyesight wasn't so good, help with little jobs and sometimes take them out for short trips. As with the flowers, the recipients were grateful.

There was almost a tension in the dining room during supper, as residents tried to finish their meal and make their way as quickly as possible to the lounge. Securing the best chairs was a constant source of disagreement, particularly as there was more than one person who thought the most comfortable chairs 'belonged' to them.

Ownership was based upon a conflicting set of criteria – who had sat in it first that morning, who had been in it the longest that day or who had been in the home for the greatest period (a factor considered by long timers to outweigh any other claims).

The commonest arguments arose when someone left their seat for a few minutes and returned to find it occupied. Such occasions had been known to build into feuds that were almost on a par with those of famous rival Scottish clans of the past. The situation was made even more complex because there were certain residents who refused to sit next to each other.

Of course, there were also friendships to take into account, where people simply *had* to sit beside a particular person, otherwise the world would implode and all life as we know it cease. The fashion show always brought this problem to boiling point and there were no concessions during the race after supper. Those with a Zimmer were simply manoeuvred around and left behind in the corridor.

A few rows of seats had been reserved for invited guests, which included the local MP and newspaper editor, plus several visitors from the business world. When everyone had finally settled themselves, Matron gave a short speech of welcome and thanks before leaving to get dressed. One of the staff dimmed some of the lights to emphasise the central area and a few moments later music could be heard over the speakers.

The first performer to enter and strut around the floor was received by a stunned silence before the audience overcame their initial shock and burst into enthusiastic clapping. Hamish, wearing swimming trunks that bordered on indecent, started posing and flexing his impressive muscles as if he was a contestant at a bodybuilding competition.

'Blimey, do you reckon that's real or has he stuck a garden trowel down there?' said Joan.

'I don't know,' replied Joyce, sitting next to her, 'but he could turn me over any time.'

'Get them off!' shouted Mrs O'Reilly in glee.

'Really,' hissed Deirdre to Mrs MacDonald. 'That woman is so vulgar. I knew she'd end up nearby.' Her friend was too busy cleaning her glasses to take any notice.

'Oh dear,' said Dorothy to no one in particular, although she couldn't stop herself from smiling at the sight.

'Off! Off!' called Mrs O'Reilly.

The cry was taken up by several of the more extrovert women and this continued until the handyman gave his final pose and left the room to huge applause. It seemed impossible for anything else to be as entertaining and that the evening must surely decline from that point onwards, but when the next person entered there was another gasp of surprise. With the top half of his body dressed in garishly-coloured clothing, and without any trousers, the man looked as though Quentin Crisp had become involved in a Brian Rix farce.

It was Mr Dunn.

A great cheer went up as people realised who it was. The undertaker, wearing a pair of red garters, walked into the centre of the room and dramatically swished back across his shoulder the bright orange chiffon scarf hanging around his neck. He turned his face disdainfully one way and then another, the large feather sticking out of his hat swaying above his head.

'Keep them on!' cried Mrs O'Reilly, which made even Mr Dunn lose his composure and start laughing. During all the years he had been involved with the home, it was the first time anyone had seen him smile and the transformation was unbelievable. It transpired that even undertakers had a sense of humour.

He was followed by an extremely elegant and quite beautiful young woman dressed in a stunning evening gown that drew gasps of admiration. No one initially recognised this apparent stranger, however, who moved gracefully around the floor like an experienced model.

'Goodness me!' said Joyce. 'It's our Anna.'

And indeed it was. The applause for the carer was on an even bigger scale than that received by the men. The next performer was known instantly, as Matron had dressed exactly as Hattie Jacques used to in the *Carry On* films.

Throughout the evening it seemed that the next act couldn't possibly be better than the previous, yet each time it had been. Not only was the fashion show declared the best ever but the evening itself was one of the most enjoyable anyone at We Care For You had known.

Eight

One afternoon a few days later a handful of residents gathered, seemingly by chance, in the conservatory. In addition to Miss Ross, Dorothy and Joan, there was Joyce, Walter and Angus. Deirdre, who hadn't been invited, had somehow heard about the meeting and wherever she went Mrs MacDonald always followed.

'We've all received a letter from the new owners,' said Miss Ross. 'Many of us can afford the increase. For others, it will be a struggle. But for some it's simply too much money. These people face the very real prospect of having to move to a cheaper care home.

'I've spoken to Dorothy and she doesn't mind me telling you that she is someone who faces having to go, leaving behind all the friends she's made over the years and the staff and surroundings that she's so familiar with. I don't need to tell you of the ... horror that such a daunting outlook would hold for any of us. The question is, what can we do about it?'

There was a great deal of agreement that something should be done, but for the moment no one had any inspiration about what this could be.

'Whatever we do, it will be more effective with a larger number of people involved,' said Walter.

'I think we had already worked that out,' snapped Angus.

The two men sat as far apart as possible and the animosity that flowed between them made the atmosphere in the conservatory slightly uncomfortable. Without making it obvious, Miss Ross had been studying them and it seemed to her that the hostility came only from the new resident. It was clear that they were linked strongly by some past event, but even Deirdre had no idea what the connection was.

'We should form a committee,' suggested Joan.

'What sort of committee?' asked Dorothy.

'An Escape Committee,' said Deirdre.

'I didn't know we wanted to actually escape,' said Mrs MacDonald.

'Not physically, but at least from the situation we find ourselves in,' said Deirdre, appearing rather irritated that her sidekick should query anything she said.

The idea of being in league with Deirdre was not appealing. The woman was difficult to like and impossible to trust. However, she couldn't afford the rise and there was no denying that this would ensure her co-operation. They were, for better or worse, all in this together.

'I think,' said Miss Ross, 'that we should form a committee of the most able-bodied of the residents and then agree how we can fight back against these fees.'

Several names were suggested, some of them discarded for perfectly sound reasons while others were challenged because of petty personal grievances, previous disagreements or insults, real and imagined. Eventually, however, they agreed on four people.

'If we're going to meet without anyone else being

involved, we need an activity, something that gives the group a valid reason to get together regularly and that doesn't look suspicious,' said Joan.

'What could we do?' asked Deirdre. 'We can't suddenly develop an interest in art or architecture. That would look odd itself.'

They sat in silence, looking at each other, the floor and the walls, trying to think of a craft, hobby or subject that would provide a plausible cover. It was Dorothy who came up with the solution.

'We should form a knitting bee.'

'Knitting?!' queried Angus.

'Well, some of us are already enthusiastic about it and I know that Joyce, Deirdre and Mrs MacDonald can knit. We can give the others lessons. These could be part of the reason for the group and we can easily provide samples for those who need to give the appearance of producing items.'

'There's more to you than meets the eye,' said Joan.

It was agreed that Miss Ross would approach the four potential members and between them they would decide on a date for the first meeting of the care home's official knitting bee.

Nine

Walter was sitting in the chair by his bed. It was a small room and, although not unpleasant, there was little of 'him' in it. There was certainly not enough space for many mementos of his deceased wife, Moira, apart from a couple of photographs and a few items she had bought him. It was not much to represent so many years together.

Near to the door was a wedding present from their best man, a beautifully carved blackthorn walking stick with the head of a Labrador that bore a striking resemblance to the dog Walter had owned at the time. It had been extremely skilfully made and was something he didn't want to part with.

He felt the room was sterile, like a bright new dressing over a wound that hadn't healed. From the outside, it looked good. He wondered how many of the residents gave a false impression on the surface, compared to what they felt inside, underneath that dressing. But then he had met Julie. How that young woman had changed his life! His thoughts were interrupted by a knock at the door and when he opened it there she was.

'Hello, Uncle Walter,' said Julie.

She kissed him on the cheek, as any niece might do with a favourite uncle.

'Hello love, come in.'

Once they were alone he hugged her tightly and she held on to him as though she was a frightened child which, in many ways, she still was. Eventually, he pulled back.

'Let me look at you,' he said, studying her face. 'How are you this week?'

'I've survived.'

'No one has hurt you?'

'They all hurt me, but, no, not in the way you mean.'

'I'm sorry.'

'Don't be. Coming here is the highlight of my week. It's the only good thing in my life.'

'That makes me pleased and sad at the same time.'

'It's not your fault, Walter. You've been nothing but kind to me.'

'Not always,' he said, looking down at the dark green carpet, remembering with shame the first time she had visited. Julie took hold of one of his hands.

'Now, we're not going over that old ground again. We agreed there's no point.'

'I wish there was something else I could do,' he said, putting both hands around hers.

'You've helped me more these past few months than anyone else in the last four years.'

'And you've done more for me since my Moira died than anybody, including family and professionals.'

'Come on, "Uncle Walter", this is the one laugh I get. Put the kettle on, I'm gasping.'

She dragged him from his morose thoughts with her cheeriness. How could anyone be positive doing what she did? He walked over and switched on the kettle, arranging the mugs and teapot. She took off her shoes and coat. He whispered across the room.

'Have a listen and see if we have an audience.'

'I did spot them near the bottom of the stairs, pretending to read tonight's menu,' she said.

Outside Walter's bedroom Deirdre and Mrs MacDonald had just arrived on tiptoe. The former put her ear to the door, close to where Julie's was pressed up to the panel on the other side.

'Can you hear what's going on?' said Mrs MacDonald.

'It's very quiet,' said Deirdre in a voice that was too low for her friend to catch.

'What!'

'I said, oh . . . shhh.'

Walter made the tea and was still waiting for a response.

'Are they there?' he said.

'It's hard to tell.'

'Give the door a whack.'

With her hand, Julie hit the panel next to Deirdre's head, making her cry out in alarm.

'Yes, they're outside,' said Julie, moving away and starting to laugh.

In the corridor Deirdre had leapt back in surprise, almost knocking into the other woman.

'What happened? Have they started already?' asked Mrs MacDonald.

'Shhh. They'll hear you.'

Walter took two mugs over to the table where the chessboard was already set out. Julie, still fighting off a fit of giggles, took her place opposite.

'Right,' he said loudly, 'I've got everything laid out. My king is standing to attention, ready for you to try and get your hands on it.'

'I must admit, I've never seen one with such an impressive crown,' she said, following his lead.

'I've even given it a polish. But I warn you, I've been studying some new moves from my book and you're going to find it particularly hard this week.'

'Well, don't imagine you're going to get your hands on my pieces easily. I'm not about to go down without a fight. And . . . I think we should do it against the clock!'

Walter tried desperately to stifle his laughter. Their performance was on a par with an extremely poor school pantomime, but they suspected that the women listening outside would fall for everything. They heard what they expected to.

'Go over and see what you can find out,' said Walter quietly.

Julie got up, crept across the room and put her ear against a panel. Deirdre, just the other side, was fighting to maintain control of the hysteria that was threatening to overwhelm her.

'Oh my God! I can hardly bear to listen.'

'What's happening?'

'They're timing themselves!'

'Timing? How?' asked the confused Mrs MacDonald.

'With a clock!'

Julie crept back to the table and relayed what she had heard. Walter almost knocked the chessboard over. It took some time for them to control themselves. When he made his first move, Julie moaned loudly, as if in pleasure.

'Oh, Mr McKenzie! That's such a classic opening, but it still takes my breath away.'

The two played their game and kept up the charade for the next fifteen minutes, building up the excitement with their comments until Walter cried out, 'Oh, Julie! I can't help myself. I'm . . .'

'Yes?'

'I'm . . .'

'What is it, Mr McKenzie?'

'I'M CASTLING!'

In the corridor, Deirdre almost fainted against the door.

'What is it? Aren't you well?' said Mrs MacDonald, who had to rely on her friend for a running commentary of what was happening.

'Help me to my room. I feel quite ill.'

'Oh my goodness. Take my arm. I'll fetch Matron.'

'I'm never going to walk along this corridor. It's simply too awful.'

The two women staggered away, one swearing not to go near that room again and the other promising her full support in whatever she decided, while both knowing they would be back the following Thursday. In the bedroom, Walter hadn't managed to castle before keeling over in his chair.

'For Christ's sake, stop it, Walter. Stop it! I'm going to wet myself.'

Ten

'We're a bit like *The Dirty Dozen*, although I don't remember any of them using needles and knitting patterns,' said Walter, when the last of the Escape Committee (the name had stuck) settled themselves into the conservatory for their first-ever meeting.

The original eight had been joined by Mrs Butterworth, slightly eccentric but generally game for a dare, two almost identical sisters known as Meg and Peg who often swapped names and clothes for their own amusement and the confusion of others, plus a woman called Stella. Her small stature and rather pious nature were misleading because she was fearless in the face of injustice.

'I'm certainly not dirty!'

'They're characters from a film, Mrs MacDonald,' said Walter, 'about a group of people who get together with a common purpose, a mission, like us.'

'It still seems an offensive description to me, saying we're dirty.'

Angus dropped a needle on the floor, the third time in the last few minutes. He reached down with a sigh. Dorothy was attempting to show him the basics of knitting and had started the first few rows so that it was easier for him to try. The lesson wasn't going well.

'I know it feels deceitful, but we must keep the real reason for our group a secret,' said Miss Ross. 'That includes friends and family, other residents and staff . . . especially staff. I know there are many we like and trust implicitly, but it wouldn't be fair on them.'

Everyone nodded their agreement, including Deirdre, who found keeping information to herself almost immoral.

'Right, we need ideas, either how to fight the rise in fees or how to raise money to cover it.'

'When I was involved in the Women's Institute, we made all sorts of things to sell for cash,' said Mrs MacDonald. 'But I suppose we can't make jams or chutneys here. I don't think the kitchen staff would be pleased.'

'The charity shops collect items and then resell them,' said Angus. 'I gather some of them make quite a bit each week.'

'You would need a lot of space for sorting out stuff and much of what's donated goes straight to the tip,' said Meg, though it might have been Peg.

'I helped out at a shop for years and you wouldn't believe the number who leave rubbish at the door to save going to the dump themselves,' added the other sister. 'We had to make a car journey every few days to dispose of it.'

'We wouldn't have an outlet to sell anything and I don't think we should compete with local charities,' said Miss Ross.

For the next twenty minutes people suggested a variety of ideas, none of which seemed to meet their needs, until they all gradually fell silent and a sombre mood settled upon the group.

'We should start by going on a protest march,' said Joan

eventually, her natural enthusiasm making the others sit up and take notice.

'A march?' queried Dorothy. 'How would that help?'

'Well, that's what people do to raise the profile of something, isn't it? They walk through the streets, waving placards, shouting slogans and making the public aware. It seems to work for all sorts of subjects. What was that bunch on the six o'clock news the other night?'

'They were going on about the plight of puffins,' said Joyce. 'Apparently their numbers are decreasing at an alarming rate.'

'Unlike us,' muttered Angus.

'I remember now,' said Walter. 'The protesters each wore a red beak and dressed in red trousers.'

'We're probably not as newsworthy as puffins,' said Dorothy.

'If we disguised ourselves as elderly folk, we wouldn't have to buy any props,' said Joyce.

'Why don't we go on a march to highlight the plight of residents in care homes facing increases in fees?' said Joan.

'Which many can't afford,' stressed Miss Ross.

The committee members looked at each other and the idea appealed to them all.

Eleven

Preparations for the march went on in secret over the next week and it began to feel like the Escape Committee was aptly named. Keeping membership limited to those who were able-bodied proved to have huge advantages when it came to making unsupervised trips, which allowed items to be obtained without arousing suspicion.

They were helped by the fact that everyone in the home was involved in making Easter bonnets, which meant it was necessary for all sorts of unusual objects to be purchased. Over the years this tradition of creating headgear had taken on such a fiercely competitive edge that Meg and Peg even kept details of what they were doing a secret from each other.

With such subterfuge going on in almost every room, it was relatively easy for Deirdre and Mrs MacDonald to buy large rolls of material unnoticed. These were made into placards, designed so that a walking stick could be inserted into each end as a means of holding them up.

Miss Ross created a leaflet and made several hundred copies at the local library. Walter and Joan went out on scouting trips to devise a route that would not be too taxing to walk but which was likely to bring them into contact with the largest number of people.

They chose the last Saturday in March and on the allocated morning left the home in small groups, having agreed to meet in a side street next to Marks & Spencer. None of the staff asked any awkward questions and by ten o'clock the committee had nearly all regrouped as planned.

'Where on earth are Deirdre and Mrs MacDonald?' said Walter.

'We'll give them a few more minutes,' said Miss Ross.

'Oh dear,' said Dorothy, 'I think I must pay a visit before we start any marching. It is rather chilly.'

'The toilets in Marks are good,' said Joyce. 'In fact, why don't we grab a cup of tea before we leave? We won't get anything once we're on the go. We can then use their facilities with a clear conscience.'

Ten minutes later the group was seated around two tables in the café, apart from Walter, who had offered to wait outside and let the latecomers know where they were.

'They do make nice bakes,' said Joyce, biting into a large slice of coffee cake that had somehow been included in her order.

'I feel quite nervous,' said Dorothy. 'I hope we don't get arrested.'

'You can't be arrested for taking part in a peaceful march,' said Angus. 'It's our right. Mind, it would get our cause quite a bit of publicity.'

'Perhaps we should have informed the police,' said Mrs Butterworth.

'I don't think twelve OAPs walking down the street is going to cause such a hold-up that the authorities need to put diversions in place,' said Joan.

Walter arrived with Deirdre and Mrs MacDonald, who

explained they had been delayed while at the post office, although why they had chosen to go there on that particular day was beyond understanding. By the time the latecomers had got their drinks, people had visited the facilities, more than once in some cases, the morning was slipping by and Miss Ross was getting agitated.

'Well, let's get to it then,' she said.

When they gathered outside, with shoppers, families and tourists strolling past, the idea of the protest suddenly seemed even more daunting. However, Miss Ross took out the banner hidden in her bag and the others followed her example. Several of them had brought a walking stick.

Walter didn't need one to get about but sometimes used his for the simple pleasure of the feel of the handle, which fitted his hand so perfectly. Angus had stared at the skilfully-made object, although he made no comment. After a few minutes of fumbling and muttering, the Escape Committee was ready.

Brightly-coloured wool had been used to create eye-catching wording. '*Fair Fees for the Forgotten*', '*Equal Rights for the Elderly*', '*We Will Be Heard Again*', '*Pensioners Have Rights As Well As Puffins*'. Others had leaflets to hand out. Miss Ross checked everyone was ready. A tense excitement hung about the little group, but they smiled back encouragingly and she felt a gush of enormous pride, even towards Deirdre.

'Let's go!'

And off they went, Dorothy and Mrs MacDonald leading, as they were likely to be the slowest and Miss Ross didn't want to risk people being split up. They came out of the side street and were soon in the thick of shoppers, many of whom looked on curiously.

Dorothy immediately handed out a leaflet. In reality, it was more of an exchange, as the man pressed one on to her, offering a '*Buy one get one free*' meal at the local pizza restaurant. Still, it was a start and it wasn't long before people were taking more notice, particularly when Walter started shouting out 'Fair Fees for the Forgotten!' as loudly as he could.

However, when they turned into the High Street they were almost swept away by hundreds of people walking in the same direction, holding up scores of placards. A handful of police kept pace along the outside.

'What's going on?' said Joan to Miss Ross.

'Heaven knows. It looks as though we've ended up in another march. Maybe we can use it to our advantage?'

'Look at all these people who've joined us,' said Mrs MacDonald to Dorothy. 'Who would have thought we would have had such an instant impact? It's marvellous.'

Dorothy, who had just handed out the '*Buy one get one free*' leaflet to a rather perplexed passer-by, smiled, then dropped back to speak to Joan.

'I'm confused. Why do these people want equal rights for a sandwich?'

'A sandwich! What do you mean?'

'Well, look what's written on that.'

Joan followed Dorothy's gaze and made a sound that could have either been despair or a stifled laugh.

'You're thinking of a BLT. That says *Equal Rights for LGBT.*'

'What does that mean?'

'Oh, love, I'll explain it to you later.'

Miss Ross, holding the other end of Joan's banner, glanced around nervously. They were already being strung out. Joyce had dropped some distance behind, talking to a stallholder selling handmade chocolates, while there was no sign of Mrs Butterworth or the sisters.

'We're getting split up, Joan!'

'I know. What can we do?'

A sudden gust of wind caught a lot of people by surprise. Deirdre almost fell over but was saved from potential injury by a strong hand taking her elbow. She turned to thank the person and stared into the face of an extraordinarily handsome young man.

'Oh, goodness me!' she said, though it wasn't clear whether this was in response to nearly falling over or to the appearance of the man. 'Thank you so much. How very kind.'

He had such clear skin, a beautiful smile and his eyes . . .

'It's nearly always windy at this part of the High Street,' he said, picking up the end of the banner that she had dropped. 'Shall I take this for you?'

'Well, I don't know . . . I suppose . . .'

'Come on, boys, let's help these elderly folk,' said the man in a loud voice.

The message passed along the marchers in an instant and the next moment all of the Escape Committee were surrounded by young people wanting to help. Even the men had their walking sticks taken from them, and although it dented their pride they were grateful not to have to carry them any further.

'Thanks, son,' said Walter to the youth now holding up his walking stick. 'I must admit my arms were aching.' He continued walking alongside in silence for a few minutes but couldn't take his eyes off the various piercings through the teenager's nose and ears. 'Did those hurt?' he asked eventually.

'Naw.'

'If you don't mind me asking, why did you have it done?'

'People should have the right to express themselves without being punished. Everyone should have equal rights, whether it's about jobs, relationships, how they want to dress. No one should be telling you what to do or think. It doesn't matter what your beliefs are, you should have the right to have those beliefs.'

Walter didn't understand what the march was about, but he couldn't argue with the lad's conviction and was impressed by the passion behind what he said.

'I'm Walter,' he said, holding out a hand.

The youth stared at him suspiciously before finally shaking it.

'Smiler,' he grunted.

'That's an unusual name,' said Walter, amused. 'Where did that come from?'

The youth glared, his face a mixture of anger, confusion, metal rings and acne.

'Right,' said Walter, nodding and wishing he hadn't asked. 'It's good to have a belief in something. Err, could you explain LGBT?'

'Are you trying to be funny?'

'No. Honestly. I haven't a clue.'

Smiler seemed to weigh up the question before replying. 'Buy me a pint when we get to the square and I'll explain it to you.'

The march had the feel of a good-natured festival and several people chatted and joked with the police walking along the outsides. By the time the crowds started to congregate in the town's main square, the Escape Committee was completely split up.

Miss Ross didn't even know what had happened to the banner she had been helping to carry. When someone tapped her on the shoulder, she turned around expecting to see one of the other residents. Instead, there were two women in their late thirties.

'Hello,' said one of the women, who looked vaguely familiar. 'It's Tiffany.'

Given a name, Miss Ross suddenly placed the ex-pupil.

'Of course. How are you?' she said, shaking the outstretched hand.

'I've never been better, thank you. This is my partner, Grace.' The two women shook hands and there was a moment's pause in the conversation. 'I guess we're all rather surprised to see each other on this march.'

'The march?' said Miss Ross, who understood what it was about. 'Yes, well my involvement is probably not what it seems. Shall we find somewhere to have a quiet cup of tea? I could do with a sit down.'

* * *

In a nearby pub, Walter carried a pint and a half of beer over to the table in the corner. He sat down and pushed the pint across to his new acquaintance. The teenager took a long drink, before setting down the glass in front of him.

'So, where are you from?'

Walter took the question to mean where did he live, rather than where was he born. He didn't think the lad was that interested in his life story.

'I'm at the care home.'

'We Care For You?'

'You know it?'

'My grandfather was there for a while before he died. That was a long time ago, when I was just a kid.' Although Walter had discovered the teenager was nearly seventeen, he didn't think he looked much more than a kid even now, but he decided it would be indelicate to indicate such a thing. 'So you'll be there until you die.'

It wasn't so much a question as a statement and Walter almost reeled from the harsh reality that lay behind the comment.

'Well, that's a blunt way of putting it.'

'That's what happens to people, isn't it?'

'The home isn't a hospice. It's not a place where the terminally ill go. It's just somewhere for people who can't look after themselves any more. They could live there for years.'

'But it's your life now.'

'Yes . . . I suppose it is,' agreed Walter, suddenly feeling rather depressed.

'So, why were you marching?' asked Smiler, draining the beer at an alarming rate.

'The new owners have put up the fees and it's more than some residents can afford. We thought a protest in the High Street might create some awareness of our plight, but we seem to have been swallowed up by your march. I don't think anyone noticed us in the end.'

Walter took his first sip. These days his bladder wouldn't allow him near a pint.

'People probably thought you were elderly gays and lesbians.'

'Would they! Why, for God's sake?'

'It's a lesbian, gay, bisexual and transsexual protest.'

'Hell, I didn't realise. Well, that should certainly upset Deirdre.'

'Who's she?'

'A resident who likes to think she's the overseer of our morals.'

Their conversation was brought to a halt by the barmen arriving with lunch. Walter could remember how hungry he'd always felt at Smiler's age, so he kept quiet while they ate. The food opposite seemed to disappear as quickly as the beer. When he considered it was reasonable to continue, he said, 'So, tell me about this LGBT parade.'

★ ★ ★

In a little café a few streets away, Tiffany was pouring tea. Now that she was sitting opposite, Miss Ross could see traces of the girl who used to attend her school. There had been so many boys and girls during her long career, although some stayed in one's mind.

'Your father was a minister, wasn't he?'

'Goodness, that was well remembered,' said Tiffany.

'Well, I recall that several teachers used to attend his Sunday services, so he is more memorable than the majority of parents. Is he well?'

'I believe so. We haven't been in touch for quite a while. To be honest, we haven't spoken since I came out, not once all the arguments and terrible accusations were over. I knew that telling him was a great risk and I had fought against my feelings for many years. However, in the end . . . well, my life was simply wasting away. Then Grace and I met and the secret had to be told. There was no longer an option.'

Miss Ross nodded and drank her tea while the two women took hold of each other's hands across the table. They looked so happy and in love. The sight unsettled her and yet was also strangely comforting.

'That is a tragedy for everyone,' said Miss Ross. 'Some people cannot accept these situations because it threatens too directly what they believe and to condone such a relationship would undermine the foundations of their own lives. It can be so frightening that even the love for a daughter is not enough.'

'There are plenty who think it's wrong, even in this day and age,' said Grace. 'We encounter abuse and intimidation on a regular basis, whether we're walking down the street, out for an evening or at work.'

'What's your opinion, Miss Ross?' asked Tiffany.

'My opinion? Well, I think . . . if you can find love, you must hang on to it with everything you have. Without love, life is so easily an unfulfilled and lonely journey.'

Twelve

Members of the Escape Committee returned to the home in ones and twos during the afternoon to be greeted with the news that Mrs O'Reilly was very poorly. The priest had been sent for, although he was busy with a funeral and was not expected until later in the day.

Miss Ross arrived by herself and was the last to get back. She thought that the leaflets they had handed out to the public would have no impact whatsoever and that the march had been a complete failure in terms of highlighting the rise in fees. She found her friends in the conservatory and flopped down next to them in an uncharacteristic mood of despondency.

'All that work, secrecy and worry and in the end I don't think what we've done will make the slightest difference to our predicament,' she said, easing off her shoes. 'Excuse my feet.'

'Where did you get to?' asked Joan.

Miss Ross hesitated for a moment, remembering the long conversation she had had with Tiffany and Grace.

'I met an ex-pupil and went for tea with her. What about you two?'

'We caught up again in the square and listened to the speeches before going back to Marks for another cup of tea and a well-needed sit down,' said Joan. 'Joyce was already there, looking almost as if she had never left and then Deidre came in.'

'We never saw anything of the others, but they've returned safely now,' said Dorothy. 'Unfortunately, the same can't be said for a lot of the walking sticks. Walter was particularly upset at losing his. Apparently there was some confusion. He went for lunch with someone and this person handed over the banner to another lad to hold, but then it got passed on again and by the time Walter emerged into the square nobody knew where it was.'

'Well, we've all got back without anyone here having the slightest idea of what we've been up to,' said Joan.

'That's the problem!' said Miss Ross. 'No one knows what we've been up to! As an exercise in raising the profile of something, it could hardly have been less successful.'

'We did,' said Dorothy, 'at least all work successfully as a team. Our knitting bee has functioned well together and survived to fight another day.'

Miss Ross sighed wearily.

'I'm sorry, I'm too tired to contribute much at the moment.'

'You do look worn out, dear,' said Dorothy. 'You might not have heard the sad news about Mrs O'Reilly. Apparently she's not expected to last the night. Joyce was quite upset. She's gone up to see her.'

* * *

Mrs O'Reilly's wrinkled hand looked tiny between Joyce's chubby fingers. The two women hadn't spoken much, one feeling a little breathless and the other a little unsure what to say.

'I've enjoyed our chats,' said Mrs O'Reilly.

'And we'll enjoy many more.'

'Oh, I'm not so sure. It's a shame not to make one hundred. I was looking forward to that.'

'You'll make your birthday. I can feel it in my bones and they never let me down.'

'Good bones those.'

'They need to be! They've been fortified by gin.'

'I should last for ages yet, then.'

'I'm sure you will,' said Joyce, suddenly becoming aware that someone else was in the room. It was the priest, standing quietly just inside the doorway. 'I'll leave you together,' she said, standing up. 'I'll see you in the morning. I bet you'll be right as rain after a good night's sleep.'

'Don't let Father Connelly hear you talk about betting. He's quite a religious man, you know.'

Joyce nodded to the priest and left. He sat down in the vacated chair next to the bed.

'How are you, Mrs O'Reilly?'

'Not too good, Father.'

'I'm sorry to hear that. I came as soon as I could.'

'I know you have. It's good of you.'

He had known her for a great many years and throughout them all she had been a cantankerous, sharp-tongued, heavy-drinking member of his congregation who would have tried the patience of Saint Monica. Without doubt, she was one of his favourites. He took hold of the hand that was still lying on the bedspread.

'Would you like me to anoint you?'

She nodded. The priest stood up and removed his coat and scarf, then from a small case he brought out a glass phial containing oil of chrism, which he put carefully on a nearby table. Laying a hand on her shoulder he prayed for several minutes while she lay quietly with her eyes closed.

Using the olive oil that had been blessed by the bishop, Father Connelly anointed her head and hands. For the next hour, they talked and prayed, occasionally reminiscing and laughing as they had done on so many occasions.

'Is there anything you would like, Mrs O'Reilly?'

'Is this a last request, Father?'

'It's not a firing squad you're facing, as well you know.'

'I suppose, now that you ask . . .'

'Just name it, my old friend.'

'Let's get pissed.'

★ ★ ★

The next morning Anna was trying to relay to Ben some information she had heard from one of the night staff. However, she was struggling to explain and put a hand to her face as if too upset to continue.

'Mrs O'Reilly was found . . .'

'Dead?' asked Ben.

Anna nodded, putting her other hand on the wall for support.

'Well, she was a great age,' said the male carer sadly. He had liked this particular resident, who was always lively and good fun.

'Drunk!'

'What?'

'Dead drunk . . . and Father Connelly! He was asleep in the chair.'

It was only then that Ben realised his colleague wasn't upset, she was laughing. Eventually Anna was able to tell the story of how the night staff had bundled the priest into a taxi and tucked up Mrs O'Reilly as best they could. This morning the old woman had been complaining that she had woken up in the semi dark and found one of the male residents asleep by her bed. She really shouldn't have to put up with that sort of carry-on at her age!

★ ★ ★

As it was Easter Sunday, the local Church of Scotland minister visited the home in the afternoon to take a short service. Afterwards he stayed behind for what was one of the highlights of the year. It was the Easter bonnet parade. The culmination of weeks of secret preparations, hard work, planning and, in some cases, spying sessions, would be revealed and judged.

There was always a high turnout of visitors for the event and as each resident made their entry into the lounge relatives and friends clapped enthusiastically and made suitable comments, much to the delight of the ageing models. The variety of headgear seemed endless, with some examples equal in imagination and skill to anything encountered during Ladies Day at Ascot.

Several had knitted their displays. Dorothy had cleverly created a teapot with tiny Easter eggs coming out of the spout, while Joan had made an enormous tea cosy with a smiling face. On top of what was meant to represent a mortar board, Miss Ross had figures of schoolchildren in a classroom. The miniature teacher, wearing tweed skirt and jacket, looked decidedly familiar.

When Joyce entered, she had a large paper dinner plate on her head and it was only when she sat down that those nearby could see a 'full English' breakfast, all made out of wool. There was soon a wide assortment of chickens, flowers, rabbits and sheep balanced, sometimes precariously, on a mixture of straw hats, top hats and unidentifiable objects.

'I do object to that sort of thing,' said Miss Ross to anyone within hearing distance. The arrival of a King Charles Spaniel wearing a fez and a pair of wings had led to her outburst. 'I may not be an animal lover, but this doesn't seem right to me.'

'I passed poor Tiddles in the corridor looking particularly fed up,' said Dorothy. 'Someone had dressed him in a mixture of ribbons and foliage. He was an awful mess. I think it may have been one of our less aware friends. As no one was around I relieved him of his burden.'

Anna left to check on Beatrice, one of the home's residents who was physically very able but whose confusion was rapidly worsening. She found her sitting perfectly still in her bedroom. It took a few moments for the carer to be able to speak and with some effort she managed to keep her voice calm when she did.

'Are you all right, love?'

The old woman smiled, careful not to move any part of her body, the reason being that her favourite hen, Mabel, was sitting on top of her head.

'Is that your Easter bonnet?'

As if in response to the question, the chicken clucked loudly, appearing quite content on its unusual perch.

'I think it's tremendous. How about we take Mabel outside and give her something to eat?'

Beatrice seemed to consider this for a moment and then nodded enthusiastically, which resulted in a great deal of flapping, feathers and fun.

People continued to add to the growing crowd in the

lounge. Using cardboard, Walter had made a quite realistic chessboard and pieces, which was very impressive until the whole thing fell to the floor. His mishap resulted in a huge cheer, which he took in good part, as he went around gathering up the pawns that had come unstuck.

It was impossible to know what Angus had tried to make, as the main item had fallen off while he was coming along the corridor and he appeared wearing a flat cap and carrying something yellow under his arm that could have come straight out of a fairly unpleasant nightmare.

The biggest round of applause by far occurred when Ben pushed in a wheelchair in which Mrs O'Reilly sat, wearing a small bonnet on which there was a simple green shamrock. The clapping and cheering were so great that Ben stopped the wheelchair in the middle of the floor and the beaming occupant slowly lifted her hat, which sent the entire room into raptures.

When everyone had arrived and been served with tea and cake, the minister stood up to speak. He felt that if there was such a thing as a poisoned chalice in this world, it was judging this event and there were few things he faced with as much dread. Reputations could be made and broken in a single afternoon, which meant that rivalry was rife and memories both long and unforgiving.

'I can say without any hesitation that you have this year outdone anything I've seen before at We Care For You,' he said, which resulted in a round of polite applause, accompanied by many smiles and nods of approval.

'Choosing the best example is an extremely difficult task because it's obvious that you have all gone to great effort and dedicated a lot of thought and time to these extraordinary displays. I can honestly say I've never seen anything quite like the sight before me now.'

The minister caught Matron's eye and she didn't know how he could keep a straight face at such a tongue-in-cheek comment. She had to scratch her nose to hide her grin.

'However, it's not the amount of money we've spent or the time we've lavished on something that lies at the centre of what is truly important in our lives. It's what's in here,' he said, putting a hand to his chest.

'I'm reminded of the elderly woman in the Bible who put into the church collection box a few copper coins, what we generally refer to today as her last penny. And Jesus, standing nearby, called his disciples to him and said, "Truly I tell you, this poor widow has put more into the treasury than all the others."

'Now, I'm not implying for one minute that the winner is a poor old widow. I'm far too fearful of incurring her wrath! But I wanted to explain that the reason she has won is because what she created means so much to her in here.' Once again the minister laid a hand gently over his heart. He paused for a moment, as he had seen television presenters do in competitions and awards. 'The winner is . . . Mrs O'Reilly!'

There followed a few seconds of silence as everyone looked at the woman in the wheelchair, wearing by far the simplest bonnet amongst them, then the entire room erupted into cheering, clapping and banging anything that came to hand. It was the first time that any of them could remember seeing the Irish woman cry.

Thirteen

Monday, 28th March

Meeting Tiffany and her partner Grace has left me feeling both confused and reassured. They seemed so happy and content in each other's company, proud to proclaim their relationship to the world. It's a freedom I will never experience. I console myself in the knowledge that I have found love and with it a sense of fulfilment that has been absent throughout my life, even though I may not have realised it. So often we do not appreciate something until we no longer have it, yet it is also true that we may not appreciate what has been missing in our lives until we find it.

Fourteen

Beatrice lay in bed, studying the ceiling in the hope that it might provide a clue as to her whereabouts. She knew that this was sometimes illusive, but her location generally revealed itself after a while and it was nothing to worry about. Matron had told her not to be frightened because there was nothing that could hurt her and she had at least remembered that advice.

When the door opened a little while later, she recognised the man who entered, which was a good sign that she was definitely in the place she was meant to be.

'Do you know what day it is?' he asked.

'Tuesday?' she guessed.

'It's our forty-fifth wedding anniversary. Don't tell me you didn't remember.'

'Of course I did,' she said, and suddenly the name of her long-dead husband popped into her head. 'Harold!'

'Well, at least you've not forgotten my name. And I think we should celebrate.'

'How?' said Beatrice, sitting up in bed, totally enthralled that Harold and she were going to do something special. 'What shall we do?'

'I'll give you a hint.'

And with that Mr Forsyth let his dressing gown slip to the floor to reveal his skinny naked body with its manhood standing to attention.

'Oh, Harold!' she said, hardly believing her eyes. 'Do you think we should?'

'What's to stop us?'

Beatrice giggled and slowly lifted the duvet.

Deirdre's nosiness had been her downfall on many occasions and it was rather unfortunate for her that she passed by shortly after. The unusual noises coming from behind the door aroused her curiosity immediately. She listened for a moment to double check, then knocked and went in. With the duvet lying in the corner the two naked occupants on the bed were visible in their entirety. Beatrice didn't even notice the new arrival, while Mr Forsyth looked over without any indication of surprise or embarrassment.

'The sow,' he said panting, 'needs servicing.'

Deirdre's scream could be heard throughout the building and within moments it seemed that everyone was either in the bedroom, stuck in the doorway or crowded in the corridor. Mrs MacDonald had to help her distraught friend outside, manoeuvring past Albert who, as if to mark the occasion, had taken out his mouth organ and was playing 'Knees Up Mother Brown'. Matron ushered the spectators out of the bedroom and shut the door, leaving the still cavorting couple with Anna and Ben.

'Blimey, he's not forgotten everything then!' whispered Joan to Miss Ross as they made their way to breakfast. Joan, being one of the first to arrive, had been granted a ringside view of the performance. 'I wouldn't have thought he had it in him to keep going like that, randy old sod.'

Miss Ross was pleased to have avoided any visual aspects of the event and would have been happy to be spared the verbal description, although she knew this was unlikely.

'It's a very sad affair,' she said.

'Do you think it's been going on for a while?'

'I don't mean an affair in that sense. If this had been going on for a while, I'm sure someone would have noticed before today.'

'I suppose so. What do you think they'll do?'

'Heaven knows. I'm just glad I don't have Matron's job.'

Deirdre, not wanting to miss anything, made a miraculous recovery and arrived in the dining room not that much later than anyone else. Having been the one to make the discovery, she was able to provide an unrivalled eyewitness account.

'Oh, but I couldn't possibly tell you what I saw,' she exclaimed several times, before going on to relate in detail the terrible scene she had been forced to see, not without a few embellishments along the way. Deirdre couldn't remember the last time she had enjoyed breakfast so much.

When the carers had finally managed to prise Mr Forsyth and Beatrice apart, they got the old farmer into his dressing gown and back to his room. Later on, Ben put down mats fitted with pressure pads that set off alarms, alerting staff to movements in and out of the bedrooms. Unfortunately, even those with severe dementia always seemed to learn quickly that they should always jump over these objects and never, under any circumstances, stand on them.

* * *

Visiting times were extremely flexible, with family and friends welcome to call any point between morning and evening. They could even appear during meals, as they were often able to help feed those with dementia or other problems.

However, most people came during morning coffee or afternoon tea, meeting residents in the lounge, the conservatory or in their bedrooms. There was a small courtyard, while the garden was very pleasant to walk around or sit in when the weather was favourable.

Joan always seemed to have a stream of guests. She had four children, six grandchildren and an undetermined number of stepchildren. Many of them were regulars and she was often whisked off somewhere for a trip out or a meal at a local restaurant. There was a huge difference amongst residents in how often they had visitors. Some had none because they didn't have a single connection with anyone outside the home.

Matron always felt particularly sorry for them, although she thought it was worse for those who had families who just didn't bother to make contact. A person could end up alone in life through no fault of their own, but if no one wanted to see you, did that mean you weren't actually worth the effort?

It wasn't clear just how much Beatrice remembered or understood about the events earlier that morning, but she seemed in an excitable frame of mind. After Ben had fitted the new mat and left her alone once more in her bedroom, she went over to the telephone and dialled 999.

'Hello,' she said when the call was answered. 'This is the Matron at We Care For You. We have a serious fire, which is spreading rapidly. There are many trapped upstairs. Can you please send the fire brigade urgently?'

When assured that they were on their way, Beatrice thanked the nice lady and set off for the lounge. It was a busy morning and on the way she passed the hairdresser, who was about to start working her way through that day's list, using the small room that had been set aside for that purpose.

The Church of Scotland minister was visiting the residents he normally called on during his fortnightly trips and one of the district nurses was also somewhere in the building. They called daily, as there were always dressings and catheters to replace, ears to syringe, blood pressures to check and a host of other medical matters to be carried out. Beatrice tried to avoid the nurses, as she had a phobia of needles and reckoned it was best to be on the safe side.

In the lounge a dozen children from the nearby primary school were singing to a packed room. This was always a popular event. When the fire engine arrived in the car park, blue lights flashing and siren blaring, the singing faded away as children and adults alike moved to the windows.

'What's that?' asked Beatrice, who had remained in her chair.

'It's a fire engine, but I'm sure it's just a false alarm and nothing to be worried about,' said Dorothy, sitting nearby.

'I wonder what's brought them here.'

The children thought their visit had suddenly become extremely interesting and they watched eagerly as two firemen jumped down from the cab and rushed into the building. Moments later they appeared in the doorway to the lounge with Matron. They glanced around before leaving to check out the rest of the home. Ben went outside and returned with the remainder of the crew, who joined everyone for coffee.

'This is like Piccadilly Circus,' said Joan to Miss Ross,

both sitting in the corner, trying to stay out of the way. Joan was waiting for family to arrive and was positioned so that she could see out of the window.

To make matters worse, the three dogs that belonged to residents, along with Tiddles, whose ownership was a mystery to everyone, decided to add to the mayhem. Then the minister appeared, having gone through his list quicker than the hairdresser.

'Shoo,' said Miss Ross to a terrier by her leg. She always thought this particular animal was unpleasantly smelly. Joan gave its bottom a tap with the toe of her foot and the dog went off in search of a more friendly reception.

Joyce was in her bedroom having her weight checked by Anna. Each resident was weighed monthly in order to spot any changes that might indicate a health problem. When she stepped on to the scales, the pointer danced danger-ously around the right hand side of the display.

'You seem to have put on another two pounds.'

'I can't understand it. I've been ever so careful what I eat. Are you sure these scales are right?'

'I think we have to take it that they are.'

'Well, it's a blinking mystery.'

The conversation was one that the two women played out almost every month and it had a sense of pantomime about it. Both of them knew that Joyce ate far too much and that she wasn't going to alter her lifestyle, but they still went through the motions.

'We really do have to get your weight in hand,' said Anna.

'Absolutely. I couldn't agree more.'

'Here's something that might help,' said the carer, put-ting down a copy of the leaflet she had left the previous month. 'I'll speak to Matron about how we might best be able to move forward.'

'Thank you, I'll read that straight away. I don't know what happened to the others. They must go to the same place as pens. They always seem to disappear as well.'

A short while later the fire crew, schoolchildren and several families left around the same time, just as other visitors were arriving. The large numbers of people moving into and out of the building gave Mr Forsyth the opportunity to slip out of the front door unnoticed. He had tried unsuccessfully on many occasions but had always been thwarted by the ever-watchful staff. With his shoes and coat on, nobody suspected anything.

Joan was now deep in conversation with some of her family, so Miss Ross went for a walk in the garden with Dorothy. With the schoolchildren gone, several other residents left the lounge. Matron took Beatrice to her office for a little chat.

Mr Adams, a half bottle of whisky hidden down his trousers, set off with his Zimmer, hoping that no one would notice the unusual bulge. Angus and Walter, who had never yet been seen to speak to each other in public, went for a game of chess in the latter's bedroom, while the various animals disappeared to find new entertainment.

It was just before lunch that Mr Forsyth's absence was noted and a thorough search instigated. However, the old man was just about to be found out. Having walked into a café and ordered tea and a scone, Mr Forsyth had gone into the gentlemen's toilet only to emerge several minutes later totally naked. He had sat at his table and begun his food quite happily, acknowledging the stares of the other customers with a nod and smile.

The owner, a mature woman of commendable common sense, calmly walked over and laid a clean tea towel over the man's credentials, as if putting a napkin on someone's lap in a posh restaurant. The ex-farmer thanked her appropriately. She then put a spare tablecloth over his shoulders, tucking in the material around his body as much as possible. Before ringing the police, she decided to make one call.

'It's Margaret at the café. Have you lost one?'

Ben was despatched to collect the escapee.

Fifteen

'The piano!' cried Walter.

'I do like a good sing-song,' said Mrs Butterworth.

'We've no time for singing,' said Joan, exasperated at how easily they could become sidetracked.

'For the barricade,' explained Walter.

Building a barricade had been the topic of conversation for the last hour, at least while there had been no staff around or any resident who was a risk of giving away their secret by innocently repeating something they had over-heard. The idea this time was that the Escape Committee should lock themselves in the lounge.

There had been a long-winded debate about renaming the group if they were going to blockade themselves into a building, but the argument had fizzled out when Miss Ross had lost her temper with them all. Walter's suggestion dragged them from their sullen silence of hurt feelings at being treated like badly behaved children.

'But it's so heavy,' said Deirdre.

'That's generally the requirement!'

'Then how will we move it?'

'We simply take off the clips on the wheels, push it into position, then put the clips back on.'

'Enemy ahead!' shouted Angus, who was on watch duty by the door.

The effect of his warning was dramatic, obviously making allowances for speed, as people dispersed. Angus joined Walter at the chessboard, while Joan and Miss Ross retrieved the needles and wool on their seats and quickly resumed activity. Dorothy hadn't stopped knitting, so simply continued. Everyone else gave the realistic impression of being asleep, apart from Deirdre, who picked up a newspaper, and Joyce, who had spotted a couple of Rich Tea biscuits on a nearby table.

Moments later Anna poked her head into the room. Miss Ross nodded, Walter gave a little wave of acknowledgement and Dorothy smiled with such innocence that Saint Peter himself wouldn't have suspected the devious plotting that had been going on only minutes earlier. The carer smiled back and, seeing nothing for her to do, left.

'Goodness, this is painfully slow work,' complained Joan, putting down her needles.

Angus stood up and crept to the door, as if he was on stage in a pantomime. Walter resisted the urge to shout out, 'He's behind you!'

'All clear,' whispered Angus.

Everyone gathered around again, apart from one.

'It's all right, Mrs Butterworth,' said Joyce, looking over at the figure in the nearby armchair. 'You don't have to pretend any more.'

'For goodness sake!' said Miss Ross. 'Someone wake her up. The piano is perfect for blocking the internal door.'

Dorothy held up her hand, exactly the way she had been taught at school more than seventy years earlier.

'Yes?'

'If we do that, we won't have any access whatsoever to the facilities.'

There was a gasp of horror from the group that could hardly have been worse had World War Three just been announced.

'I've thought of that. We'll block the door further along the corridor, so we'll be able to use the toilet just outside the lounge.'

'There's only the one, though.'

'We won't get through this without some hardship,' said Joan.

'Maybe we can set up a rota,' offered Mrs MacDonald.

'A rota . . . oh dear.'

'What about the doors leading into the garden?' pointed out Deirdre. 'There'll be no way of blocking those. They open outwards. The staff will simply walk in and all this planning and effort will have been for nothing.'

Was the woman ever positive about anything?

The group fell silent, apart from the clicking of Dorothy's needles. It was Walter who came up with a possible solution.

'Superglue.'

They all looked at him, then at the patio doors, as if slightly surprised to see either.

'It will only work if we lock them first,' said Miss Ross.

'Yes,' agreed Walter.

'Which means,' added Joan, 'we will have to get hold of a key.'

The next five minutes were taken up writing out a list of all the people they knew who carried the relevant key and where the spares were kept. The conversation then took on a wider context.

'We'll need supplies,' said Deirdre.

'Like food,' said Joyce.

'We'll have access to water so can make as much tea and coffee as people want,' said Joan.

'Not too much, I hope,' muttered Dorothy.

'They might turn off the water and electricity.'

'Good God, Deirdre, we're not terrorists!' cried Walter. 'They're hardly going to starve us out or send in armed police for a group of care home residents with an average age of eighty.'

'I was just saying. No need to be so shirty.'

'The success of this whole exercise,' said Miss Ross, trying to restore order, 'lies in getting the media to the home before the staff have a chance to enter.'

'What do you mean?' asked Angus, who was following the conversation from his lookout post.

'If we barricade ourselves into the lounge but no one outside knows, then we'll achieve nothing. Eventually the staff will gain entry one way or another. But if we can get the media here, then we'll have the upper hand. The new owners wouldn't dare use force to enter if there are television cameras and reporters monitoring everything they do and it will give us the chance to put forward our case against the rise in fees.'

There were murmurs of agreement and nods at the suggestion.

'Could we get that nice Craig Anderson to come along?' asked Dorothy. 'I'd be ever so chuffed to be interviewed by him.'

'Or that young girl who does the six o'clock news, the one on the *Antiques Roadshow*,' said Mrs MacDonald. 'She's always pleasant. I could show her my grandmother's watch. I'm sure it's quite valuable.'

'We can't dictate who'll come,' said Miss Ross. 'We need to form subcommittees.' However, before she could say anything further, Angus called out, 'Enemy ahead!'

* * *

It took more than a week of secret conversations, scribbled messages hidden in knitting patterns and snatched meetings of the Escape Committee for Miss Ross and Joan, now officially the two in charge, to be satisfied with the arrangements.

Every member had been given a specific task. Walter was to devise a way of 'borrowing' a key to lock the patio doors, while Angus had to obtain a sufficient quantity of the correct type of glue to seal them. Deirdre and Mrs MacDonald were to gather food and make sure that the little fridge in the lounge was well stocked. Joyce had to smuggle in extra blankets, while each of the others had lists of small items to collect: tea bags, coffee, loo rolls . . .

'We can't include anyone who is not fully in charge of their faculties,' said Miss Ross. They were once again in the lounge, Angus keeping lookout at the door.

'What?' asked Mrs MacDonald.

'Faculties,' she repeated a little louder. 'Everyone has to have them.'

'I don't think I've had one. When were they given out?'

'Heaven help us,' whispered Joan.

'We can't include any resident who is too frail or who doesn't fully understand what is happening, otherwise we're effectively kidnapping them, which would give the owners an excuse to break in using force.'

'I think Matron is going to be ever so cross if we cause

damage,' said Dorothy. 'We might all get a bill to put things right.'

'We're committed now,' continued Miss Ross.

'Committed!' cried Mrs MacDonald in horror.

'Oh, for goodness sake! Anyone who doesn't want to go through with this can pull out. No one will be thought any the less for doing so. It's a very serious thing we're intending.'

Miss Ross surveyed the group, but nobody flinched at her gaze. She was pleased. Their bodies might be a collection of repairs, spare parts and bits that no longer worked efficiently, or in some cases not at all, but there remained a steely determination to fight against a common injustice.

'Right, then. We just have to start putting our plans into action.'

Sixteen

For several days, a strange tension hung in the corridors alongside the smells of cooking, disinfectant and flowers. The staff sensed an underlying excitement but couldn't pin anything down to an individual or event. Matron was like a bloodhound, sniffing around for leads, enquiring more than usual if everything was 'all right'. She got nowhere, which increased her curiosity to bursting point.

Matron didn't miss the odd little nods and knowing smiles that some people gave each other while they were going around. Deirdre could hardly look her in the eye, and one morning Mrs MacDonald had actually turned around and scuttled off in the opposite direction when she had seen her coming. Yesterday, Angus had walked past carrying a knitting pattern! His sudden interest in making items out of wool was definitely strange. She hadn't run the care home for all these years not to spot when there was something going on.

As the plans progressed it became clear that the committee would need help from other residents and these were gradually made aware of the plot, apart from those too confused to understand. Everyone wanted to play a part, no matter how small, and it took quite a while to allocate the various tasks in sufficient detail so that people knew exactly what was required.

Then the morning was upon them. Miss Ross had barely slept, pacing around her room most of the night in her slippers and dressing gown. In the dim glow of the bedside lamp the whole idea had appeared completely mad. How had she become not just involved but the ringleader of such a scheme against authority, against so much that she stood for?

But it wasn't everything, because she believed in justice, fair play, friendship and helping others, as well as standing up to bureaucratic bullies. There was one other reason for making the protest, a reason which no one would ever know. And as for the 'knitting bee', they were a bit like the POWs in *The Great Escape*. Metaphorically, at least, their forged papers were all stamped with the same date. It was now or never.

Breakfast seemed to drag out desperately slowly and as Miss Ross looked around the dining room she caught nervous glances from the others. Walter and Angus, now openly speaking in public, were making forced conversation about something on television the previous night. Meg and Peg looked extremely concerned, while Stella appeared even more stern than usual and Mrs Butterworth knocked over a glass of orange juice as well as a cup of tea.

Joyce was the only one acting normally, tucking into her usual selection of food as if the day was set to be like any other. Opposite her Joan had a mischievous expression, which was almost as unnerving as those who appeared terrified. Deirdre and Mrs MacDonald had been too scared to leave their bedrooms and Miss Ross cursed them for such unnatural behaviour, which could attract the attention of staff. She doubted that either would stand up to any sort of questioning.

Eventually people started to leave and wander about. That morning had been chosen because there were no classes in the lounge. During the early stages of the plan there had been various discussions about how to overpower the OTAGO teacher or the old gentleman who played the accordion, but the suggestions had bordered on the absolutely ridiculous until Miss Ross pointed out that it would be easier to simply pick a morning when there was no activity.

By ten o'clock more than half of the committee were in the lounge. Angus, his pockets bulging, sat at the chessboard as if waiting for Walter. Dorothy, Joan and Miss Ross were knitting while others pretended to sleep, chat or read. The tension was unbearable and indigestion was almost stopping Miss Ross from thinking clearly.

Anna had tucked up Albert in an armchair and was still chatting to him at quarter past with no sign of leaving. Joyce ate another digestive biscuit. Dorothy put down her knitting and went to the toilet. Joan got up and left the room.

God, this is desperate.

Walter had walked past the office three times and he doubted he could do it again without looking like the criminal that he felt inside. The spare key for the patio door hung with several others on a wall by the filing cabinet, but Matron had been talking on the telephone without a break for almost twenty minutes. Joan walked casually up to him.

'What's the delay?' she hissed.

'Matron's still on the phone.'

'We've got less than fifteen minutes before the diversions start!'

'I know,' said Walter miserably. 'What are we going to do?'

As if the word 'diversions' was a magic spell, Mrs Campbell materialised from around the corner, steering her Zimmer for the toilet along the corridor. She slowed down, which was almost the same as stopping. Joan answered her enquiring glance with a tiny nod, imperceptible if you weren't seeking it, and Mrs Campbell increased her pace to a level that, for her, must have felt like breaking the sound barrier. Walter hoped the old woman didn't reach such a velocity that bits of her started to fly off. Then the first of the alarms sounded.

'Christ, that's too early,' said Joan.

In the lounge, everyone, except Anna, stopped what they were doing and stared at Miss Ross.

It all has to happen now. Don't wait for ten-thirty. Do it now.

On the upstairs landing, Mr Sutherland was helped onto the floor by a couple of other residents. As soon as he was lying in a position that gave the appearance of him having collapsed, they hurried off in different directions to fetch members of staff.

A similar ploy was being carried out in the dining room, where Betty Wilson, reliving with delight the many years spent enjoying amateur dramatics (her Cleopatra was apparently still talked about), was now sprawled half underneath a table. A couple of chairs had been positioned carefully on their sides for extra effect.

Her accomplice, rather carried away in the heat of the moment, pushed a pile of plates off the table, which resulted in such an almighty crash that Betty cried out in surprise before remembering that she was meant to be unconscious.

Mrs Campbell steered herself into the allocated toilet, where she locked the door and manoeuvred herself onto the seat. She sat looking at the thin red cord hanging from the ceiling. Not for the first time over the last few days Mrs Campbell marvelled at how rebellious she was about to be, how terribly naughty.

Slowly, she reached out her hand. The alarm joined bells ringing outside almost every toilet in the building, as well as several external doors. The loud crash from the dining room had Matron rushing out of her office and down the corridor.

'Go on, Walter,' cried Joan before heading off in the opposite direction.

Several people in the lounge had stood up in response to the various noises. Anna left to investigate what was going on. Joan rushed in and for a moment the Escape Committee looked at each other, stunned into inaction. Joyce was the first to react.

'Come on, come on, we can't stop now!'

Tubes of superglue emerged from various pockets about Angus's body and he thrust them all at Miss Ross before getting down on the floor by the piano. Walter burst in, out of breath and waving a key as if it was a winning lottery ticket.

'I've got it!'

'I can't undo these clips,' called Angus.

Joan and Miss Ross led their team to the patio doors, while the two men struggled to free the wheels of the piano. Dorothy walked slowly over, still clutching her knitting.

'I always used to find it's more effective to kick the clip with your foot,' she offered. Seconds later the piano was mobile.

'This is heavier than I thought,' said Angus. 'We need help here!'

Joyce led the remaining committee members, who joined Dorothy and the two men. They each took hold of or leant against part of the piano and slowly the instrument was shoved bit by bit across the carpet and into the corridor.

The quiet care home, where lives rumbled along week after week with nothing too exciting happening, was suddenly a place echoing with noise and frantic confusion. Shouts and running feet could be heard in other parts of the building, while several of the alarms continued to ring. The atmosphere was electric and they all felt themselves being swept up in the drama that was unfolding, the drama that they themselves had put in motion.

'Where are Deirdre and Mrs MacDonald? Dorothy! Mind what you're doing with those needles.'

'Sorry, Walter.'

'They're meant to be bringing the food,' said Angus. Everyone was panting and people had to raise their voices to be heard. 'We'll have to block the doors, even if they're not here.'

'Wait! Wait!' cried Joan, running down the corridor after them.

'We can't,' shouted Walter. 'There's no time.'

'Albert's still in the armchair.'

They looked at each other in horror, as the piano slowed to a halt.

'Damn, damn!' cried Walter, heading back to the room. 'We've got to get him out.'

Albert looked up in surprise as the two men took an arm each and tried to lift him out of his chair.

'Is it supper time? I can hear the gong.'

'That's right, mate,' said Walter. 'You don't want to be late. It's your favourite.'

'Haggis! Lovely. I knew a girl once called Haggis.'

'Please try to stand,' said Angus.

The male carers lifted and moved residents as if they were almost weightless, but it was so much more difficult now that they were attempting it and particularly with their 'target' deciding not to help. Joan appeared, immediately assessing what had to be done. She stood in front of Albert and took hold of the lapels on his jacket.

'On three,' she said. 'One . . . two . . . three!'

The old man was hauled to his feet.

'Come on, you don't want to keep a tasty girl like Haggis waiting,' said Walter.

'Ah, Haggis,' he said, letting himself be manhandled by the three accomplices. 'Haggis has a sister, you know.' They squeezed past the piano and committee members, who were standing around unsure what to do. 'She's a Swede. Hee, hee, hee.' Albert, still laughing, was deposited safely on a chair beyond the door, just as Deirdre and Mrs MacDonald arrived, each struggling to balance several large tins.

'Where have you been?' said Walter.

'It's madness everywhere,' said Deirdre. 'There are people running and shouting. We had to be so careful.'

'Come on, there's not a moment to lose,' said Joan.

Once they were on the correct side of the doors, the piano was pushed up to them and the clips put back on the wheels. They stepped back to examine what they had achieved. The instrument suddenly looked far too insignificant.

'This is not enough,' said Joan.

Moments later there was a human chain passing items along the corridor. Lamps, small tables, wooden chairs, the piano stool – all ended up on top of or around the piano. To finish, they dragged three armchairs and put them side by side across the corridor, the backs tightly up against their makeshift barricade.

Then the last of the alarms stopped and a silence descended upon the building such as none of them had ever known.

Seventeen

Once everyone had gathered again, they stared at each other in utter disbelief. They had done it! Their crazy plan had worked and there was a collective feeling of achievement and excitement they hadn't known in years.

Some of them might still be gasping for breath and leaning on furniture to stay upright, but they had gained a feeling of power over their lives that they had not believed was now possible. The only casualty was Mrs Butterworth, who had a tube of glue stuck firmly to one hand. It was Dorothy who stirred Miss Ross into action.

'Well, what do we do now?'

'Angus, keep watch on the barricade. Deirdre, you and Mrs MacDonald check that all the windows are closed and locked. Joyce, can you shut all the blinds?'

'The blinds?'

'Let's keep the staff guessing as to what's going on. Dorothy . . .'

'Oh, I was just . . .'

'All right. Perhaps Peg . . .'

'I'm Meg,' said the woman.

'Sorry,' continued Miss Ross, not entirely sure she wasn't

being misled. 'Perhaps you and your sister could make everyone a cup of tea? Joan, you've got your list and mobile?'

Her friend nodded, retrieving both items from a pocket. Miss Ross took a big breath then produced her own mobile, along with a sheet of paper.

'Right, let's get ringing.'

The two women found the quietest spots they could. Joan was the first to get through.

'I need to speak to the news desk,' she said. 'It's urgent.'

★ ★ ★

Angus and Walter stood side by side in front of the barricade, straining to hear any movement on the other side of the doors, the former looking even more dishevelled by the neat figure of Walter, today wearing his mauve-red blazer and tie.

'I can't believe we're actually doing this,' said Angus.

'It makes a difference to listening to that bloke play the same five tunes each week on his bloody accordion. I didn't believe that I could ever wish myself to have dementia, but when he strikes up "Mairi's Wedding" . . .'

'I don't know what we've done to upset him so much.'

'Maybe he just doesn't like old people.'

The building had a strange stillness about it and they stood for several moments without speaking.

'It's odd how alone it feels standing here, waiting for the storm and wondering what will happen when it hits. I guess this is a good opportunity for me to apologise, Angus. I know saying sorry is hardly sufficient for what happened. It's way too little and far too late.'

'It was a long time ago. Now my Norma's gone and your Moira. I was very sorry to hear about her death.'

'Thank you. Likewise . . . with your Norma . . . extremely sorry. I hadn't realised she had passed away until you arrived at the home. You never had children?'

'No.'

'Were you able to forgive?'

'I never forgot, but I forgave her for what happened. What about your Moira?' asked Angus.

'It was very difficult for a while, as I'm sure it was for you. I don't think she ever forgot either, but we didn't speak about it again, not after the initial rows. Then Becky was born and, well . . . life moved on. Moira and I were meant to be together and I tried to be a good husband, the best I could possibly be.'

The two men stood in silence for a while. Watching the barricade meant that they didn't have to look at each other, which made talking easier.

'I betrayed Moira and your friendship,' said Walter. 'Even when I was . . . with Norma, I just kept thinking how wrong it all was. I don't believe I could forgive the way you have.'

'Look at us. Two old farts in a care home. What am I meant to do, call you out for claymores at dawn? When I walked into the dining room that first day and saw you sitting there, all I could manage was to chuck bread rolls at you. How pathetic is that?'

'You've shown great dignity, Angus.'

'Dignity!'

'Yes. You always did. It's one of the things I admired about you.'

Through the crack between the doors they could just make out figures further along the corridor.

'Did you see that?' said Angus.

'The storm is about to break.'

'This is it, then.'

'I don't think they'll be coming at us with muskets.'

'Well, you never know . . . what with the cutbacks and everything.'

Their banter ceased as one of the doors was pushed. It moved only a fraction before being stopped by the piano. They could hear male voices, then there was a slight pause before both doors were suddenly shoved with such a determined force that the whole barricade started juddering along the floor.

'Hell, this isn't going to keep them out!' cried Walter, learning against an armchair to add his meagre weight.

Angus rushed back into the lounge.

'To the barricade! To the barricade!'

For that moment – that one glorious moment, which none of them would ever forget, would never afterwards quite believe happened – they were young again. Arthritis, wobbly legs and hip repairs were all forgotten, along with discarded sticks and walking aids, as they rushed forward in a great surge that sent tea cups, saucers and a plate of bourbon biscuits flying across the carpet.

Angus had to flatten himself against the wall, while Walter was knocked into an armchair. Before he could regain his wits someone sat on top of him. People wedged themselves into seats, while others sat on knees or perched on the arms of chairs. In an instant they created a solid wall of determined humanity. That barricade wasn't going to move a single millimetre.

'I do apologise, Walter. There wasn't really time to ask if I could sit on your knee. You must think me very forward.'

'Please don't give it another thought, Dorothy. It's my pleasure, though you could perhaps be careful with your needles.'

'I am rather keen to finish this.'

'There's no point in letting a small matter like a siege get in the way of your knitting.'

Dorothy smiled and continued with the large red scarf, although the feeling of his thighs against her bottom was a bit off-putting.

Angus didn't know whether to laugh or cry. There they all were, from seventy to infinity, piled on top of each other in what had to be one of the most ridiculous, and simply marvellous, sights he had ever seen.

Joyce had Peg and Meg each balanced on one of her knees, as though they were children and she was Father Christmas. Mrs Butterworth now had both hands stuck to the tube of glue and looked as though she was praying – and maybe she was. Then there was Dorothy, seemingly oblivious to the situation, needles flashing so fast you couldn't follow the patterns they made in the air, while Walter watched on nervously.

When it was obvious that the barricade was not going to move any further and they all started cheering and clapping (Mrs Butterworth stamping her feet), Angus couldn't prevent the tears that leapt from his eyes. He was enveloped by a feeling of such pride that in the end he had to take out his hanky and blow his nose quite loudly.

In a corner of the lounge, Joan was speaking to someone from *The Sun*.

'I can hear cheering,' said the reporter.

'Get used to that noise, young man. In fact, you can tell your readers to get used to it. It's the sound of people who are no longer willing to be ignored and forgotten, who will once more stand up and be heard by a society that has become deaf to their needs!'

When Miss Ross finished her call, she walked over to the

patio doors, as she could see figures moving outside. She peered around a blind and looked straight into the worried face of Matron. A few feet away, Hamish was trying to move the handle on the door, but this had been wedged firmly with a chair before being glued and was unlikely to ever move again. Miss Ross pulled up a nearby blind and opened a small window at the top.

'What on earth is going on?' shouted Matron, whose usual calm professionalism had been badly shaken by the morning's events.

'Sorry for the inconvenience. We're protesting against the rise in the care home fees.'

'The fees? A protest! You can't.'

'But we are. We're doing it. We've barricaded ourselves into the lounge and won't come out until the fees have been reduced.'

'I have no control over such things.'

'I appreciate that, so I assume you will have to contact the new owners.'

'Please think what you're doing. You have old, vulnerable and frail people in there who need regular medication and professional assistance.'

'We are the most able-bodied of the residents and everyone here has volunteered. They all have their full faculties, although we do have one urgent request.'

'Oh my goodness, what is it?'

'Could you please obtain something to release Mrs Butterworth from the tube of glue she's got stuck to?'

'Glue?'

'Here,' said Miss Ross reaching up to the open window, 'is a spare tube so that you can get the right solution.'

'I've never known anything like it. There will be serious repercussions.'

'I certainly hope so. We haven't done all of this not to make a change.'

'We might have to force an entry. There will be damage that will have to be paid for and residents may well be upset.'

'I don't think anyone will be doing anything to cause upset, not now.' Miss Ross had seen what Matron hadn't yet spotted, the arrival of a BBC van. 'I would suggest that you contact the owners and pass this responsibility on to someone else.'

The other woman turned around and gave a little cry of alarm when she saw a TV crew disembarking in the car park. Miss Ross felt quite sorry. After all, it wasn't her fault that the fees had gone up and now she was faced with a desperate situation that was certain to get worse. Matron rushed off and Hamish, his face beetroot with exertion and frustration, gave up trying the door.

* * *

By lunchtime the grounds were awash with newspaper and radio journalists, as well as TV crews, several police and an ambulance. There was even a film crew from China, which had been making a documentary about the Loch Ness monster and had hurried north when word had reached them about a group of rioting old-age pensioners. The elderly viewers back in China would be far more interested in this human-interest story than anything about a legendary dragon.

The staff had long since given up trying to push open the doors in the corridor and so everyone had returned to the lounge, where a strange calm had descended. Chairs had been turned around to face the car park and the blinds pulled up so that people could watch the activity outside. Walter couldn't remember when the television had last been turned off and was being so resolutely ignored.

Joan and Joyce had cleared away the knocked-over cups and made a fresh brew, while Mrs Butterworth had been unstuck, so no longer appeared to be in a permanent state of religious fervour. People sat drinking tea and eating the cakes that Deirdre and Mrs MacDonald had smuggled out of the kitchen.

It was the most interesting day any of them could remember. They had had far more aerobic exercise, mental stimulus and fun than all the classes and group activities of the whole of the last year put together.

'Isn't it exciting?' said Dorothy. 'Do you think we'll be on television?'

'Looking at that crowd, we'll probably be the main news item,' said Joan.

'I wonder if my Andrew will see it?'

'That's Craig Anderson, isn't it?' cried Joyce.

This revelation resulted in everyone moving to the windows to get a better view of someone they felt they knew, although had never met.

'He seems much smaller in real life,' said one of the sisters.

'Everyone appears smaller than they do on television,' announced Angus.

'Do they?' said the other sister. 'How very odd.'

'It's something to do with the tubes,' said Joyce.

'I could do with a bit more to eat than cake,' said Walter.

Deirdre immediately took this as an attack on her efforts to provide food supplies.

'What did you think I was going to bring, a selection of hot meals on a trolley?'

'Don't get your knickers in a twist.'

'Tell them to leave your knickers alone,' said Mrs Mac-Donald.

Walter and Angus started giggling. Since the success of the blockade they had been like naughty schoolchildren, although the men weren't any worse than many of the women in this respect. Looking at the others, Miss Ross hardly recognised them as the same stooping figures who'd been shuffling along the corridor only the previous week, complaining about their long list of ailments, poorly fitting teeth and squealing hearing aids.

'Still,' said Joyce longingly, 'look at that catering van. You can almost smell the cooking from here.'

There was a moment of silence as everyone's attention focused on the extremely well-stocked van. A queue had formed not far from where a representative of the care home owners was being interviewed by someone from the local radio station.

'This is all just a little misunderstanding that will soon be cleared up,' said the man. 'There's really no need for all this fuss. No need at all.'

The queue to interview him was even longer than the one for food. It was the best 'human' story to emerge for ages and the reporter was keen to give him a grilling.

'You say this is a little misunderstanding, but surely it's unprecedented for a group of elderly UK residents to barricade themselves into a building. This is a major incident. They must have been driven to extreme levels of anguish to have reacted in this way.'

'We're here to listen to their needs and sort out any problems . . .'

'But what about the fees? Haven't these recently been increased significantly? And wasn't this done without any consultation? Isn't this what the protest is all about?'

'Well, of course . . . all such establishments are facing rises in their costs.'

'So do you think we can expect to see people in other care homes protesting in this manner?'

'Others?'

'Are we at the start of a revolution amongst the elderly of this country?'

'A revolution!'

'Do you believe what's happening here will be the catalyst for pensioner riots similar to the Poll Tax Riots of 1990?'

'Oh God, no!'

The man looked around, searching for an escape, for anything that would give him an excuse not to be where he stood. He was saved, at least temporarily, by the arrival of Matron, carrying a sheet of paper. Unfortunately, in his agitation her name completely escaped him.

'This is the manager of the care home. I'm sure she will give us an update on the unfortunate situation that has occurred while I wasn't here.'

Matron glared at the man before speaking into the microphone that was being held out in front of her.

'I have a list of demands from the residents,' she said, hesitating before unfolding the sheet and adjusting her glasses. 'They want ten bacon rolls, four brown and six white, plus two white rolls with sausages. No seeds on the rolls and plenty of brown sauce.'

* * *

'Ahhh . . .' sighed Walter contentedly. 'Why does this bacon taste so much better than anything we usually get?'

96

No one could answer, though they all agreed that it *did* taste so much better.

'Maybe because it's free?' offered Joyce.

'It was nice of them to give us our lunch,' said Dorothy.

'What now?' asked Joan.

The question was directed at Miss Ross. She had been dreading this, but it could no longer be avoided. They had done well. The barricade had held, the media were outside and now it was down to her to present their case. She dabbed her lips with the paper napkin provided by the catering van.

The care home representative was seething, but he could hardly prevent someone from speaking to the media, even if they were all on private land. It would have appeared as though the 'service users' were prisoners if he had forbidden the press. So, after Miss Ross had announced that she wanted to make a statement, a small forest of microphones had been set up on stands outside a lounge window that opened at waist height, which allowed for a more dignified delivery of her speech.

Eighteen

'This is the six o'clock news ...'

They had moved their chairs and were gathered around the television. The novelty of watching all the different people going about outside, and in turn being constantly on display, had worn off and the blinds were once more closed.

'A group of elderly residents in a Highland care home have barricaded themselves into the building in protest at an increase in fees ...'

'Who's she calling elderly?' said Joyce.

They had to listen to the highlights of several news items before coming back to a report from the BBC journalist who had been in the car park for most of the day.

'There's our home!' cried several voices together, as a television camera panned across the front of the building before stopping at a reporter standing on the lawn.

'Around a dozen elderly residents ...'

'Now he's doing it!'

'Shhh.'

'... have barricaded themselves into a Highland care home in protest at a recent rise in residential fees. Staff were caught

completely unawares by the unprecedented action, which involved other residents setting off alarms and pretending to have collapsed in various parts of the building, while those in the lounge blocked an internal door and sealed the patio doors with superglue. Edith Ross, a spokesperson for the group, which has been in the lounge since this morning, gave a statement to reporters.'

'There you are!' said Dorothy. 'You look quite regal, a bit like the Queen on her balcony.'

'*We have not undertaken such drastic action without giving considerable thought to the consequences. We are making this protest to bring to the attention of the wider world the problems facing people in care homes where fees are being increased to levels that cannot be met, where hard-working, honest people are being forced to move from what they have come to think of as home, and at a time in their lives when they are most vulnerable.*

'*It is happening not just here but throughout the country. Grandparents and parents, those who have helped to make Great Britain what it is today, are being treated disgracefully by politicians and businesses. We are not assets to be squeezed dry and discarded when the savings have gone, to be deposited in small, dark rooms until it's time to be taken away by Mr Dunn ... or another undertaker ...'*

Her speech was full of passion and anger, and the Escape Committee burst into applause when she finished. Her face on the screen blinked back at them in surprise, as she was lit up by dozens of flashes. The BBC reporter was the first to ask a question.

'*How long do you think you can last out?'*

'*As long as it takes, young man!'*

With that, Miss Ross shut the window and closed the blind. The journalist completed his report before handing back to the studio and an item about a dispute surrounding the proposed colour of a Town Hall's windows. Walter turned off the television.

'I wanted to see the weather forecast,' said Deirdre.

'Does it matter?' he said. 'Were you planning on going somewhere?'

She glowered but didn't reply. They all sat in silence for a while until Mrs MacDonald, not generally an instigator of conversation, spoke.

'Maybe it was because of the pig.'

Everyone turned in her direction and even Deirdre seemed to be completely taken aback by the comment.

'The pig?' she asked.

'Yes . . . why the bacon tasted so much nicer this morning. It's because of the type of breed.'

Nobody quite knew what to say until Walter, feeling increasingly mischievous, broke the silence.

'I reckon it's because the pig was happy.'

'Happy?' repeated Mrs MacDonald, bewildered at such information.

'Oh, yes,' chipped in Angus quickly. 'I've read that can have a huge effect. If an animal has had a pleasant life, then the meat tastes completely different to one that has been miserable.'

'I didn't know that.'

'It stands to reason,' said Walter, continuing the windup. 'Next time you're in town, Mrs MacDonald, you call at the butcher's shop and I bet he'll tell you that he gets a certificate with every carcass, confirming that the beast was smiling right up to the end.'

'Boys,' said Miss Ross. She spoke quietly yet her voice, finely honed during decades of teaching, carried an authority that few would oppose. She didn't mind some leg-pulling, but she wasn't prepared to let them confuse Mrs MacDonald to the point where she actually would call into the butcher's. The two men sat grinning at each other, like naughty schoolboys who knew they weren't going to get into any serious trouble for their misdeeds.

'Maybe the bacon tasted so good,' said Dorothy, clicking away in her armchair, 'because *we* were happy.'

Miss Ross shook her head at how these gems could come from someone who so often seemed not to understand at all what was going on around her. The conversation got Joyce thinking about food. In fairness, most subjects did.

'I guess we should do something about an evening meal,' she said.

'What I wouldn't give for an old-fashioned fish supper,' said Angus.

'With proper mushy peas,' added Walter.

'Wrapped in newspaper, with lots of salt and vinegar,' said Joyce wistfully. 'What you get today in those plastic dishes just isn't the same. It's another example of the dumbing down that has gone on in society.'

'It's all about health and safety,' said Walter.

'Health and safety?' queried Dorothy. 'When did a fish supper do anyone any harm?'

'It's the ink off the newspaper,' said Walter. 'They reckon it's bad for you, although I never heard of it harming anyone.'

'There'll be a regulation somewhere preventing it,' said Angus.

'Well, I think it's a silly regulation and if we want a traditional fish supper, then we should get it,' said Dorothy.

'Hear, hear,' shouted several voices.

'Goodness me, at our age a tiny bit of ink isn't going to make any difference,' continued Dorothy.

Ten minutes later Joan was talking over the telephone to the local fish and chip shop.

'We'll have to pay you when you deliver the order. We're at the care home.'

'The care home!' said the man, suddenly animated. 'Are you the ones barricaded in the building?'

'Yes, we are.'

'What you're doing is marvellous. Marvellous! Wait until I tell my wife, Doreen. She'll be so excited. I wouldn't dream of charging you. I'll deliver them myself as soon as they're ready. I'll send Doreen to the newsagent's the moment I put down the phone. Are there any particular newspapers you would like?'

Half an hour later the lounge was filled with the smell of fried fish, chips and vinegar. The order included a couple of loaves of bread, butter and bottles of sauce. The excitement of earlier in the day was replaced with a feeling of general contentment as people tucked into their meals.

'I can't remember when I last had one of these,' said Joyce, munching her way through an enormous chip butty.

'I can't remember ever eating so much,' said Dorothy, showing no signs of slowing down. 'What did that nice man call these?'

'Moby Dicks,' said Joyce, pushing a chip back into her mouth.

'Well, I've certainly never had such a big one.'

'As the actress said to the bishop,' whispered Joan, which set Walter and Angus off giggling again.

'There's nothing wrong with my hearing.'

'Sorry, love. You enjoy your Moby Dick.'

'I will, don't you worry.'

'It's amazing how building a barricade gives you an appetite,' said Walter. 'Maybe we should make one every day, then Matron can cancel the classes – like that bloke with the accordion.'

'It could go national,' added Angus. 'Build a barricade for a better life.'

'Barricades – the building blocks for healthy bones,' said Walter.

'What a day it's been,' said Joan.

'We'll certainly not forget it,' added Angus. 'Pass the salt, please, Joyce.'

'I don't think anyone here will forget it,' added Miss Ross.

There had been a stand-off with the owner's representative and a more senior manager was due to arrive the following morning. A truce had been declared and once it was clear the committee were determined to stay overnight, Matron and her staff had spent nearly an hour collecting items from bedrooms and passing them through the window.

Holders for false teeth, dressing gowns and slippers, books, glasses, a hearing aid battery . . . the list had seemed endless, and it wasn't long before there was some good-humoured banter going on between the carers and the residents.

'Aren't you going to finish those chips, Deirdre?' asked Joyce, deftly moving the newspaper containing the unfinished supper across to her own knee before the other woman could answer.

'What are we going to do now?' asked Mrs MacDonald.

There was a silence, before Walter replied. 'Do you know . . . we can do exactly whatever we want?'

'Well, what do we want?' asked Deirdre, watching with amazement at how quickly her uneaten chips were disappearing.

'How about a dance?' said Joan.

'How about a drink?' added Angus.

'Why don't we have a party?' suggested Joyce.

'Angus,' said Walter, 'would you be kind enough to help me compile the drinks order?'

'Babycham,' said Meg and Peg together, which at least solved the problem of which one wanted what.

'Mine's a port and lemon!' shouted Joyce.

'Stout.'

'Hey, there's no need for that sort of comment, Dorothy. I'm just big-boned.'

Everyone waited for Dorothy to take the bait. It took quite a few moments.

'Goodness me. No, Joyce. I meant that stout was the drink I wanted.'

Joyce hung on for as long as she could before doubling over in laughter, her chins vying with each other to wobble the most.

'Oh, you're pulling my leg! You are awful.'

'But I like you,' cried Joyce, slapping her thigh with delight and sending several chips onto the floor, one going down the inside of her slipper.

'Hey, never mind a chip butty, you've got a chip footy,' said Walter.

'Pity to waste it,' she said, stretching down and only just managing to retrieve the chip, which she popped into her mouth.

There was an instant of disbelief before everyone burst out laughing and soon several of them were trying to outdo each other with jokes and stories, while so many people shouted out their drinks orders that Walter couldn't write them down fast enough.

'Hold on, hold on,' he cried. 'Was that Martini shaken or stirred?'

'I'll give Matron a ring and get a CD player sent around,' said Joan, but as no one appeared to hear above the surrounding din, she shouted, 'WHAT MUSIC DO WE WANT?' which set them all off down another avenue of debate.

Glenn Miller won the day, and while one of the night staff organised a selection of the required CDs from a friend who lived nearby, Walter called the local pub, which was quick to deliver free of charge two boxes of assorted bottles, cans and packets of crisps, plus a wide selection of glasses.

Word of what the residents were doing had spread and they had gained a lot of local sympathy and admiration. Angus set up a bar on one of the tables, while Walter helped to move chairs and furniture to create a space for dancing.

When they all had their correct drinks, Walter stood up and raised his glass.

'To the Escape Committee!'

There was a chorus of 'To the Escape Committee!' before Joan jumped up and said, 'To Miss Ross!'

There were so many toasts in quick succession that everyone's glasses soon had to be refilled and then refilled again. It seemed as though each minute that passed eliminated another year from their age and an hour later anyone listening outside would have been forgiven for thinking the lounge contained a group of boisterous teenagers.

Angus put on a CD and as 'Moonlight Serenade' filtered across the room Joan dimmed the lights and the atmosphere took on a different tempo in every sense.

'Miss Ross, would you do me the honour of giving me this dance?' said Walter, who had walked up to her chair and bowed politely.

'Well, I was never a great dancer,' she replied, for once

appearing quite flustered; indeed, she was more taken aback then when she had faced the television cameras.

But everyone was watching and smiling, while Walter was holding out his arm, and there was simply no way she could refuse, not after everything they had been through. Their first steps were greeted with a huge round of applause. Angus followed his example and was soon dancing with Joan. Joyce stood up and waddled over to Dorothy, where she bowed, at least as far as she was able.

'I would be most extremely grateful if you would put down your knitting and give me the honour of this dance, the music of which I am particularly fond.'

'Well, I am most touched by your kind offer,' replied Dorothy, playing along.

For the next few hours the well-known tunes of Glenn Miller floated from the lounge and beyond the barricade, beyond boundaries of age, status and beliefs. 'Sunrise Serenade', 'A String of Pearls', 'Little Brown Jug' . . . the music seemed to bind them all together in a mood of reflection.

People in other parts of the building thought about the protesters and what they were trying to achieve. They thought about family and friends, alive and dead, and about their own lives and what they themselves had achieved or were perhaps trying to achieve.

In a bedroom along the ground floor Mrs Campbell tapped her fingers on the duvet and remembered when she was young and was considered quite a catch, and the fun she had enjoyed before allowing her dear husband to catch her. Mr Sutherland, too excited to go to bed following his part in the earlier subterfuge, sat in his chair, nodding in time to the music and reliving the moment he asked his future wife for a dance to 'Tuxedo Junction'.

Even those residents who lived in a haze of confusion

were transported back to their youth and an era when they were strong and healthy and whole. They smiled joyfully in the semi-dark of their bedrooms, and when laughter filtered throughout the otherwise silent building they joined in as if at the party themselves.

Nineteen

As Miss Ross and Joan surveyed the scene in front of them the next morning, it was obvious that the protest couldn't continue. The lounge looked dreadful and so did the people in it. Empty bottles, glasses, crisp packets and balls of newspaper were scattered amongst the figures still asleep, whilst the place had an unpleasant odour of which the fish supper was not the only culprit. Those who were awake moved about gingerly, the result of either too much alcohol or having spent the night in a chair.

'This can't go on,' said Joan.

'No,' agreed Miss Ross. 'It wouldn't be fair. No one wants to be the first to admit it, but everyone is desperate for a shower, a change of clothes and to get out into the fresh air. I know I am.'

'But we did well.'

'Yes. I just wonder what good it will do in the end.'

There were some tense moments as people queued for the one toilet, but once everyone had been given a cup of tea they gathered around and agreed to stay put until the care home owners had come back with a response. People tidied themselves and the surroundings as best they could and at nine o'clock Matron appeared at the window with a more senior representative.

He agreed to meet everyone individually and discuss their situation on a case-by-case basis. As a further gesture of goodwill, none of the residents would be charged for the cost of repairing any damage. There was little more that could be done. The man read out a brief statement to the reporters who had gathered again outside and they quickly dispersed, heading for the next story.

'We're already yesterday's news,' said Miss Ross, watching the media leaving. The Chinese film crew had already headed south to resume its search for the 'water dragon'.

'Our fifteen minutes of fame!' said Joan. 'It's not much over the course of your whole life.'

A couple of male carers climbed through the window in order to dismantle the barricade and by ten o'clock the members of the Escape Committee were being shown back to their rooms. There was a mixture of conflicting emotions. Deirdre and Mrs MacDonald almost looked as if they were about to claim to have been kidnapped, while the sparkle that had captured them all the previous night was fading in the bright light of the morning.

They were once more elderly people in a care home, waiting for families to make contact, passing time until the next outing. Not everyone was crestfallen. Walter and Angus tried to hang on to the magic that had been created and a few in the committee gave a thumbs-up or a comment to other residents, many of whom applauded as they walked by, along the corridor.

Miss Ross felt that everything they had achieved was slipping away, but she kept her misgivings to herself. There was one encouraging development. The previous evening a taxi driver in Inverness had set up a website called

'Save our Seniors' to raise funds. Over the next few days this generated support from people throughout the UK, although by the weekend the donations dried up, with the total at almost £8,000. The residents at We Care For You were extremely grateful. When split evenly between them, the money would pay for their rise in fees for almost a fortnight.

Twenty

Thursday, 14th April

Have I been foolish? I'm powerless, unable to help the one person I most want to. All I've achieved is to cause delay and disappointment. No one openly blames me for the failures, but I feel it inside so keenly. What good is my education now? What good is my love? My nights are filled with despair.

Twenty-One

'Oh, Mr McKenzie! That pawn!'

'Julie! My Queen!'

'It's disgusting, a man of seventy-eight with a woman in her early twenties . . . And every Thursday afternoon, as frequent as semolina!'

Deirdre, listening outside Walter's bedroom door, was beside herself with indignation and had to fight to keep her voice low as she spoke to Mrs MacDonald and Angus, the latter having been unwillingly dragged into the spying session. The home's moral judge could be extremely domineering at times.

'Well, at least he's regular,' said Angus.

'It's not right. Not fair to everyone else.'

'Matron should be told,' chipped in Mrs MacDonald. 'You're a man, Angus. What do you think?'

He wanted to say 'Lucky bloody bugger' but held back and replied, 'I'm sure Matron already knows.'

'Keep your voice down,' hissed Deirdre. 'They might hear us.'

'Between *The Archers* and their noise, I don't think Walter and his niece are likely to notice anything we do out here.'

'She's no more his niece than I am. We have to put a stop to this.'

'What someone does in the privacy of their own bedroom is up to them,' said Angus.

'But it's not his. It belongs to We Care For You.'

'Yes,' added Mrs MacDonald. 'It's part of our home, all of us.'

'The space between those four walls . . . it's the only place left where we have some control. As far as I'm concerned, while he pays his fees it's his domain.'

'It's not residential fees he's paying for with that woman! We can't simply do nothing.'

Angus thought he heard a different sound from the other side of the door.

'Quiet! I think someone's coming.'

'Again!' cried Mrs MacDonald. 'It's not natural.'

'To the stairs, quickly.'

He ushered them along the corridor, but they hadn't got far when the bedroom door was flung open and Walter emerged. He called after the scurrying figures, forcing them to stop.

'All right, folks?'

'Err . . . yes, thanks,' said Angus.

Walter nodded politely to the women.

'Deirdre, Mrs MacDonald.'

'Hello,' replied Deirdre, forcing a smile. 'We were . . . going for a walk.'

'Ah, along the corridor?'

'It's wet outside,' she replied.

'Oh, I hadn't noticed.'

Under her breath Deirdre whispered, 'I bet you hadn't.'

It was then that Julie walked out of the bedroom. She

looked so stunning that Angus couldn't take his eyes off her, even though he had seen her on many occasions.

'Thank you, Uncle Walter. I've really enjoyed myself.'

'That's all right, love.'

'You might have given me a beating this time, but I'm going to give you such a thrashing next Thursday.'

Deirdre put a hand to her mouth in an attempt to hide her gasp, while Mrs MacDonald's legs went so wobbly that she had to take hold of Angus's arm for support. The couple seemed unaware of the effects their comments were making and carried on amicably.

'I can't wait, Julie.'

She reached up and kissed him lightly on the cheek, then walked past the others, politely acknowledging each of them. They automatically returned her greetings and a few moments later the sound of high-heeled shoes could be heard clip-clopping down the stairs.

Deirdre's indignation had never been so indignant.

'Well! What have you got to say for yourself?'

'Say? Nothing, except that I'm going to lie down,' said Walter, giving a rather over-theatrical yawn. 'I'm suddenly feeling rather tired.'

'I'm not surprised,' whispered Angus.

'I'll see you all later,' he said, going back into his room. As he closed the door, they could hear him say, 'Enjoy your walk.'

'I can't believe the nerve of the man!' spluttered Deirdre when they were alone.

'She's so young,' said Mrs MacDonald.

'And so pretty,' mused Angus.

'It's not just . . . you know . . . but beatings as well.'

'Beatings?' queried Mrs MacDonald.

'I dread to imagine what sort of obscene objects the

114

poor cleaners come across. It's a wonder they've not complained.'

'Well, I still think he has a right to his privacy.'

'And our ears have a right not to be inflicted with this depravity.'

'You don't have to listen at his door.'

'That's not the point. Come along, Mrs MacDonald. Let's find a quiet spot to decide a plan of action. You'll be joining us?'

'No, I need some fresh air. I'm off to the pub.'

'You men! You're all the same.'

Angus watched the two women walk away, one propelled by righteousness and the other by loyalty.

'I wish we were,' he said quietly to himself.

As the women reached the top of the stairs, Mrs MacDonald could be heard asking, 'What sort of objects, Deirdre?'

Twenty-Two

Later that evening, Walter was sitting near the piano with a book in his lap. It was difficult to concentrate on the text and he constantly picked up the paperback only to lay it down again. He kept thinking about Julie's visit that afternoon and the day when the Escape Committee had barricaded themselves into the lounge. Was it really only a couple of weeks ago?

It seemed to him that the two events were somehow connected, perhaps because they both represented examples of injustice and hurt, fear and determination. He looked up as a figure sat down beside him.

'All right, Angus?'

'I suppose so. Recovered, have you? I don't know how you do it.'

'What?'

'Don't play the innocent. The entire care home knows what goes on in your bedroom on a Thursday afternoon.'

'Well, it's none of their business, is it?'

'Don't get on to me, I agree with you. Anyway, that's not really what I meant.'

'What then?'

'How do you . . . do it? At our age.'

'What's wrong, can't you get it up any more?'

Angus looked away, crestfallen, and Walter suddenly felt terrible that his banter had overstepped a mark and hurt his friend. He had hurt him more than enough already during his life.

'Sorry, mate. I meant that as a joke, but it just came out wrong. It was totally out of order.' Angus remained silent. 'There's no shame in it, if that is the case.'

'Are you on something?'

'Medication, you mean? Crikey, no, I'm already a walking advertisement for the pharmaceutical industry.'

'Aren't we all? So you're not using anything to enhance your . . . performance?'

'No. I guess I've been lucky.'

'You might not feel so lucky if your Becky found out. I can't see her being chuffed at discovering her ageing father is having sex once a week with a prostitute.'

'Ah, Becky and I haven't spoken for a while.'

'Sorry to hear that.'

'Oh, we've not had an argument or anything. Becky and John and the girls just seem constantly busy these days. Before coming into the home I used to be close to Heather and Penny.'

'Your grandchildren?'

'They're lovely girls.'

The two men fell silent, watching the others in the room. Dorothy, Joan and Miss Ross sat in one corner, their needles a blur as they carved out patterns in the air. Joyce was eating her after-supper snack and a few others had gathered around the television to watch a documentary. Walter's attention eventually landed on his adversary.

'What are Deirdre and Mrs MacDonald up to? They're

117

looking even more suspicious and devious than usual. Interfering old . . .'

'They're planning your downfall, that's what they're doing.'

'Oh, are they?'

'There's a petition going around to put an end to Julie's visits.'

* * *

'Now, Beatrice, you're a sensitive, intelligent woman, just like myself and . . . and . . .' Deirdre was going to say Mrs MacDonald, who was nodding her head vigorously, but somehow the words just wouldn't come out. 'I know you feel strongly against what Mr McKenzie gets up to every Thursday. I mean, I'm broad-minded, of course. We don't reach our age without seeing a bit of the world, do we? But really, this has got to stop.'

'What has?' asked Beatrice.

'Mr McKenzie's goings-on.'

'What's he going on about?'

Deirdre's expression, which she hoped conveyed that of a sensitive, intelligent woman, didn't change, but inside she was screaming with frustration. So much of her life was dominated by frustration.

'Dear me, this is a very delicate matter. I'm referring to the visits that he gets from that young woman.'

'Oh, his niece. She's very nice. She helped me only last week.'

'What did she do?' asked Mrs MacDonald.

'I can't rightly remember, but I do know that she helped me with something and I was very grateful at the time.'

'Well, that was kind of her.'

118

'Perhaps it was a couple of weeks ago.'

Deirdre's expression faltered.

'Please! Could we stick to the matter in hand? Look, I tell you what, Beatrice, why don't you just sign your name here, on this bit of paper, and then Mrs MacDonald will fetch you a nice cup of tea.'

'Will I?'

'Yes, you will.'

'Is it time for tea, then?'

'I think I can hear the kettle boiling. You just have to sign here first . . . on the dotted line.'

But Beatrice had lost interest in the conversation because she really liked tea . . . at least, she was fairly certain she did.

'No, don't go!' cried Deirdre, but the other woman was already walking away.

'You do have to catch her at the right moment,' offered Mrs MacDonald. 'But I fear they're increasingly rare.'

Deirdre looked around the room.

'This is going to be a lot more difficult than I had expected. How many signatures do we have now?'

Her friend counted up the names on the petition that they had gathered during the day.

'Seven. That includes us and Mrs Pierce, who thought she was signing for the delivery of a new washing machine/ tumble dryer. She was quite looking forward to using it. There's the three that we gave up on altogether and we've had six flat refusals.'

'Yes, all of the men we've asked!'

'Even Mr Forsyth seemed to understand the point straight away. He was amazingly lucid and vocal in his reply.'

'Incredible, isn't it? Most of the time he's trying to find a herd of Friesians or telling us that the sow needs servicing, but when we explain about the petition, oh suddenly there's this miraculous connection with reality, with some animal instinct to reproduce. He's immediately one of the men again. They're like rampant bulls, all sticking up for each other.'

Mrs MacDonald's head, in its attempt to convey solidarity, was almost a blur. The other woman carried on without noticing.

'Well, Mr McKenzie might be giving out beatings, but we're not beaten yet. Come on, there's Mrs Weaver by the bookcase and I don't think she's landed on planet cuckoo yet . . . although I wouldn't be surprised if she's in orbit.'

* * *

'I don't honestly know if I can get it up,' said Angus. 'It's been so long since I tried. I might just need the right circumstances . . . in order to be able to perform again. Christ, even Forsyth does better than me. Maybe I should pretend to have dementia, then I can go around squeezing breasts or patting backsides whenever the fancy takes me. It's staggering what he gets away with.'

It was a bizarre conversation to be having, sitting in the corner of the lounge with other people nearby, doing their usual evening activities . . . a bizarre conversation to be having anywhere.

'Well, I can't help you there,' replied Walter.

'That's the point. I wondered if you could.'

'How the hell am I meant to help get your willy up?'

'Shh! Not so loud. They're not all deaf.'

'Sorry, but I don't understand why you think I can help with your . . . problem.'

'I wanted to speak to you about Julie.'

120

'Why?'

'How did you find her?'

Julie was someone Walter didn't want to talk about and this time it was his turn to become quiet. She was so much a part of his life, closer to him than his family in many ways.

This strange, beautiful young woman off the street was the only person in his life whom he could be totally honest with. He said things to her that he had never even spoken about to Moira. God, how he missed his wife. If that evil illness hadn't taken her away, they would still be living happily in their little cottage.

'Walter . . . look, I can see this is a private matter to you . . . but it means so much to me. I have to know if I've lost that ability. Whether I'm still a man or not.'

Walter had first looked into the face next to him when they were six years old. Friends forever. That's what the two of them used to say. And they could have been, if Walter hadn't slept with the other man's wife. He didn't regret anything more than that. All four of them had been destroyed by his actions. Now there were just the two of them again but this time their lives were behind them, not stretching ahead into an unknown and exciting future.

'I asked the taxi driver.'

'The taxi driver?'

'Not the regular guy, that other one we sometimes get. He seemed a sort of sleazy bloke who might handle such a request. I had to agree that he got the fare to bring her to the home every week and then do the return journey.'

'That's why he's always the driver on a Thursday. I thought it was a bit odd.'

'I resent it, but he did stick to his side of the bargain.'

'So . . . do you have to pay her much?'

'Oh, Angus.'

'It's just that with the fees going up I hardly have any spare money.' They both fell silent. 'Perhaps she has a friend ... someone she could speak to, who might visit me?'

'Whether your willy works or not isn't what makes you a man.'

'I know that.'

Walter still didn't want to continue the conversation.

'I have to know. Please help me out.'

'You could speak to the taxi driver.'

Angus looked aghast at the suggestion.

'I couldn't do it. I just couldn't.'

'No, seeing his smug expression wasn't a pleasant experience. It made me feel dirty and then you're always concerned he has a hold over you and whether he might try to use it someday.'

'I wouldn't want to give him the satisfaction,' said Angus. 'I only know Julie well enough to say "Hello" to in the corridor. I couldn't approach her direct. Will you help?'

Twenty-Three

The financial situation was steadily getting worse for several of the residents and worry was making Dorothy unusually pessimistic. As the plans to reduce the fees hadn't worked, the only option remaining, if she was to stay, would be to raise money. Dorothy was in her bedroom with Joan and Miss Ross. Every now and again one of them would wipe away a tear or make some comment about the injustice of the situation.

'Is this what I've worked, scrimped and saved for all these years . . . to be forced to leave my friends behind and end up in a dingy room surrounded by strangers where you can't even hear the birds singing?'

The brochures for several other care homes had been circulating over the past few weeks and a couple of copies lay on the bed.

'For the first time in my life, I can understand why a woman might despair so much that she sells her body.'

'Dorothy!' cried Miss Ross. 'What a dreadful thing to say.'

'I think we would make more selling egg cosies,' muttered Joan.

They fell silent, and one by one resumed their knitting. There was no sign of Tiddles, who had sensed the huge change in the atmosphere and had taken to hiding in unusual places, as though he too feared being forced to move somewhere. Joan looked particularly thoughtful, as if a memory had given her an idea.

'Though mentioning prostitution,' she said, causing Dorothy to drop her ball of wool, 'I once worked in a newsagent's. If the shop was empty, I sometimes looked through the men's magazines. You wouldn't believe the things I saw.'

'I hope you're not going to suggest that we get photographed in the nude,' said Miss Ross. 'I was once shown a calendar of naked WI members in various poses behind vases of flowers and bowls of fruit. There was more than one who could have done with a few extra apples.'

'I couldn't pose nude,' said Dorothy, looking fondly at the photograph next to her chair. 'My Willie would never have stood for it.'

'No, not pose,' said Joan. 'In the pages at the back there were always lots of adverts. Some of them were from women offering to talk to men over the telephone.'

'Talk?' said Dorothy.

'Well, you know, in a particular way.'

'I can assure you,' said Miss Ross, 'I have never talked to any man *in a particular way* and I'm not about to start at my age.'

Their knitting was completely forgotten by the unexpected topic.

'I don't understand. How do the women make money?'

'They put a telephone number in the advert, one that people pay a lot to use. The women keep most of the cost of the call. All they have to do is keep the men on the line for as long as possible.'

'Talking dirty!' stressed Miss Ross.

'Talking dirty?' repeated Dorothy, trying to work out what this signified.

She had never discussed subjects like this with Willie and would certainly not have asked for an explanation about such matters. It was all so different these days. Couples seemed desperate to disclose the most intimate details about their lives in as public a way as possible.

'Is that what's meant by oral sex?'

Miss Ross decided that she didn't want to be involved in any discussion about 'oral sex' and busied herself with her knitting. By an enormous effort of will, Joan managed not to burst out laughing, as she didn't want to hurt her friend, whom she knew was feeling vulnerable. However, it was a close thing and it took several moments before she could reply.

'It's that sort of idea, love.'

'My Willie never wanted to talk dirty. He was a clean-living man.'

'Yes, but there are lots of men who do and many of them want to do it with a mature woman.'

This was too much for Miss Ross.

'Do you mean to say there are men who actually want to ring up some deaf old wrinkly, sitting in her cardigan and slippers, and shout down the telephone to them about sex?'

'Probably a lot more than you might think. All of the men's magazines carried similar adverts. I reckon there's an opening for us.'

'I don't like this reference to us.'

'The same adverts appeared for years. It must have been worthwhile for those women to keep paying to have them in.'

Miss Ross was increasingly uncomfortable with the direction of the conversation. She put her knitting on the chair and walked over to look out of the window.

'You can count me out of this venture,' she said without turning around.

The weather was heavy and overcast. It felt as though every day had been grey and damp since they had abandoned their blockade of the lounge. In the end, what had they achieved? A free fish supper? A flurry of media interest that died away just as quickly as it had arisen. Nothing had altered with regards to the fees. They were running out of options, time and hope. Joan's voice brought her back to the present.

'But think what's at stake. We'll need your help if we're going to do something.'

'I still don't understand what the idea is, but would it mean that I could stay where I am?'

Dorothy's simple innocence . . .

Miss Ross turned around and sighed.

'Of course I'll help, only don't expect me to speak to men on the telephone. When I was headmistress, I would skelp a lad if he was caught in the school with one of those publications.'

'So, what do we do now?' asked Dorothy.

'We'll have to install a telephone, with a number set up at a premium rate,' said Miss Ross, once more taking charge. 'I'll look into it.'

'There'll have to be some sort of advertising,' pointed out Joan.

'It won't be cheap,' said Miss Ross. 'There's a risk that we might not even get back what we pay out.'

'We could save money by just writing out cards and putting them around town,' said Joan.

'If we're going to do this, it has to be done properly. We'll have to put together a business plan so that we know how many minutes of telephone calls are required to cover the rise in Dorothy's fees. Then we can calculate budgets and targets.'

Dorothy, still trying to follow everything that was being suggested, looked at her friend with great admiration.

'I don't know what I would do without you.'

Miss Ross was moved by the comment. She took hold of one of Dorothy's hands.

'You are my dearest friend in the world. What else am I meant to do?'

Twenty-Four

If Deirdre wasn't so keen to hear her own voice, she would have been speechless with outrage. Unfortunately, this had never been known to happen. She had been in the office for the last ten minutes, Mrs MacDonald nodding vigorously by her side.

'I understand your concerns,' said Matron, 'but there's really nothing I can do. All residents are entitled to have visitors to their rooms.'

'But surely not prostitutes!'

'No, not one of those women,' added Mrs MacDonald.

'I cannot make any comment about this particular visitor. In fact, Julie is extremely popular. Several people have mentioned how helpful she is and how they look forward to chatting to her once she's visited her uncle.'

'Her uncle!' Deirdre spat out the words. 'Goodness me, you surely don't believe that story.'

'I can only stress again that what someone does in their bedroom is up to them. I've had no complaints other than yours.'

'What about the petition?'

'I think we all know that many of those who signed your

paper would not have understood what they were doing.'

'It's not them who have to listen to the terrible goings-on,' said Deirdre.

'Do you listen?' asked Matron, knowing well that this was one of her main pastimes. 'Your room is nowhere near Walter's.'

'Well, one sometimes can't help it, if you happen to be passing along the corridor at the time.'

'Deirdre has been very upset by all this,' added Mrs MacDonald.

'Maybe it would put your mind at rest if you were more involved in some of the activities or interest groups. You could even form your own and meet on a Thursday, so that you had a distraction when Julie visits.'

With this suggestion, Matron achieved a world first when Deirdre opened her mouth but no words came out.

* * *

For several weeks, there had been an atmosphere of great excitement. Some of the crew from HMS *Ross-shire*, which was due to be anchored for three days at the nearby Invergordon harbour, had proposed a visit. An hour or so after Deirdre's meeting, a large taxi pulled into the car park.

When the two naval officers and three crew members walked into the reception area, they were rather surprised to be greeted by staff dressed as pirates. Having signed the visitors' book and sanitised their hands using the wall-mounted dispensers inside the front door, they were escorted to the lounge, where the residents were waiting.

Matron made a short speech of welcome and this was followed by one from the senior officer, a lieutenant.

However, he had only just finished when two kitchen staff accompanied by a cleaner came rushing in and surrounded the junior officer.

'This man's pretending to be Captain Cook . . . but I'm Captain Cook around here,' said the cook, with a great theatrical wave of her plastic cutlass. Everyone thought this was a tremendous joke and while the young man looked about him in surprise they all started cheering. 'What shall we do with him, shipmates?'

'Make him walk the plank,' shouted Mr Adams.

'Get him to scrub the kitchen,' cried Joyce.

'Hey, my feet could do with a massage!' said Mrs O'Reilly.

The three ratings were grinning widely, while the lieutenant and Matron discreetly moved away from the limelight.

'I say off to the brig with him while we have tea and cakes and decide his fate,' shouted the cook. 'What say all of you?'

There was an immediate chorus of 'Aye, aye'. With that, the young man was manhandled out of the room, along the corridor and locked in a cupboard alongside dozens of boxes of incontinence pads. The 'kidnappers' returned to great applause and began to help serve hot drinks and treats.

Beatrice slipped away, anyone noticing simply assuming that she was going to the bathroom. Her first destination was the chicken coop. She quickly found Mabel and tucked her tightly under an arm before heading upstairs. Beatrice stepped over the mat inside her bedroom, quietly closed the door and, still holding the hen, dialled 999.

'You must come immediately to We Care For You,' she said with great desperation in her voice. 'A man is being held at knifepoint. He's been kidnapped!'

Beatrice thanked the person on the other end of the line when they confirmed that the police were on their way. She put down the receiver, smiling.

The people at the emergency services were always so pleasant, as well as taking you seriously. It was such a real pleasure to speak to them that she was already looking forward to the next time. Before leaving the room, she tucked Mabel up carefully within an old cardigan at the bottom of the wardrobe.

Representatives from HMS *Ross-shire* visited the care home whenever the ship was nearby and there was a huge camaraderie between the residents and crew. The ratings were excellent ambassadors, immediately sitting down and chatting to those who were less able to get out of their chairs, while the lieutenant took around cups of tea and plates of baked treats, much to everyone's delight.

Seeing that the visit was going so well, Matron nipped back to her office for a few minutes. However, she was rather concerned to spot through the window a police car, with its blue light flashing, driving at speed into the car park. As she walked into reception, two policemen came hurrying through the doors.

'We've had a report of someone being held at knife-point,' said the older of the two men, already suspecting that this was a false alarm.

'Ah,' said Matron, completely forgetting for the moment that she was wearing a pirate's hat and had a large stuffed parrot on her shoulder. 'There is some truth in that, although it's nothing to be alarmed at. Shall we go to the lounge?'

As they entered, the lieutenant was walking past with a plate of biscuits.

'I'm afraid someone has called the police to report that one of your crew is being held against his will,' said Matron.

'Goodness me, I do believe he is,' said the lieutenant, holding out the plate to the nearest policeman. 'Chocolate biscuit, officer? I can recommend those round ones.'

'Thank you very much, sir. I don't mind if I do.'

Twenty-Five

The fun during the day gave way that evening to sadness with the impending departure the next morning of Mrs Campbell. She had been at the home for longer than any of them and residents and staff alike felt it was a crime that she was being moved away because of the fees. The cook baked a cake and people tried to make a little party of it, to celebrate the happy times she had experienced there, rather than look to the despair that was now her future.

She put on a brave face, but her apparent joviality didn't fool anyone. Most people felt that she would be a great loss. Even Miss Ross held her in high regard and she wasn't impressed easily.

The old lady made a valiant effort to speak to everyone in the room, wishing them the best and thanking them for their friendship over the years. She was particularly kind to Albert, to whom she chatted for quite a while, holding his hand and nodding intently whenever he said something.

When Albert experienced one of his periods of clarity, he not only talked sensibly and could remember accurately, he also knew that he had dementia. Miss Ross thought it must be a terrifying condition to have, yet to actually know you have it must surely take that fear to a new level. She sat quietly in a corner and watched the others.

Walter and Angus were playing chess, each with a wee dram next to the pieces they had captured. It was quite common for residents to have a tot after supper. For some, it represented more than a simple pleasure, and Matron kept alcohol owned by these residents safely locked up, with staff doling out a set amount. Sometimes family members would smuggle in bottles, thinking that they were doing no harm and it was a bit of a laugh. Of course, they were never around to clear up the physical and emotional mess afterwards.

Near the piano, Deirdre and Mrs MacDonald were deep in conversation and gave the appearance, as they generally did, of plotting. Joyce was happily munching into a second slice of the leaving cake. Miss Ross suspected there was much more to the comical larger-than-life woman than met the eye, although she knew very little about her past. Maybe that was what made her so intriguing. Still, everyone was entitled to their secrets.

Then there was Dorothy in the next chair, knitting of course. Her innocence of so many things gave her an air of vagueness that didn't do justice to the wisdom hiding behind those big NHS glasses. Every now and again she would come out with such a perceptive observation that at times it was impossible to know what was going on in her head.

Anna was helping Beatrice with a jigsaw: the image on the lid showed Highland cattle with Ben Wyvis in the background. It was the third evening they had been working on the puzzle and although the carer was doing most of it she made the older woman feel it was her who was putting the pieces together.

A few people were asleep and a couple were sitting in front of the television, although it was on fairly quietly, so perhaps they were asleep as well. Joan was in her room, talking to one of her sons, who had called in after work.

Miss Ross only had a couple of distant relatives. She kept in touch via letters, though they rarely met. One of the few visitors she had was an ex-pupil who was now a minister. She had always lived her life alone, which had suited her well enough. When there is no alternative to a situation, there isn't much point in railing against it. Coming into the home had resulted in a huge life change. She had lost so much yet gained something she had never known.

★ ★ ★

Miss Ross and several of the others were sitting in the dining room the next morning when Matron entered, looking quite shaken. She tapped a glass with the end of a teaspoon and the high-pitched clinking resulted in an almost immediate hush.

'I'm very sorry to have to tell you that . . . Mrs Campbell passed away during the night. She died peacefully in her sleep.'

The general intake of breath was accompanied by several gasps and cries of 'Oh no'. A couple of residents started to cry. Miss Ross wondered how Matron knew the old woman had died peacefully, unless someone had been with her at that very point and, as Mrs Campbell had appeared in normal health the previous evening, it seemed unlikely that this was the case. She suspected it was a standard comment, designed to put people's minds at rest.

'Mr Dunn will be here later and anyone who would like to pay their respects should gather in reception at eleven. I

know this is a great shock to all of us. She was a very well-liked and much-loved member of our little community.'
Matron left to inform people in other parts of the building and her departure was followed by an awful silence.

Almost everyone – residents, carers, kitchen staff, cleaners – waited patiently for the body to be brought from the bedroom. All of the men had dressed smartly. Even Albert, standing near the exit, was wearing his best clothes.

Anna and Matron had washed Mrs Campbell and dressed her in the 'going away' outfit which had been hanging in the wardrobe. When people reached their nineties, they were generally very practical about the end being near and many of them had given instructions about what they wanted to wear for their funeral. More than one woman had a shroud, carefully packed away in a drawer.

The care home always prepared the deceased as much as possible in this way. After all, the staff had cared for them, often for many years, helping them out of bed in the morning, back to bed at night, and aiding them with their most intimate needs in between. They had laughed with them at funny events, hugged them when they were sad, met their families and rejoiced when there was happy news.

And then there was Mr Dunn, steering the trolley on which the coffin had been placed, his assistant at the far end pushing. Their movements were slow, precise and dignified. The undertaker was nearing the end of his long career. When they reached the centre of the reception area, the two men stepped away and stood at the back of the group.

'I know we are all very sad at the sudden loss of our dear friend,' said Matron. 'We had expected to be saying goodbye to her this morning, as she left for another home. Many of you spoke to her last night and I had a long chat with her earlier in the day.

'Mrs Campbell felt that she had lived a long and good life. She had loved and been loved by her dear husband, and was extremely grateful for the care she had received here over many years. She would not have wanted us to be sad. Perhaps we could have a few moments to reflect and remember.'

Matron bowed her head and the others present followed her example. There was complete silence for several minutes and then, almost magically, soft music could be heard.

It was Albert.

He had brought out his mouth organ and was playing 'The Last Post' with such extraordinary feeling that the sound was haunting. Many heads turned in his direction, but no one said anything. When he finished, even Mr Dunn reached up and wiped his eyes.

Still nobody moved or spoke. Albert walked up to the coffin and gently laid the shiny silver instrument on the burnished mahogany, before stepping back to stand next to the double doors that led outside. The moment was so intense with emotion that there wasn't a single person present who wanted to destroy it by moving or speaking.

Eventually, however, Matron looked over at Mr Dunn, who took the gesture as an instruction to continue. He moved forward with his assistant and together they slowly pushed the trolley towards the doors. As the coffin drew level with him, Albert saluted, the smartest salute he had ever given.

Then they were past him and outside, the automatic doors closing behind them, as if signalling the end of an era rather than one individual life. Albert, tears streaming down his face, slowly dropped his arm. Joan was the nearest to him and gently laid a hand on his shoulder. He had such an expression of misery that she felt her own eyes filling up again.

'I loved her,' he said simply.

'I know, sweetheart,' said Joan, reaching up and tenderly wiping away some of the tears from his cheeks. 'We all did.'

'She was so kind to me.'

'Mrs Campbell will be greatly missed.'

'Now she's gone, nothing will be the same.'

Joan was rather at a loss as to what to say, so hugged the old man who was so upset at the resident's death.

'You played that music beautifully,' said Joan, eventually pulling back from him. 'She would have been pleased.'

'I'll never play again.'

'You mustn't say that. Come on, love. It's not warm by the doors here. Let's go to the lounge and have a cup of tea together.'

Joan, with her arm around Albert's waist, led him away, his sobs clearly audible as they walked down the corridor. Everyone else had dispersed, except Matron, Dorothy and Miss Ross, who were standing nearby.

'I've never heard Albert play anything so beautifully,' said Dorothy.

'He's very upset at Mrs Campbell's death,' said Miss Ross.

'Yes,' said Matron, 'it's not surprising. They had been married for more than sixty years.'

The significance of what had just been revealed was so staggering that neither of the women could respond straight away.

'Married?' said Miss Ross finally. 'You mean . . . Albert and Mrs Campbell were husband and wife?'

'I never knew,' said Dorothy, astounded that after being a resident for so long she had still been unaware of the relationship.

'Yes. You see, everyone who was around when they

came here has gone. Albert's dementia got worse and Mrs Campbell didn't appear to want to tell later arrivals that they were married. The staff knew, of course, and we all respected her decision. I think she was concerned that he might be put under pressure by not always being able to remember that she was his wife.'

'But she was leaving him behind,' said Dorothy.

'The rise in fees meant that they couldn't afford for both of them to stay and Mrs Campbell believed it would be detrimental for him to be removed from the surroundings he was familiar with and the people he knew. She spoke to me about it and I had to agree with her conclusion.'

'So she was leaving him?' said Miss Ross.

'It was the kindest thing to do,' said Matron. 'She was totally committed to him. When he had his lucid moments, the two of them could still connect with each other. At other times, she was content to know that he was close by and being well looked after. She was with her husband every day, even if he didn't always know she was his wife.'

Dorothy brought out a hanky and dabbed her eyes.

'She gave up,' said Miss Ross. 'She lived ninety-three years and died the very morning she was going to be separated from everyone she loved.'

'I think her spirit decided it was time and the body simply obeyed,' said Matron, putting a hand on Miss Ross's arm. 'I've seen it before and on every occasion it's always seemed to me to be the best way.'

Matron left the two women alone. Dorothy was sobbing quietly. Miss Ross, in a rare display of physical affection, put her arms around her friend, hugged her tightly and wept.

Twenty-Six

Deirdre was, in every conceivable way, 'thin'. Her long thin nose stuck out too far from her thin head, which balanced precariously upon a neck that looked unable to support anything at all. Her thin body had thin limbs and the thin limbs had thin fingers and toes. When she spoke, her voice was thin, but the 'thinnest' thing of all was her mind.

'Thank you all for finding the time in your busy schedules to come along to this very important meeting.'

Deirdre had managed to persuade a small group to gather in the conservatory to discuss the woman claiming to be Walter's niece. She knew there weren't likely to be many on her side and that it would take all of her skills to win around sufficient of them to stand a chance of being able to prevent Julie from entering the building.

The promise of fresh éclairs from the local bakery had ensured the attendance of Joyce, while Angus had come along without any bribery, although Deirdre suspected he might be spying for Walter. Dorothy was already in the conservatory, so had simply stayed on, and Albert had wandered in then refused to leave. In reality, only Mrs MacDonald could be relied on to support the cause and she could be terribly vague at times. This was going to be very tricky.

'We have gathered here today,' said Deirdre, who thought it might be impressive if she tried to sound like a minister in the pulpit, 'to put a stop to the visits that are taking place by someone who is not suitable for We Care For You.'

'We car.'

'I'm sorry, Mr Adams?'

'In the high winds the other day, the 'e' fell off the sign outside. It's now *We Car For You.*'

'I prefer small cars,' said Mrs Weaver. 'They're more economical, don't you think so, Mrs MacDonald?'

'Oh, yes. I'm sure you're right. We have to consider the environment and future generations.'

'The young these days,' continued Mrs Weaver, 'they have so many pressures and now there are rising water levels.'

Deirdre was horrified at how quickly she had lost control of the debate. Within moments they were discussing cars, the environment and water levels when they were supposed to be talking about THAT WOMAN.

'Please! I'm sure Matron will soon have the sign repaired. We must keep to the subject of the meeting.'

'What's that, then?'

Deirdre groaned. Now Albert was involved. She should have been firmer about not letting him stay.

'To put an end to the visits by that woman.'

'What woman?' said Albert. 'Not Haggis?'

'She calls herself Julie, although I bet that's not her real name.'

'She's ever such a nice girl, helped me out just last week,' chipped in Mrs Weaver.

'She's a prostitute!' shouted Deirdre in frustration. This

wasn't going to plan at all. The room fell silent, apart from the clicking of Dorothy's needles, as they all absorbed the information in various ways.

'Can't they still be nice?' asked Mrs Weaver.

'How do you know she's a prostitute?' said Joyce sharply. 'It's a serious accusation to make.'

'Well . . . well, you only have to look at her.'

'I didn't know you could tell such a thing by looking at someone.'

Deirdre was taken aback. It was completely out of character for Joyce to be angry at anything or anyone. In fact, it was more than anger. There was almost a threat in her voice that transformed the person they all knew as a natural comedian, someone who was happiest when making those around her laugh.

'The young today . . .' said Mrs MacDonald. 'They wear such extraordinary clothes.'

'It was never like that for us,' said Mrs Weaver. 'We had to wear sensible items that were hard-wearing and kept you warm. Fashion was only for the famous.'

'I have endured great personal distress in order to gather the information that confirms it,' said Deirdre, trying to impose some sort of authority.

'Confirms what?' asked Mrs Weaver.

'That she is not Walter's niece but a prostitute.'

'She could be both,' said Angus, 'in which case she has a perfect right to see a relative.'

'Prostitutes have rights as well as puffins,' said Dorothy.

'We cannot have the morals of our home being corrupted by such a person,' shouted Deirdre.

'I'm probably past corrupting, but I don't mind if someone wants to try,' chuckled Mr Adams, who was actually past most things. 'What do you reckon, Angus?'

142

The other man didn't want to get involved in the discussion but he was happy to scupper this particular scheming if possible.

'I don't mind, although someone might have to remind me what it is I have to do. What about you, Mrs Weaver, fancy a bit of corrupting?'

This set several people laughing, including the target of the joke, who knew it was meant in fun and willingly played along.

'Oh, I'm all for it!' she said.

'Are you?' cried Mr Adams. 'Quick, help me up to my Zimmer. I have to strike while the iron's hot! Goodness, I can't even remember when it was last warm!'

Now everyone was laughing and Deirdre was desperate to regain control.

'This is not getting us anywhere! There are important decisions to be made, decisions that affect everyone. Angus, you know what I'm saying is true.'

The laughter died away. He was angry at being dragged into this and remained silent. It was Dorothy who saved him from answering.

'Isn't there something in the Bible about he who is without sin throwing the first stone?'

'This is hardly the occasion to be quoting the Bible,' said Deirdre.

'I didn't know it was only relevant on certain occasions. Whatever Julie may or may not have done, I know that I don't have the right to condemn her and I doubt that anyone else in this room has either.'

Several people looked with surprise at Dorothy, who wasn't known for giving speeches and because she spoke with such simple conviction it seemed that her words were all the more powerful. Even Mrs MacDonald was nodding her head in agreement. Deirdre was on the verge of losing the debate. However, she had listened to enough church sermons over the years to know that a good 'fire and brimstone' speech could yet win the day.

'Look at yourselves!' she shouted. 'Don't you have any standards left at all? Where has decency gone, our belief in right and wrong? Our home, it's a . . . a microcosm of society. Evil men walk our streets because the hands of the government and police are bound by insane bureaucracy, just as Matron's hands are tied in this instance. Evil has walked straight through our front door and sat down beside us, joined us at meals and gone into our bedrooms. And what do we do? Nothing!'

Whatever else he thought of her, Angus had to admit that Deirdre had the ability to perform in front of an audience. He could see that the group, apart from perhaps himself, Dorothy and Joyce (whose earlier outburst still puzzled him), were being won around. They were like branches blowing in the wind, first leaning one way and then another.

'What about live and let live?' he said.

'No one ever says that to us,' countered Deirdre, now in full flight and unwilling to let anyone alter the course she was steering. 'When did we last get the chance to live as we want? Have we fought so many battles in our long lives just to . . . to eat éclairs and knit while the enemy strolls unchallenged amongst us?'

There was a lot of nodding of heads and a couple of people said, 'No'. Joyce looked as though she was considering walking over and punching Deirdre on the nose.

'Are we so in our dotage that we don't care enough to do anything?'

This had several people shouting out. Now most of them were egging each other on to agree.

'It's up to us to act, to show these modern liver-faced bureaucrats that we won't have our hands tied. We will once again make a difference in a world that has forgotten us. Others will no longer do what they want to us against our will, stuffing us with food and pills we don't need. We will be heard and count for something.' Deirdre raised both hands to the ceiling, as if beseeching God. 'We will once again be YOUNG!'

The group exploded into cries of agreement, clapping and banging tables for all they were worth.

Twenty-Seven

Walter was sitting in his room analysing his life, something he had found himself doing a lot recently. Was Smiler right? Was he only marking time until there was none left? His melancholy thoughts were interrupted by frantic banging on the door. Startled, he got up quickly and opened it. Angus was bent over, gasping.

'Christ, mate! Are you all right?'

'Yes,' said Angus, although he didn't sound it.

'Come in and sit down, man.'

'No.'

'You look awful.'

'I've run up the stairs.'

'What possessed you to do such a daft thing? Get your breath back. I'm just waiting for Julie.'

'She's at the entrance. You'd better get down there.'

'Why? What's going on?'

'Deirdre's wound up a bunch of them into a frenzy and they're preventing her from coming into the building. It was starting to get ugly.'

* * *

'Please let me in,' cried Julie.

Deirdre was unmoved by her tears or pleading, however the others were stunned at how unpleasant this encounter had so quickly become.

'I need to be with Walter.'

'Hah! I see the pretence of him being "uncle" Walter has finally gone. More lies. More corruption, just as I've been warning people.'

'I've never done you any harm, any of you.'

'Your very presence harms us. It's an affront to everything that we've stood up for over a great many decades: honesty and hard work.'

'You don't understand.'

'No, it's time for you to understand. You're not welcome here. We don't want your sort in our home.'

'Hey, I didn't come here to terrorise the girl and make her cry,' said Mr Adams.

'Pah! A typical man's reaction. At the first sign of a few tears from a pretty girl your resolve turns to water. Didn't we all agree on actually doing something, on taking action, instead of watching what's left of our lives disappear into a meaningless . . . nothing! Well, didn't we?'

'This is not making me feel young, just sad,' said Mrs Weaver.

Deirdre was deaf to everything except her own determination to make a difference, almost to the point that it didn't matter what it was. She needed to be noticed, needed proof that she still had the power to make change, that she was actually still alive.

'Is it true that you are a prostitute?'

The young woman physically flinched at the shouted accusation, made in front of so many dear friends.

'Come on, girl! Are you or are you not a prostitute?'

The reply was almost inaudible, yet Julie felt it could be heard throughout the whole world, by the pleasant man in the corner shop, by all her relatives, by her old teachers at school, by her parents.

'Yes.'

'Hah! Condemned out of her own mouth. And she expects us to let her wander amongst the frail and vulnerable, those too confused to understand the danger they're in. Well, there comes a point when you have to make a stand and I'm going to protect them even if no one else will.'

'Please don't send me away. This is the only place where people are kind. It's the only time when I'm safe. Is it so much to ask?'

Julie would have begged on her knees if she thought it would have done any good, but Deirdre's hard expression had changed to one of triumph. She was still able to make a difference.

'You should have thought of these things before entering your chosen profession. No woman these days has to sell her body to survive. We're not in the Dark Ages. If you choose this life, then it's because you want to.'

What Deirdre didn't notice was that the more adamant and animated she became, the less support she had around her. Even Mrs MacDonald wanted to distance herself from what had turned into simple cruelty.

'This is disgraceful,' said Mr Adams, banging his Zimmer on the floor to emphasise the point. 'Let the girl in.'

'She can come to my room,' chipped in Mrs Weaver.

'Deirdre!' said Mrs MacDonald, with a force that took everyone by surprise. 'You've gone too far.'

Deirdre stared in shock at her friend, but didn't have time to react to the betrayal because Walter was shouting and thrusting his way into the group.

'What the hell do you lot think you're doing?'

'Walter!'

He took Julie in his arms with great tenderness, but his face was blazing with anger.

'Here comes the knight in shining armour,' said Deirdre, trying to maintain some sort of control and moral high ground. 'Well, it's a bit rusted now and you're too late.'

'They won't let me in. They're going to send me away. What will I do?'

'No one is sending you anywhere, you'll be all right now,' said Walter kindly, before turning on Deirdre with such ferocity that the entire group stepped back. 'And you can stick your caustic comments back down your throat before I do it for you.'

'Really! I'm not being spoken to like that. Matron shall hear.'

'She certainly will,' shouted Walter. 'Look at you all. Proud, are you, ganging up to frighten a girl who is young enough to be your granddaughter?'

'You should have thought of her age . . .' Deirdre was desperate to hang on to something, anything.

'Shut up! This girl survives the only way she's able to. There's not one of you here that's faced a fraction of her problems. She's been let down by everyone who should have cared . . . seen more heartache in her short life than you lot have in four times that length. You complain about your aches and pains. You've no bloody idea of the desperation and despair there is amongst young people out on the street. Well, shame on you. Shame on you all.'

And everyone did feel terribly ashamed. This wasn't anything to do with the grand ideals that Deirdre had told them about in the meeting the other day.

'Give me space!'

The new voice belonged to Joyce, who was forcing her way none too politely into the rear of the group. She still had a couple of curlers in her hair and it was obvious that she had rushed there part way through a hairdressing appointment. Deirdre, rather unwisely, made a move to stand in her way.

'If anyone tries to stop me, I'll flatten them, whoever they are, man or woman!'

As if to demonstrate her seriousness, Joyce balled her hands into fists, which looked as though they were indeed quite capable of knocking any one of them to the floor. Deirdre decided that preservation was more important than principle and stepped out of the way. Joyce stopped in front of Julie and Walter, immediately eyeing up the situation and making a snap decision.

'Come with me,' she said. 'Let her go.'

'But . . .' said Walter miserably.

'Let her go. Come here. Dry your eyes. We'll go to my room.'

Julie looked for guidance to Walter, but even he appeared to hesitate and after a few moments of indecision he removed his arms. She let herself be guided through the crowd and along the corridor, looking like a child next to the much larger woman.

The group dispersed in silence, a feeling of sadness weighing down heavily on them. Within moments only Walter was left in reception. He was still standing there when Angus came down the stairs towards him.

'Sorry, I had to sit on your bed for a while to get my breath back.' When he reached his friend, he realised he was crying, a stream of huge tears flowing freely down his face. 'Whatever has happened?'

'I've done a terrible thing, a stupid, terrible thing. I

didn't mean for people to be hurt. Everything's gone so horribly wrong and it's all my fault. I'm no better than I was fifty years ago, when I caused so much pain to the people I loved.'

'Hey, this is not like you. Tell me what happened?'

But Walter couldn't speak, so Angus made the decision for him.

'Come on. Let's go for a beer.'

Twenty-Eight

Joyce closed the door firmly behind her and physically placed the sobbing Julie in an armchair. Then she waddled over to a chest of drawers.

'I've only got sherry.' She poured a generous measure into two glasses, then handed one over before sitting on the bed. 'Now, drink that. We've got some talking to do.'

'You don't understand . . .'

'Oh, don't I? Let me tell you something. I've been watching you closely over the last few months and in my job I became a very good judge of character. So I'm going to trust you with something I value more than my life.'

'What do you mean?'

Joyce, still with two curlers in her hair, drank some of her sherry and went back over to the chest of drawers. Not without a little difficulty, she retrieved an envelope that was hidden under clothing in the bottom drawer. Once sitting back down, she opened the envelope and withdrew two photographs.

She stared at the image of one, which showed a striking young woman, scantily clad and standing in an alluring pose. With a little sigh, she passed it to Julie, who studied the shot without understanding at first why she had been given it.

'It's you! But you were stunning.'

'Hard to believe now,' said Joyce, patting her ample tummy. 'Did you never consider that women who work the streets are just as likely as the rest of the population to become old, get ill and end up in a care home? There aren't special places for ex-prostitutes.'

'You were . . .'

'I worked the streets for eight years before going a bit more upmarket with my own flat. Age is a great leveller. Someone who has been a prostitute can end up in a care home along the corridor from the judge who used to condemn her in court decades earlier. Come to think of it, I had quite a few judges to my flat,' said Joyce with a smile that almost magically transformed her into the familiar character everyone was so fond of. 'Word must have got around the chambers!'

'I've never considered what happens to women afterwards.'

'No one ever does. There's not exactly a recognised career path. And people like me are hardly likely to advertise what they did for a living when they were younger. I told the others here I was a secretary and I've kept everything else fairly vague. But you need to make up some sort of story about your past for residents like Deirdre, otherwise they become too suspicious.'

'Where were you?'

'I went to Manchester. I wasn't going to work around the area where I grew up. I was always careful, including what I did with the money I made. When I got out of it, I was ok, then when I reached the stage when I couldn't cope on my own, I stuck a pin in a map of Scotland and here I am.'

'Why Scotland?'

'Ah, I reckoned that there was almost no chance of me meeting an ex-client up here. Now, they wouldn't recognise me if they did, so I don't worry any more.'

'I don't know what to say,' said Julie. 'Did you never want to marry?'

Joyce became reflective and didn't answer straight away.

'Oh, there was a man. There were always men, of course, but I loved Jimmy. He wasn't a client. We met one morning at the local corner shop. I'd been up all night and was desperate for something to eat and he was in there buying sausages for his breakfast. Strange how some trivial facts stay in your mind, while important ones are often easily forgotten.'

They were quiet for a while. Julie had been so stunned by the news that she had stopped crying.

'We can only play the cards we're dealt in life,' said Joyce. 'Some people seem to get a royal flush and others, they get the joker. Though that hand rarely makes you laugh.'

'What's the other one?' said Julie, indicating the photograph that was still face down on the older woman's thigh.

'I guess this was my royal flush and joker in one,' she said, handing it over. Julie studied the image and couldn't stop tears forming again. 'He was called George. You never saw such beautiful eyes. He could look right inside you and tell if you loved him or not.'

'What happened?'

'Jimmy knew what I had been, but I left that life behind when we got together and he accepted me for what I was. I fell pregnant amazingly quickly, all things considered. We were so happy together. Then when George was only three months old Jimmy was crushed to death in an accident at work.'

'I'm so sorry.'

'George would be forty-five now. I think about him every day and I always do something special on his birthday, even if it's just a little trip out. No one here knows or would notice that I always mark the date in some way.'

'You didn't keep him?'

'No choice, really. He was adopted, all proper and above board. I gave the woman at the agency a photograph of Jimmy and me holding George, along with a letter that explained pretty much everything,' said Joyce, sighing. 'Adoption was the best thing for him. What life would he have had with me? Jimmy and I hadn't even married. We were going to. It broke my heart. I lost the man I loved, my beautiful baby boy and then went back on the game. Jimmy was from Scotland, which was another reason why I stuck my pin in that map . . . perhaps it was the real reason. Here, drink that sherry.'

Joyce put the photographs back in the drawer and refilled both of their glasses.

'Firstly, there's one thing you can do for me.'

'Of course. What is it?'

'Sit on the bed so that I can have the chair. It's moulded to my shape.' Joyce handed over a glass and settled herself in the armchair. 'Now, if I'm going to help I need to know your story. Whatever you say will go no further. Not even to Walter.'

'He already knows. He's been very kind.'

'You're very fond of each other, aren't you? You could easily pass as his niece. Take your time,' she said, when Julie hesitated. 'Take as long as you want. I'm not going anywhere.'

They sat in silence for almost ten minutes before the story began.

'I came from what everyone would consider to be a good family. My parents were very strict, but they loved me and we were comfortably off, so I didn't have much to complain about. Not really. I was just so lonely. At least it felt like that. The truth was I didn't have any idea what loneliness meant.

'I was an only child and it wasn't easy to bring friends home, not that I had many. Anyway, by the time I was fifteen they were all involved with boyfriends and I felt rather dumped. Then I met someone on the Internet. My parents didn't understand anything about computers and always thought I was doing homework.

'Daniel was gorgeous. It wasn't long before we were writing and texting each other constantly. I was madly in love with him. Everything was so exciting . . . so romantic. Of course, when he finally asked to meet I agreed instantly.'

'And were the photographs he sent really of him?' asked Joyce.

'Yes, but taken about fifteen years earlier. However, by that stage it didn't seem to matter.'

'You were hooked.'

'Totally. We started meeting in secret whenever possible. On my sixteenth birthday, we made love. My parents thought I was celebrating with friends. I was a virgin. He was so kind and tender, very experienced, and I thought myself to be so lucky.'

'How long did it take before he wanted you to sleep with other men?' asked Joyce. Julie looked surprised. 'Do you think grooming is a recent thing? It might have a new name and get lots of publicity these days, but it's been going on for a very long time. I saw a great deal of human nature when I was in the business, and a lot of it wasn't pleasant.'

Julie let out a long sigh, her shoulders sagging even further.

'Six months. He was so clever about it. We went back to his place one day and he plied me with more drink than usual. Then one of his friends happened to drop by. He was good-looking and could only have been in his early twenties. Daniel kept on about how marvellous it would be if he could watch while . . .'

'I know love,' said Joyce, reaching over and taking hold of one of Julie's hands. 'He had you well and truly controlled.'

'Eventually I gave in and had sex with this stranger. I was really upset afterwards but Daniel kept saying how pleased and proud he was of me and that all grown-ups did this sort of thing. It was normal, only I was still too young to understand. Then . . .'

'Then there was often a friend popping in while you happened to be there and they gradually became older and less attractive, until you reached the stage when there would always be more than one friend calling.'

Julie nodded her head and started to cry.

'One day, when I was seventeen, I read an article about grooming and suddenly realised this was what had happened to me. I confronted Daniel. He was livid and threatened to expose me to my parents. I had lied to them so much and become so deceitful that we had drifted apart, but they were still all I had. I begged him not to, but at the same time remained adamant that I wasn't doing it any more.'

'And he carried out his threat?'

'I came back from school one day to find my father waiting in the hallway, standing next to a couple of suitcases. There was such a coldness about him it frightened me. My mother was nowhere to be seen. He grabbed my arm and marched me into the sitting room, where he pushed me onto the settee and said that we were going to watch something together . . .'

She couldn't continue. Joyce heaved herself out of the chair, stood in front of Julie and hugged her so tightly that the younger woman seemed to disappear into folds of flesh.

'You don't have to go on. I understand it well enough. Hush now, you'll make yourself ill.'

It took a long time for the heartbreaking sobbing to stop and for the tiny frame to cease trembling. Julie looked up, her pretty face a mask of blotches, tears and despair. Joyce wished that she could have had five minutes in a room alone with the man behind this. She might be getting on, but by God she would have made him regret what he had done.

'When I was a child, I used to cuddle up to my father on the settee and we'd watch children's programmes on that old television. Only this time I was on the screen . . . naked . . . doing such terrible things with these disgusting old men. And all the while my father sat there, screaming at me to open my eyes when I couldn't bear to see any more. I wanted to be cuddled by him so much.

'When it was over, he dragged me to the front door. I begged him to let me stay. In the end I was hanging on to his legs, but he pushed me into the drive and threw the cases out before closing the door.'

'And you never saw them again?'

Julie shook her head in reply.

'How long ago was that?'

'Four years,' she said, before burying herself back into the folds of Joyce's body, as if the warm flesh of the older woman offered a chance of hiding from the pain and desperation, of hiding from everything and everyone.

Twenty-Nine

The pub was almost empty and it was easy to find a quiet spot. Walter looked like a condemned man, head bowed, staring unseeing at his hands spread out on the table. Angus returned with two half pints of beer. He sat opposite, pushed one across, then remained silent, taking small sips and waiting for the other man to speak.

'When my Moira died, there was no warning at all. She only went out to buy something for dinner. I said I'd have the coffee ready at eleven and she better not be late or I would have it without her. It was a bit of a joke we had. She smiled and left. That was the last time I saw her alive. The doctor called it an aneurysm of the brain. He said she wouldn't have known anything about it.'

Walter stopped and Angus felt he should say something. After all, the four of them had all been close friends when they were young – in another life.

'I've never been able to decide whether it's kinder that way, or whether it's better to have a chance to say your goodbyes, settle everything up.'

'My grief turned into a depression that overwhelmed me. I fell to pieces.'

'That's how you ended up at We Care For You?' asked Angus.

'You know, I've always been a practical bloke, but I couldn't even boil an egg. I would put one in the pan and simply watch the water steam away until there was nothing left.'

'Everyone always used to comment how you and Moira were like two halves of the same person.'

'I can't remember exactly how it all happened. Becky meant well, but without me having much say in anything the house I had shared with Moira for so many years was sold and I was stuck in the home. It was like waking up from a nightmare only to find it was real. Don't get me wrong, the staff are fantastic and I'm very grateful for their kindness during those early months, but I had lost everything.'

Walter finally picked up his glass. Angus watched a family getting up from a table across the room. They all looked so happy.

'The thing is, Moira and I were still both very active and had a regular sex life. When I first arrived, it was the last thing on my mind. After a while I simply assumed that side of my life was over.'

'But the urges came back, only now you were surrounded by a bunch of elderly people you barely knew,' said Angus.

They both stopped speaking when a barman came near to their table to take away some glasses.

'I tried to ignore the feelings, but it got to the point where I started thinking, well, it's my money and my body and if I paid a professional then no one would be hurt. It would just be a business arrangement until I didn't feel the need any more.'

'Then you found Julie, or rather the taxi driver did?'

'That first time . . . I don't know how to describe it, Angus. It was extraordinary, tender, passionate, believe it or not. Anything any normal man could possibly wish for.'

'She's an extremely attractive woman.'

Walter became withdrawn, as if deciding whether to go on, or rather knowing that he had to but was reluctant.

'Yes, but it was also grotesque . . . obscene. There was a part of me that was revolted. The shame was so great that I couldn't sleep at night and in the end I couldn't even look at myself in the mirror when I shaved.' He put down his glass and wiped his eyes.

'All right,' said Angus. 'Don't upset yourself.'

'I realised that I wanted peace of mind more than sex. When Julie visited that second Thursday, I told her we couldn't continue.'

'But she's been visiting for months.'

'I was taken aback at how upset she was. I made a pot of tea and sat her down. We spoke for hours – about how she came to end up doing what she did, about my Moira. I said that if she wanted to return the following week we could talk again.'

'And that's how it's gone on ever since?'

Walter nodded. Angus took a long drink of his beer, studying the other man over the top of his glass. However, everything he said appeared to be genuine.

'Despite her age, Julie understands more about the despair I sank into after the death of Moira than anyone else and speaking to her every week became the most important thing in my life. After a month, we came to an agreement. I would pay her enough so that she didn't have to work at all on a Thursday. She would visit me for a few hours and do what she wanted for the rest of the day.'

'But not work.'

'No, that had to be her side of the bargain.'

Angus put his glass down with a bang.

'Hang on a minute. What about the noises from your bedroom, bloody moans and cries of "Oh, Mr McKenzie! Julie, my queen!" Explain all that!'

'It was just a game.'

'Is that what you call it?'

'I guessed that certain residents would start listening at the door.'

'Go on.'

'I always have a chessboard laid out in my bedroom. That's what we were doing.'

'You've lost me.'

'One day Julie challenged me to a game.'

'Of chess? You don't imagine . . .'

'Don't imagine that someone who sells their body could sit down and enjoy such an intellectual hobby?' said Walter, finishing the other man's sentence. 'She slaughtered me that first time.'

'Crikey, she must be good.'

'People always assume things of others, don't they? Anyway, it ended up that we would always play when she visited. We decided to have some fun when we suspected that the home's moral judge was listening at the door, but to make it more difficult everything we cried out had to relate to the game we were playing.'

'You devious devil! They were all chess moves!'

'The thought of Deirdre almost fainting because I was about to castle . . . well, it made us laugh. Only . . .' Walter put down his glass and began to cry. 'Now it's gone horribly wrong and I don't know what's going to happen – to any of us.'

Thirty

Friday, 20th May

Dorothy doesn't complain, but I know the extra costs are eating into her savings and that time is against us. I have to do something to enable her to stay. Do we both move to a cheaper home? My heart tells me we must stay together, but my head tells me that leaving is not the solution.

Thirty-One

'Speak to a granny today,' said Dorothy.

She was in her room with Joan and Miss Ross, the latter sitting with a pen and paper. Following their decision to set up a sex line, they were trying to think of appropriate wording for the advert. Tiddles had emerged from hiding and was sitting in his favourite lap.

'I can't see that causing a stampede of mackintosh-wearing men rushing to their mobiles,' said Miss Ross.

'Mature women for sale?' suggested Joan.

'I am certainly not for sale! It sounds like an advert for a second-hand car: one careful owner, some bodywork required!'

'Big end may need looking at!' said Joan.

'You can leave my big end out of this,' replied Miss Ross.

'The big end . . .' said Dorothy in such a way that the others immediately knew she was about to start reminiscing. 'It reminds me of when Willie and I had to think of a name for the little converted church we were living in. The building was right at the end of a lane and it had a bell, so we called it—'

'Please tell me you didn't!' interrupted Joan.

'Well, what's wrong with The Bell End?'

Joan put a hand to her mouth, but the laughter escaped anyway. Miss Ross tapped the notepad with her pen. They weren't getting anywhere and recounting tales wasn't going to help.

'Can we *please* get back to the matter in hand?'

As though they were pupils in her class who had been caught doing something wrong, the two women replied together, 'Sorry, Miss Ross.' They fell silent again, thinking about the wording.

'How about,' said Joan after a while, 'dirty talking?'

The three of them looked at each other and the phrase was written down.

'I think we have to be more specific,' said Miss Ross.

'Ring an elderly woman for a dirty talk,' suggested Joan, who was increasingly getting into the spirit of the occasion.

'I suppose that's more informative, but it's not exactly catchy.'

'Dial Dorothy for a dirty ditty.'

'Oh! I'm not keen to have my name mentioned.'

'Dial to hear a dirty ditty about a ti—'

'We're not trying to write a limerick,' said Miss Ross, holding up a hand. She didn't really have to hear it all to know what was being suggested. 'And that doesn't give anything about age. I don't think we're on the right lines.'

'We have to get men on the telephone somehow.'

'But we mustn't mislead people,' said Dorothy. 'Our old minister, the Reverend McBain, was forever saying we should treat each other fairly because everything was seen by the Lord and we would have to answer for our actions on the day of judgement. He was a very religious man.'

'That's generally a good sign in a minister,' said Joan.

'When I was a girl . . .'

Miss Ross moaned silently, put down her pen and leant back in her seat. There was no stopping Dorothy when she got going. One simply had to let her tell whatever story she had dug up from the past.

' . . . my friends and I would sneak to the manse on a Saturday evening to watch him try to catch the cockerel.'

'Why did he do that?' asked Joan.

'The Reverend McBain didn't believe in . . . physical contact . . . on the Lord's day, so it was always locked up on a Saturday night. Seeing the minister scrabbling around the yard was a sight to behold, his black coat billowing as though he was a huge bat, the bird screeching, feathers flying in every direction.'

'I wish I had seen that,' said Joan laughing.

'That bird really didn't want to be caught.'

'The minister's cockerel isn't going to help us get the right wording for the advert! Joan, what did the advertisements say in the men's magazines that you read?'

'It was ever so long ago, I can't remember. Did you never look at the ones you confiscated?'

'Certainly not! Whenever I came across such an offending item I would instruct Mr Jackson, the janitor, to burn it in the school boiler-house. When he retired, we found them all stacked in his locker – the leaning tower of pornography.'

'We need to look at one to get some idea of the proper wording,' said Joan.

'Buy a magazine!'

'You said we had to do things properly.'

'And who's going to walk into a newsagent's and make such a disgusting purchase?' said Miss Ross, as if the proposed deed was one of the worst things a person could possibly do.

Joan stayed quiet, meeting the gaze of the ex-headmistress, who turned to Dorothy hoping for support, but she was also looking at her. Heavens, even the cat was watching her.

'Oh no. Not me. Never!'

Thirty-Two

After the morning handover from the night staff, Matron went to her office. It looked like being a normal day, that is to say it was going to be frantic, with a score of minor emergencies and probably a few major ones, at least one substance running out (riots were only just avoided the previous week when there was no marmalade for breakfast), people complaining and residents having fallouts.

The person taking over Mrs Campbell's room was due to arrive during the morning and settling in new people generally took a lot of extra effort. Albert's dementia appeared to have taken a turn for the worse and it was impossible to tell if this was due to feelings of bereavement, the fact that his wife wasn't constantly around talking to him and providing stimulation, or whether the cause was a purely physical one.

Mrs O'Reilly had become poorly during the night and the local surgery had already been contacted and asked to send a GP as soon as convenient. Matron would wait to hear what the doctor had to say before deciding if the priest should be sent for.

On top of this, she had agreed that if it was a nice day

anyone wanting to go to the beach would be taken for a treat. This would stretch the carers, who were already working shorthanded and looking tired. Finding good staff was a constant headache and the home had been running under capacity for the last two months.

The list of other items to sort out seemed endless and included a hoist that had broken down the day before. This had left Mr Adams, having just been lifted out of the bath, dangling naked several feet off the floor. He had considered the situation very amusing, largely due to the fact that his son had left him another half bottle of whisky during an earlier visit and the old man had consumed much of it.

Trying to convince some families that sneaking alcohol and cigarettes to residents wasn't always in their best interest was an ongoing issue. The son had been almost abusive in his insistence that it was his father's right to drink and puff away if he wanted to. She had tried to explain that other people had the right not to have to breathe in the smoke, but the man had an extreme case of selective hearing. It was not an uncommon problem.

Despite these many trials and hurdles, Matron moved around the building conveying a sense of unflappable calm and professionalism that was guaranteed to restore peace in situations of conflict and find solutions to impossible problems. However, even her heart sank a little when the new resident arrived.

It was obvious that Mrs Winchester-Fowler suffered from quite severe dementia and they had been assured this was only a mild condition which would not require any special or extra care. There was a growing trend for those going into homes to be much frailer and in need of help than years ago.

The one bright thing that day was the sun, so after lunch

fourteen residents were loaded into the minibus and taken to the beach, a trip that was only possible because several friends of We Care For You came along to help. From the level of excitement, singing and general noise during the short journey, outsiders could easily have thought they were off on a week's holiday.

A message had already been sent to the man who hired the deckchairs and these were waiting for them when they arrived. Most were used only to deposit items of clothing, as the lure of the sea was like the sound of Sirens, threatening to infect them with a spell of madness.

'Let's go!' cried Mr Adams, who was in a wheelchair, a Zimmer across his lap. 'Don't let them win.'

This last comment, directed to Hamish behind him, was in response to the more mobile folk who were already walking away from them. The handyman's solid muscles were put to the test across such a soft surface, but he soon began to catch the slow-moving group.

'Hey, look at this,' said Joan, spotting the approaching pair. 'I'm not being beaten by some old sod in a wheelchair.' With that she increased her pace to as brisk a walk as she could manage and was instantly followed by Meg and Peg.

'Angus, we can't be left behind by a bunch of women!' said Walter.

Then the Sirens sang again and suddenly people who had difficulty getting out of an armchair were charging ahead as fast as their limbs would let them. Cries of 'Dirty foul!' from those who were hindered, or 'Get off!' from those held back by someone grabbing their clothes, were joined by an almost hysterical Mr Adams shouting, 'Faster! Faster!'

'The winners!' declared Hamish, as he stopped the wheelchair at the water's edge.

Moments later several others arrived beside them, more out of breath because of laughing than exertion.

'What age are they?' said Miss Ross, who had declined to join in the race and was following with Dorothy at a sedate pace.

'Well, you do have to wonder at times.'

They stopped when they reached a large figure, lying prostrate on the sand.

'Are you all right down there?' asked Miss Ross.

Joyce looked up at them, tears streaming down her face, too overcome by a fit of giggles to reply.

'We'll ask Hamish to stop by, dear,' said Dorothy before moving on.

Ten minutes later everyone had their shoes off and their trousers rolled up. Even Mr Adams was in the sea, hanging on to his Zimmer and calling out in delight every time the water rose up his legs. The coolness around them disguised the fact that the heat was fierce and Anna ran around with sun cream, trying to smear it on exposed areas of flesh.

When the novelty wore off, people gradually made their way to the deckchairs. Eventually they all ended up back there, eating ice creams, putting the world to right and having one of the best days out they could remember.

By the evening almost all of them had sunburn and the carers were kept busy going around rubbing moisturiser onto noses, heads, necks and arms. Their feelings of joy were tempered by the news that Mrs O'Reilly had become worse during the day and the outlook seemed bleak.

Having examined her that morning, the doctor had told Matron that the resident was very ill. However, Mrs O'Reilly had made it clear from the beginning that she didn't want to be taken to hospital or resuscitated, if that situation ever arose.

'It's so much easier if we know the patient's wishes on these matters,' said the doctor, once he was in the privacy of the office. 'If there are no instructions, then we have to presume a person wants us to try every option possible to keep them alive, when often . . .' He shrugged his shoulders.

'Often the kindest thing is to make sure they're comfortable and let nature take its course,' said Matron, whose experiences had left her with some strong feelings on the matter. 'It would help us if more doctors took the bull by the horns and actually asked the patient what they want, instead of ducking the issue because it's difficult.'

'We're all human. The reality is it's a lot simpler not to enquire.'

The doctor was a regular visitor and one that Matron liked and respected. He said not to hesitate to get in touch, if necessary. She thanked him and then contacted the priest, who said he would call that evening.

★ ★ ★

'How are you feeling, Mrs O'Reilly?' said Father Connelly, having taken off his coat and made his way to the bed.

'I'm not too good, Father. I don't think a half bottle of gin will help this time.'

'I'm still trying to forget that particular visit. I didn't feel right for several days.'

'I was grand by the next morning. I even won the Easter bonnet competition.'

'Well done, you. I wouldn't have had a chance of winning anything.'

'Not bad for someone who was dying the night before, eh?'

'I would never doubt your determination, although sometimes I suspect it's just plain stubbornness.'

She laughed but immediately started coughing. He picked up the beaker on the nearby table, tenderly lifted her head and helped her to drink a little water. Her skin felt hot and she looked feverish even to his untrained eye. There was so little fat on her that the cat he had passed downstairs looked as though it weighed more.

'Thank you, Father,' she said, once he had laid her back down. 'Would you anoint me again?'

'God doesn't require it, Mrs O'Reilly. But if you want me to I will gladly do so, if it helps to give you peace of mind.'

Thirty-Three

Joan sighed. No matter how many versions she produced – hens, pigs, dogs, a clown (this came out rather sinister, so wasn't repeated), a jester – she was heartily sick of knitting egg cosies. However, the local charity shop, to which almost all of the items were given, was adamant that they sold really well. 'Small, low-cost gifts are very popular,' the grateful volunteer had stressed.

Dorothy, sitting opposite in the armchair by her bed, was working on a jumper for Angus. She simply couldn't bear to see him going around in such an ill-fitting garment and had refused to take 'no' for an answer when she had asked to take his measurements the previous week. Tiddles was keeping his head down, having learnt that it could be a dangerous thing to look up while the needles were clicking.

'I'm sure you could make something else, you know, dear, if you're really bored with them.'

Dorothy hadn't looked up or slowed down. She had knitted for so long that the act appeared as automatic as breathing and it was only with the most complex patterns that she could visibly be seen to concentrate on the task.

Before Joan could answer, the door opened and a figure entered, dressed as though impersonating a spy from a badly made 1960s television drama. The large dark glasses, tightly pulled down hat, long raincoat and gloves looked completely out of place in the hot weather. Even Dorothy stopped what she was doing at the unusual sight, while Tiddles gave a tiny *meow* of fright.

'I take it that's you under there,' said Joan.

'I've never been so embarrassed in all my years!' said the figure, closing the door and taking off her hat and glasses.

'Whatever happened, dear?'

'Nigel Ridley! That's what happened. I used to teach English to the man behind the counter. I knew he never paid attention in class.'

Almost hesitantly, Miss Ross unbuttoned her coat and took out the magazine hidden underneath. It was wrapped in a grey plastic cover. There was a clear strip at the top to display the title, but otherwise everything was hidden to protect innocent shoppers from unintentionally stumbling upon bits of naked flesh while browsing the gardening or cooking titles.

Holding it away from her body as if it was a bowel screening sample for an elephant, she laid the magazine on the small table next to Joan's chair.

'That's awful,' said Dorothy, full of sympathy. 'Did he recognise you?'

'He gave me a very strange leer.'

'But you got a magazine,' said Joan.

'I still can't believe I've done such a thing.'

'Desperate times,' said Joan.

Having rid herself of the item, Miss Ross removed her gloves and hung up her coat by the door. She let out a small moan while sitting in her chair, as though no longer able to contain her agitation. All three of them stared at the recently purchased item.

Miss Ross eventually broke the silence.

'It needs to be opened.'

Joan picked up the magazine and ripped off the plastic to reveal a close-up photograph of a naked young woman.

'Oh dear,' said Dorothy, putting a hand over the cat's eyes, feeling instinctively that Tiddles – or her, for that matter – should not be subjected to such images. 'If you don't mind, I'll let you two look through it and read out any suggestions. It's not the sort of thing my Willie would have liked me to see.'

With that she resumed her knitting and the cat buried his head. Miss Ross sat further back in her chair, as if the extra distance would somehow make anything she was about to experience a bit less traumatic. Joan flicked through a few pages.

'If I had known that Mr Jackson was looking at this sort of thing at school, I would have skelped his backside, janitor or not.'

'Mmm, he might have liked that,' said Joan, appearing not to be bothered by the intimate body parts flashing before her eyes.

'They're so young,' said Miss Ross. 'Why do they let themselves be photographed like that?'

'I guess for the money, maybe the fame,' suggested Joan.

'We need the advertisements,' said Miss Ross, waving a finger at the magazine to indicate her friend should get on with the business in hand.

Joan turned to the back and the two of them were silent, Miss Ross's face looking increasingly disgusted. Eventually Joan read out the heading above an advert showing the image of an elderly woman lying on a settee proudly displaying her private parts.

'*Granny Fanny.*'

The stillness that followed the comment felt almost physical, until a small voice piped up.

'That's not a name you hear these days.'

The two women slowly turned their heads to stare, not quite believing what they had heard. Even the cat risked looking. Dorothy carried on, engrossed in her knitting and quite oblivious to their gaze.

'When I was at school, we had two Fannys.'

Joan mouthed the words 'Please God no', but her friend carried on unaware of the silent prayer.

'The odd thing was that although they weren't related, they both had bright ginger hair. If we ever talked about one, we would refer to them as little ginger Fanny . . . and big ginger Fanny.'

Tiddles rested his head again and laid a paw over the top. As if in sympathy, Joan laid the magazine on her lap and put her head in her hands.

'If only there were more people like you in the world,' said Miss Ross.

Dorothy, missing Joan's desperate attempt at regaining control, smiled at what she took to be a compliment. Her friend picked up a notepad and pen and elbowed Joan, who finally retrieved the magazine again and read out some more adverts, although with difficulty.

'*Older ladies know how to handle a hard . . .*'

'Yes! Thank you, I can read it,' said Miss Ross. '*Fat, fifty and filthy.*'

'Almost a limerick,' said Joan.

'Do men really want this sort of thing?'

'*Mature X-rated lady.*'

'I can't argue that she's mature, but I doubt very much that she's a lady.'

'*Big and Bouncy.*'

'*Listen to Granny Moan,*' said Miss Ross, giving a groan herself at such an unwholesome situation.

For the next twenty minutes, the two women immersed themselves in the magazine, writing potential text for the advert, crossing it out, turning to new pages, pulling faces and going through the whole process again. Finally, they came to an agreement.

'That was the most unpleasant experience I have ever known,' said Miss Ross.

'Have you come up with something?' said Dorothy, putting down her knitting.

'Mature granny, waiting for your call,' said Miss Ross, reading from her notepad.

'Oh?'

'I simply couldn't bear to write anything worse.'

'So,' said Dorothy, 'if someone rings, what do we say to them?'

'I won't be saying anything, but you two need to decide how to start off the conversation. Joan?'

'Why are you asking me?'

'For some bizarre reason, I have a feeling you might have more idea,' she replied, pulling the magazine out of the other woman's hands and putting it forcibly on the table.

'I don't know. We probably have to say something about their willy.'

'Oh dear,' said Dorothy.

'Well, it's bound to come up at some point in the conversation . . . if you see what I mean.'

Though she tried to control it, Joan started to laugh

again, not having completely got over Dorothy talking about Fannys. She wondered if she ever would.

'You need to practise your opening lines,' said Miss Ross, thinking that she was forever going to sound like a headmistress, no matter where she was.

'We don't even have a telephone,' pointed out Dorothy.

'Well, we'll have to improvise,' said Miss Ross, looking around the room. Her eye came to rest on a nearby bowl. She pointed, wagging her finger until Joan got the message and passed over a banana.

'There you are – your telephone,' said Miss Ross.

Dorothy looked suspiciously at the banana before laying it gently on her thigh near to the cat's head. Tiddles lifted his paw to examine this new object, although quickly lost interest.

'What do I say?'

'How about calling them big boy? They always like that sort of thing,' suggested Joan.

'Right. Don't hold back.'

Dorothy sat looking at the yellow fruit, its curve fitting neatly around her leg, but didn't speak. Joan tried to encourage her.

'If you don't practise, then you'll be terribly tongue-tied when it happens for real.'

'I was waiting for it to ring.'

Joan felt another loss of control coming on, while Miss Ross, still recovering from the distasteful experience of having to buy the magazine, was becoming increasingly exasperated.

'Oh, for goodness sake! Ring-ring. Ring-ring.'

Dorothy slowly lifted the banana and put it to her ear.

'Hello, dear . . .'

'You can't say "hello dear" like that,' said Miss Ross.

Dorothy put her hand over the end, as if it was a real telephone.

'But that's what I would say,' she whispered.

'You have to talk in a way that pleases the caller,' said Joan, trying to explain the point of the exercise. 'They might want to speak to a mature woman but they don't actually want to feel that they're talking to their granny.'

'I don't understand,' said Dorothy, shaking her head and putting the banana back down on her leg, as if she was replacing a receiver. 'I'm never going to be able to do this.'

'Here, give me the phone,' said Joan, now so enthusiastic that it had become real in her mind as well.

After a moment's hesitation Dorothy handed the banana to Miss Ross, who passed it on to Joan, the latter laying it gently on her thigh. They all sat in silence until Miss Ross, suddenly realising the reason for the delay, cried out in despair. 'God give me strength! Ring-ring. Ring-ring.'

Joan lifted the banana to her ear before speaking in a breathy, sexy voice that stunned the other two women.

'Hello . . . big boy. I've been so lonely waiting to hear your deep, masculine tones caressing me from a distance. I hope you're going to make me feel . . . less lonely. I bet you're really good at making women feel better.'

The demonstration over, she held the banana away from her head and with a triumphant expression waited for her friends to say something. Tiddles, who had grown used to a gentile, refined lifestyle amongst the elderly residents, jumped onto the floor and hid under the bed.

'Are you sure you haven't done this before?' said Miss Ross.

'Here, you've got to try.'

The 'telephone' was passed along, Miss Ross holding it out to the reluctant recipient.

'It's for you.'

Dorothy looked at the photograph of Willie as though seeking forgiveness for what she was about to do and put the banana to her ear.

'Hello . . . big boy. It's . . . Delilah here. So, tell me . . . tell me . . . how is the weather where you are, dear?'

Thirty-Four

Joan, Miss Ross and Dorothy had been sitting in silence in the latter's bedroom for the last ten minutes, staring at the shiny new telephone which had been placed on a small table positioned within reach of the three chairs.

'It hasn't rung,' said Dorothy.

'It only went live this morning,' pointed out Miss Ross. 'I suppose we'll just have to wait for the right person, or rather the wrong sort, to see one of the adverts.'

'I hope we haven't done all this for nothing,' said Joan.

'It's all in the Lord's hands now,' said Dorothy.

One by one, they resumed their knitting. Joan had progressed to tea cosies, while Miss Ross was working on a baby's cardigan, not out of any maternal instinct or because she had relatives with new arrivals but rather to enjoy the challenge.

'I'm going to make this a really large scarf,' said Dorothy, who constantly swapped between projects, depending upon her mood. 'My Willie would have liked it. He didn't have a scrap of fat on him and where we lived was a wild place in the winter. Poor Willie was often frozen stiff.'

The room was suddenly filled with ringing. All three of

them cried out in surprise, their needles frozen as though they were delicate ice sculptures, wool part on and part off, a tiny sleeve stopped at the cuff, the row on a tea cosy half completed. The sound seemed to echo until Miss Ross broke the spell they had fallen under.

'Go on, someone pick it up!'

'Joan, this was your idea.'

'It's your telephone. You've got to do it. Just remember the phrases we agreed.'

'For goodness sake! I've not put up cards in every sleazy public house in town for no one to answer when it rings.'

Miss Ross picked up the stopwatch that was on the floor by her chair and held it ready to start when the conversation began. Dorothy looked at the photograph of Willie for guidance, but the image simply smiled back. She put down her knitting, laid the picture frame on its face – the first time she had ever done such a thing – then lifted the receiver. The room was immediately still and tense, like the atmosphere in a wildlife documentary where the stalking lion is on the verge of rushing out to kill its prey.

'Hello?'

Joan and Miss Ross mouthed the words 'big boy' and eventually Dorothy took the hint.

'Hello . . . big boy.'

The others seemed pleased. Dorothy listened intently, looking with increasing confusion at Tiddles asleep on a cushion by her feet.

'Just a moment, dear,' she said, before covering the mouthpiece with her hand. 'This is rather odd.'

'Why? What did he say?' asked Miss Ross.

'He wants to know if Tiddles is well behaved.'

'The cat!'

'Yes.'

'What exactly did he say?' asked Joan.

'He said, did I have a naughty old pussy.'

'No, he doesn't mean . . .'

Even though she really did try, Joan couldn't finish the sentence. Waves of laughter welled up inside her and hovered just below the surface, like an over-full dam where a single extra raindrop will result in disaster. It took every ounce of willpower to stop herself losing control, which would not have helped the situation at all.

'Speak to him,' said Miss Ross almost frantically. 'Say anything. Keep him on the telephone.'

'Hello, dear, sorry to keep you. Well . . . it does have a tendency to wander. Yesterday Mr Adams found it waiting for him in his bedroom . . . it gave him quite a turn. On the whole it's well behaved, although there are times when it can be rather naughty. Oh, it's been known to settle itself in the flowerbed and leave an impression amongst the petunias. You know for ages afterwards where it's been . . .'

Joan was losing the fight and had stuffed part of a tea cosy into her mouth. Dorothy listened some more, then covered the mouthpiece again.

'This is not what I expected. He's ever so interested in the cat. Now he wants to know if it's friendly. Is Joan all right?'

'Ignore her. Keep talking to him.'

'Hello? Yes, I would say that by the end of each day dozens of people will have given it a stroke. Mmm. Yes, we always seem to be busy. There are thirty rooms and it's very popular with all the staff.'

Dorothy listened some more to the caller, but the raindrop had fallen and the strange wailing noises coming from across the room were a bit distracting.

'Yes, we have staff. And it's popular with visitors as

184

well. Sometimes there's almost a tussle over who gets their hands on it.' Dorothy looked surprised. 'Oh, he's gone. But he thought I was extraordinary. That was nice of him, wasn't it?' she said, replacing the receiver.

No one answered. Miss Ross was busy working out figures on a calculator. 'Well done. We've made two pounds and thirty pence.'

'Really! From that one call? How marvellous. I never thought it would be so easy. Shall I make us all a cup of tea to celebrate? Perhaps it will help Joan. She doesn't seem to be herself at all.'

Thirty-Five

There had been no calls for several days. The three friends began to wonder if all of their efforts were going to be for nothing and their sleepless nights unnecessary. The scheme wasn't looking positive. It had cost more than a hundred pounds just to get the line installed.

When Miss Ross entered Dorothy's bedroom to retrieve her knitting, she wasn't thinking at all about the telephone and so when it unexpectedly rang she couldn't prevent the cry of alarm that escaped from her lips. This was a scenario she hadn't considered. Apart from Tiddles on a chair, there was no one else around.

She had been against this entire venture from the start and it was only to help that she had agreed to be involved – but not like this. The other two women were in the lounge, too far to fetch. The ringing continued. Perhaps she should ignore it, collect what she needed and leave. Nobody would know. Maybe it would stop soon and then she wouldn't have to make a decision.

But it didn't. Whoever was on the other end was not giving up easily. Miss Ross walked over to the little table and stared. She reached down with her hand, then pulled it back. To lift the receiver would expose her to a sleazy world of perverted desire and lust of which she had no knowledge.

But there was only two pounds thirty pence . . .

'Hello?'

Her voice sounded unnaturally high and squeaky, almost cracking with tension. She took a big breath. This time it came out surprisingly low.

'Hello.'

She mouthed the words 'big boy' as she had done herself to Dorothy only a few days earlier. But it was no good. She couldn't utter them.

'Can I help you?'

'I expect better than "Can I help you?" How about something a bit more exciting.'

'Yes . . . well, I suppose . . . big boy.'

'Is that it? I'm not paying good money just to be called big boy!'

This was too much for Miss Ross.

'What more do you expect me to say? I have better things to do than stand here and think up rude conversation for your titillation.'

'Go on, then. Tell me about your tits.'

'You leave my bust alone, young man. I've never heard such a suggestion. If you had been in my class at school, I would have given your backside a skelping you wouldn't forget in a very long time!'

'Oh, yes, now you're starting to earn your money. I could wear my school uniform.'

'Your school uniform!'

'I'll book us a room at the Station Hotel for Friday afternoon, under the name of Fraser.'

'You can book what you like at the Station Hotel, Mr

Fraser, if that's your name. I can assure you that you'll be having a very lonely time.'

'Look, I don't want sex or anything like that . . . just a spanking. I promise, you can keep all your clothes on, even your coat, if you want. I'll give you a hundred and fifty pounds.'

The conversation was becoming so surreal that Miss Ross felt quite dizzy. How could she possibly be talking about such a subject to a complete stranger? She had never had any sort of conversation like this with anyone. And he sounded well spoken rather than sleazy, which somehow seemed to make it all the more bizarre. Without realising, she started to pull the string of pearls through her fingers.

'A hundred and fifty pounds . . . for a spanking?'

'Do you have a credit-card machine?'

'No, I don't have a credit-card machine.'

'How about a reduction if I book a session of them?'

'No, there isn't a reduction if you book a session of them. There isn't going to be a session of them, not even a single one of them.'

'All right, then. I can tell you're a hard negotiator – two hundred, in cash. You can have the money when you arrive. I can't say fairer than that.'

'Two hundred pounds! That's an absurd amount.'

'It'll all be yours, to do whatever you want with. Just for half an hour. I'll buy you a cream tea afterwards.'

'A cream tea!'

Miss Ross was so taken aback by what the caller was suggesting that she didn't know how to react. She wanted to swear at the man, something she had very rarely been known to do (and never really bad words), but she was completely lost for words.

As if taking her silence as agreement, the man continued. *'Right then, three o'clock on Friday. Don't be late.'*

The line went dead. Miss Ross was so shaken that even though she knew he had gone she started shouting.

'How dare you! Don't . . . don't you ever speak to me like that again, you obnoxious, horrible little man!'

She slammed down the receiver and collapsed in her chair. The hand that was pulling at the pearls was trembling. Tiddles watched intently. Although the cat had little to do with this particular resident, he was always a good listener and, at the time, he was the only one there to confide in.

'Oh Tiddles, what a dreadful experience. But two hundred pounds . . .'

Thirty-Six

Friday, 1st July

Can I do such an unspeakable thing? Will I betray so much of what I hold dear? Never in my life have I faced such a dilemma. The possibility of considering such an act is unthinkable. Yet as I sit here writing this I'm trying to convince myself that the good intention outweighs the hideous act, and the deed can be forgiven because of the reason behind it. Despite all my education and learning, am I simply a fool? I can't think logically and there is no one to turn to.

Thirty-Seven

Father Connelly had proclaimed on more than one occasion that Mrs O'Reilly was the most stubborn person who had ever been a member of his congregation. Almost as if to demonstrate his point, she defied the predictions of her impending demise and made a gradual recovery. As the hot days of summer passed into July, she was back to her usual self, perhaps a little frailer but with a mind and tongue as finely honed as ever.

Her ill health had at least allowed her to avoid having any contact with Mrs Winchester-Fowler, who had managed to irritate everyone several times over. Even Tiddles avoided her, despite the regular announcements that she adored cats and used to own two very expensive Siamese.

People had been astounded at the quantity of elegant clothing squashed into her bedroom and she spent much of each day changing outfits, generally appearing for lunch or in reception for a trip wearing something completely unsuitable. However, the obsession helped to keep her occupied so no one felt inclined to point out that this wasn't necessary.

She wore a gown more appropriate for an evening dance to attend that morning's service. The Church of Scotland minister held one at the home on the first Saturday of each month. These were attended by the majority of residents, regardless of individual beliefs, although they also had access to representatives of other denominations who visited from the Free Church of Scotland, the Scottish Episcopal Church and the Baptist Church.

Walter didn't go to the service. He had distanced himself from religion since Moira died and, anyway, his daughter and granddaughters were coming after lunch so that was the main priority for him that day.

Heather and Penny, at thirteen and fourteen, were turning into very attractive young women, but they still had frequent displays of utter childishness that he found both delightful and worrying. Walter had secretly arranged for Dorothy to take them outside and so after everyone had had their hugs and kisses his accomplice happened to pass by and innocently ask if they might like to see the garden.

'You're looking well, Dad,' said Becky, once the two of them had found a quiet spot in the conservatory.

'I feel well,' he said. 'The girls are growing up. I can see a difference even from the last time they were here.'

'All too fast. I can hardly keep up with them. John sends his regards and apologies for not being able to come.'

His son-in-law was a decent man, although the extremely long hours he worked running a small accountancy business meant that he wasn't as involved with his family as he should be.

'I'm glad we've got this opportunity to speak alone,' said Walter. 'I wanted to talk to you about a decision I've made.'

'What's that, Dad?'

'I'm going to leave We Care For You.'

★ ★ ★

Later on, when Dorothy was bringing the girls back inside, they encountered Mrs Winchester-Fowler stroking something that Ben was holding and initially assumed it was one of the pets.

'This is such a lovely cat,' she said, upon seeing them approaching. 'He's so friendly, aren't you, my beauty? Yes, just like my Siamese.'

The carer appeared as though he didn't know whether to be slightly sheepish or amused.

'Tiddles has been rather reluctant to meet, so I thought I would bring him along,' he said with a wink, before looking down at the wig that was folded over his arm. It was one of Beatrice's spares.

'He is very friendly,' said Dorothy, reaching over and patting the brown hair.

It was too much for Heather and Penny. The mature, sophisticated impression they had tried so hard to convey for the last half an hour was gone in an instant as they held onto each other, utterly helpless. They were still unable to talk sensibly when they finally caught up with their mother and grandfather and sat on the settee like two miniature versions of the laughing policeman at the fair.

Dorothy explained the circumstances. Walter smiled fondly, yet he couldn't help thinking how vulnerable they both looked in their make-up and adult clothes. It made him all the more determined to put his plan into action.

★ ★ ★

The next week was set to be even busier than usual and as Matron sat in her office that Monday she accepted this was largely her own fault. A few months earlier she had suggested that each resident create a bucket list and from this highlight the two or three things they would most like to do. There was no need to add 'before you die' and it was also obvious that any suggestions had to be realistic. No one was about to start climbing Munros.

Some of the activities had been so fairly ordinary that Matron couldn't help wondering why people simply hadn't done these things years ago, when they were fitter. Perhaps age and impending death gave a freedom and a permission to be honest in a way that wasn't possible before.

Sociologists refer to people born between 1925 and 1945 as the *Silent Generation*, categorised usually by their respect for law and order, alongside a willingness to work hard, conform, accept sacrifice and be patient. Maybe the latter became a bit harder when there was so little time left.

Making scented candles, going to watch a ballet, getting a tattoo and driving a fire engine (in reality, Stella only sat in the driver's seat and sounded the horn) had been relatively straightforward to organise.

Meg and Peg had both wanted to be bridesmaids, something they had never done, and an editorial piece in the local newspaper had resulted in a couple about to be married offering for the elderly women to be theirs. A minibus full of residents had gone to the church and the two women had played their part tremendously, the event attracting quite a lot of media attention.

That coming Wednesday Mrs O'Reilly was going to be taken to the public swimming pool, where they had a hot tub, an experience she wished to try, while Joyce had said she would like to learn to swim. Today a group of them were going to a nearby farm. Two residents had included this on their list and someone else had said they wanted to ride a horse, so fifteen were scheduled to go as a special trip.

The health-and-safety issues had been a nightmare. Matron, sitting in her usual short-sleeved top, was checking through an email relating to this when Mrs Winchester-Fowler stormed in.

'You hussy!' she shouted, pointing at the bare arms. 'All you do is sit watching television. It's not fair.' Before being able to prevent her, she quickly stooped down and unplugged the computer. 'There. Now you can get off your backside and do some work!'

* * *

Miss Ross sat in her bedroom that evening, having told the others that she had some correspondence to reply to. This was true, although the real reason was that she needed to be alone. The conversation with the caller who'd asked for a spanking hadn't been far from her mind over the past few days and she had been in a state of terrible apprehension ever since. She sat at her writing desk, nervously fingering the string of pearls.

The excited chatter at every table over supper had been about the entertaining visit to the farm, but she had listened without any enthusiasm, forcing a smile or nod now and again merely to appear as if interested. Being unable to decide about something was a feeling Miss Ross hated and she went to bed knowing that she would have another poor night's sleep and wake up in the same troubled frame of mind.

There were no outings on the Tuesday, but the place was

soon bustling nonetheless. At nine o'clock the hairdresser set herself up in the tiny salon, which had been designed to convey a different atmosphere to the rest of the building. There was even a pile of magazines for 'customers' to read while waiting.

She came two mornings a week and in this small room would cut, wash, shampoo and set, blow dry and perm. Two women had their hair dyed, including Joan, who remained a bright blonde. All of the men got their hair cut in the salon except Walter, who preferred to walk to the men's barbers in town.

By coffee time, the chiropodist and optician were working their way through that day's list, while the library van and district nurse had been and gone. The local GP was seeing to Mr Adams, who had tripped coming out of the dining room and hurt his leg. Falling was the biggest cause of injury amongst the residents; despite the best efforts of the staff, sometimes these things just happened.

Two committee members of the Friends of We Care For You were in the office going through plans for a fund-raising fête scheduled to take place in two weeks. Matron, although extremely grateful to them for what they did, wished they would stick to the matter in hand, as there was an inspection of the care home due to take place on Thursday and these visits always generated extra work.

And so the week went by. Mrs O'Reilly entertained everyone around her with shrieks of delight during her time in the hot tub, while Joyce eventually managed a few unaided strokes in the pool nearby and declared upon achieving this that she could swim well enough. A string of professionals, families, friends, delivery men, taxis and a host of others passed through reception, did what they had to and left. The inspection went well, despite Mr Forsyth slapping the female official on the bottom.

On Thursday evening everyone sat happily in the lounge, recounting with excitement the recent events. There was one figure not present: Miss Ross.

Lying quietly on her bed, looking up at the ceiling as if in a trance, she felt an overwhelming sense of dread. Her days and nights were so dominated by this feeling that it was difficult to tell them apart. She feared trying to sleep and feared waking up. And tomorrow was the day when she would have to make a decision . . .

Thirty-Eight

Every step she took along the pavement was like a stab to her soul, as though an invisible knife was cutting off parts of her with each yard covered. A sliver of morality fell off while going over the zebra crossing. By the post box she left a hunk of dignity. At the grocer's shop, a slice of sensitivity rolled away, coming to rest in the gutter.

Miss Ross had never known such fear. Her indigestion was awful. She would have to find a toilet as soon as she got to the Station Hotel. She kept trying to convince herself that she wasn't on her way to meet this frightful man, that there was still the option to turn back.

But in her heart she knew she couldn't. Two hundred pounds would let Dorothy stay in the home for a week. The telephone calls to the sex line had brought in some money but nowhere near enough to cover the rise in her fees. Something more drastic had to be done. This would be the most unpleasant experience of her life, but if she wasn't prepared to make such a sacrifice, then what was the value of her love? Was it so shallow that she faltered at the first true test?

The arguments about the rights or wrongs of what she

was about to do flew around inside her head like hornets, right up until she reached the building. Then they seemed suddenly irrelevant: she was standing outside the Station Hotel and whatever was about to take place would happen regardless of the morals behind it.

She hated lying. She told the others that an old cousin had unexpectedly been in touch. He had just moved to the area and they were going to meet up for afternoon tea. Miss Ross had caught a bus near the home and then walked the rest of the way. It wasn't a part of town that she visited, yet she still checked there wasn't anyone nearby whom she recognised and while walking up to the counter she looked carefully at the receptionist. The face was unfamiliar.

'Can I help you?' said the young woman pleasantly.

'Yes, I'm meeting my cousin . . . Mr Fraser. Could you please tell him that I'm here?'

The woman called a number on the internal telephone. She explained that there was a visitor, listened for a brief moment, thanked the guest and hung up.

'Mr Fraser says would you mind going up to his room?' she said. 'It's number twenty-nine on the first floor.'

'Thank you. I'll just visit the ladies.'

'Certainly, madam. Third door on the right.'

Miss Ross muttered a 'thank you' and followed the directions given. A mature woman dressed in a smart tweed skirt and jacket could hardly have appeared more dignified and she considered that, on the surface at least, no one could suspect anything untoward. Even so, she worried that the young woman knew what was going on.

Had the man done this sort of thing here before? Why on earth had she not considered this? Miss Ross stepped into a cubicle, locked the door and almost collapsed against it. If he used this hotel regularly, then the staff would know that something unwholesome was happening! She felt sick and later on, when she stood outside room twenty-nine, she almost threw up in the corridor.

Leave now, while there's still a chance.

She raised her hand.

There must be another way to raise the money.

The hand hesitated.

Dorothy would never want this.

The hand knocked.

The door opened and the man, her client, studied his new arrival before breaking into a grin.

'I do appreciate that you've come. Please,' he said, stepping aside and beckoning her into the room.

Condemned without hope, she walked in and he closed the door quietly behind her. Miss Ross walked over to the window to put some distance between them before turning to study him. He was doing the same of her. He didn't look . . . well, she hadn't known what to expect. He appeared fairly ordinary, in his early forties and a little podgy around the middle, but well dressed and with an intelligent face. The room itself was a normal hotel bedroom. There was a double bed but that meant nothing these days.

'Would you like a drink?'

He was well spoken. She knew that none of these 'ordinary' characteristics was any sort of guarantee that the man didn't pose a threat. After all, how 'ordinary' was it to want to meet an elderly woman in a hotel bedroom for what they were about to do?

Was he really going to wear a school uniform?

Miss Ross shook her head. Her voice, which had in its time been famous for its ability to control an entire hall of unruly children, had deserted her. The man poured himself a whisky then removed his wallet and slowly counted out several crisp £20 notes, which he put on the table by the bed.

'I think we agreed two hundred pounds.'

He was so calm he could have been merely paying for a meal at a restaurant. There was certainly no obvious sign of emotion. Miss Ross, trembling from head to foot and running her necklace constantly between her fingers, was on the verge of fainting.

'I prefer a hand, if that's all right?' said the man.

A hand?

He remained silent, waiting for a response. Eventually she cleared her throat. Her voice sounded like it belonged to a stranger.

'I've never done this before . . . I don't know what to do.'

'A virgin?' he said, showing excitement for the first time.

She assumed he meant to this situation, not that she was actually a virgin. But did he know? Was her secret obvious to a person like this?

'I'd like a spanking with a hand, not a strap or belt, nothing artificial.'

Her legs felt as though they were about to buckle and send her falling to the floor.

Hands? Belts? What am I doing here? DOROTHY!

'I'll leave you for a moment to get ready. Please make yourself comfortable. You might at least want to remove any clothing that may hamper your movements.'

He put down his glass and walked into the bathroom, closing the door behind him. Miss Ross put a shaking hand to her face and forced herself not to start crying. The man, she suspected, wanted to be dominated and to show weakness might be unwise. He was a great deal stronger than her and it could be a dangerous move to make him angry.

For an instant, she considered leaving while he was in

201

the bathroom. It would just be possible. But by knocking on the door she had surrendered to her fate, handed it over to someone she had never met. Reluctantly, she took off her jacket and put it over the back of a chair. Almost immediately she picked it up again. Walking over to the table, she stuffed the money into an inside pocket, then hung the jacket on the bedroom door.

When the man emerged from the bathroom, she stared in disbelief. Not only was he wearing a specially made school uniform, including carefully ironed grey shorts, but his mannerisms had altered completely as well. Here was a small boy, his exposed knees almost touching as he stood awkwardly just inside the doorway.

'Please, miss. I've been terribly naughty. I should be punished.'

Miss Ross had never seen a sight like it and for a moment hadn't a clue what to say. The man looked down at his feet, just as a child might do, expecting to be told off.

'Yes,' she eventually replied. It seemed the only comment to make.

Without another word, the man walked over, head bowed, and stood by the bed before bending over. Miss Ross simply gazed in amazement. What was she meant to do now? Then to her horror he undid his shorts and let them drop to the floor. He wasn't wearing anything underneath. She had never touched a man's bottom.

'I've been very bad,' said the small voice again.

Think of Dorothy.

Why hadn't she brought gloves? Could she do this? The money was already hers. She moved around into position, only just managing to control an urge to sob, then raised her hand, holding it in the air for one last moment of – what . . . innocence? There was a slap and the chubby pink cheeks wobbled as if mocking her.

'You don't know how naughty I've been.'

Dear God.

Each brief contact seemed to destroy a tiny part of her. In the whole of her life she had never 'known' another person, had never lain naked next to someone and held them close. That this perverted act with a complete stranger should be her most intimate experience filled her with utter despair.

Miss Ross had always led a respectable life, worked hard and saved as she had been brought up to do. But even after all those years she didn't have enough reserves to pay for her own and Dorothy's rise in fees. That's why she was there, because some faceless bureaucrats were bleeding the residents without even visiting to assess the impact of their decision. Her despair was edged aside by anger.

This time she pulled her arm further back and then hit the man with all of her strength, grunting with the effort. He moaned and she did it again. Then she hit him and hit him and hit him until room twenty-nine, on the first floor of the Station Hotel, rebounded with slaps and grunts, moans and sobs.

Her hand stung, she was gasping for breath and her crisp white blouse stuck to her with sweat, yet she carried on relentlessly as if she was no longer human and what she was beating was not a naked bottom but injustice, unfairness and the desperation of unfulfilled love. Through her tears the world around her was a blur of confusion and misery and ecstasy and pain.

* * *

Downstairs the receptionist was talking on the telephone to a friend. She was laughing.

'Yeah, that's why I always put him in the room above here. You should hear the noises this time and the woman who turned up was ancient. I wouldn't have believed she had it in her. This one must be a real pro to keep going like that. She even arrived dressed as you'd expect a retired headmistress to look.'

Thirty-Nine

Miss Ross sat alone in Dorothy's bedroom with Tiddles on her lap. The cat, sensing her great sadness, had jumped up onto knees that were not generally very welcoming. Still trembling from her encounter that afternoon, she stroked the soft fur with gratitude for this innocent affection. The building was relatively quiet, as a group of residents had gone to the garden centre. They had an extraordinary capacity never to tire of the place.

Miss Ross tried to block out the images that forced their way into her mind, overwhelming her with shame and grief. She was still battling with them when the bedroom door opened.

'Oh, you're always beating us,' said Dorothy, starting to taking off her red hat and coat.

'What! What did you say?'

'You've beaten us back from our trip out.'

'Yes . . . just by a short while. Did you have a pleasant time?'

'It was lovely,' she said, as though it had been a completely new experience. 'They're very good to have us old fogies going around en masse. And we had a nice tea. Did you see your cousin?' She walked over to her friend. 'Is everything all right, dear?'

'Yes . . . I saw him.'

'You don't look at all well. Shall I put the kettle on?'

'No, thank you. I think I'll lie down for a while.'

'That's probably the best thing to do.'

Miss Ross put Tiddles on the floor and stood up, but she didn't move away.

'I told my cousin . . . about your situation. He has made a lot of money in his life and he gave me this for you.'

With that, she pulled out the money from her jacket and handed it over.

'My goodness! I can't possibly take this. There must be a hundred pounds here.'

'Two hundred.'

'That's extremely kind of your cousin. I've never known such generosity, but you must of course return it,' said Dorothy, holding out the money.

'No!' said Miss Ross, taking a step towards the door as if to emphasise that the gift could not be taken back. 'It can't be returned.'

'But . . .'

'You have to accept it.'

'It's so much.'

'Your friendship means so much.'

'My dear, whatever's the matter?'

'I'm sorry. I've got a terrible headache. I'll be better later.'

With that, Miss Ross rushed out of the room, leaving the other woman staring in confusion at the wad of £20 notes.

Forty

Walter and Julie walked along the seafront. They had agreed to meet away from the home following her previous disastrous visit when Deirdre had tried to prevent her from entering. Since then the pair had only spoken on the telephone and he had missed her terribly.

'I've always loved the sea, with its smell of seaweed and the freshness of the wind,' she said. 'It makes me feel clean.'

'I've been so worried about you these last few weeks. We could have met before now.'

'I'm sorry. I needed some time to myself. Well, not that I get much of that.'

'Joyce didn't give anything away concerning what you both spoke about that day. I could have throttled Deirdre for what she did. And she's a funny old fish.'

'Deirdre?'

'No, Joyce. I can't work her out at all. I think there are a lot of deep waters running through her past, but I appreciate that she was trying to be kind to you.'

'She was extremely kind. I know you wanted to look after me back in your room, but it was better that I went with her.'

She linked an arm through one of his and they walked on in silence for a while. A couple of gulls flew overhead and a small group of oystercatchers waddled about at the water's edge. Apart from them they were alone.

'I told her about my past.'

'Did you?' said Walter, surprised. 'Well, it's your secret to tell or not tell. How did she react?'

'With great tenderness. I cried like a baby for ages and she just held me without speaking, like my mother used to when I was little. She thinks I should speak to Matron and explain what's happened.'

'I don't see how that will help.'

'Nor do I, to be honest, but, do you know, I think I will.'

'Well, Matron's a wise old bird and knows how to keep something to herself. If you feel comfortable about it, then I don't see that it will do any harm. The damage, as far as the home goes, has already been done.'

'Does everyone know what I am?'

'They know what you do, not what you are. There's a big difference.' The wind off the sea was chilly and Walter pulled up the collar of his coat. 'Is it an option to consider speaking to your parents?'

'I don't know. Whatever way you look at it, they were very cruel. At the period in my life when I needed them more than ever, they banished me from my home.'

'If they were like me, they wouldn't understand anything about grooming and how an innocent young girl could be so entrapped. Maybe you should give them another chance?'

'Perhaps one day, but not this one. This is for us.'

Julie stopped and threw her arms around his waist. He held her tightly. Walter knew the desperate need she had for physical affection that wasn't connected in any way to sex.

He had been surprised, after Moira died, at how much he had appreciated the touch of another person and how Anna and the other carers would often put their arms around him when they could see he was upset or looking forlorn. He held Julie until she was ready to pull away and resume walking, which they eventually did without making any comment.

'You know,' he said, 'I had quite a soul-searching conversation with Matron myself the other day.'

'Did you? What about?'

'Leaving.'

'But what will you do?'

'When I went into the home, I had sunk into such despair that, frankly, I did need looking after. But I'm so much stronger now and the things that have happened over the last few months with you – us – it got me wondering what on earth I was doing there. I'm still a relatively fit and active man, certainly capable of taking care of myself for a few more years.'

'What was her opinion?'

'Oh, she had been thinking along the same lines. However, she said it was completely down to me whether I remained or moved out. She didn't want to be an influence in any way.'

'So, you'll go?' said Julie.

'Not until I find somewhere to live.'

'But you'll move away from here?'

'After the things that you've told me about grooming I want to be near to my granddaughters. They're reaching the age when it happened to you and to be honest I don't think Becky and her husband have much idea about these things.'

'You want to move to Aberdeen to keep an eye on them?'

'If I can help to keep them out of the clutches of evil men until they're old enough and sufficiently streetwise not to be so vulnerable . . . well, I can't imagine a better use of my time. I've still got sufficient money to buy a property . . . something with two bedrooms.'

She stopped to look up at him.

'Why two?'

'It would be a chance for you to start again in an area where no one knows you. There would be a place where you would be totally safe and I could keep us both until you've found yourself a job.'

'How would it look to your family? They're going to suspect something regardless of what you tell them and you know you're a terrible liar, Walter.'

'Don't worry about my family. What we have to decide is what's best for you.'

Forty-One

Dorothy entered the bedroom to find Joan trying not to laugh, the receiver to her ear and a caller obviously on the other end. She walked quietly over to her chair and began working on the jumper for Angus, which was nearing completion.

'You have specially made trousers! Your tailor is very understanding . . . doesn't charge for the extra material.'

She knew the conversation was being repeated for her benefit but would have been just as happy not to hear.

'Yes, it must be terrible having to fight off all these women. Some people are so inconsiderate. No, no, of course you don't brag about it. Oh, well, goodbye then,' said Joan, putting down the receiver.

'Are you having fun?'

'That one was supposed to be in the more-than-a-foot club! I don't know where these men get their tape measures from.'

'I think decimalisation caused a lot of confusion.'

Joan shrieked at this and Dorothy couldn't help smiling at her friend's amusement. She put down her knitting and picked up the photograph of her husband.

'I only ever knew Willie. We were childhood sweethearts. Happy in each other's company from the first day we met. Then along came Andrew and our joy was complete.'

'I'm sure he was a good man.'

'He was. But my life with him hasn't prepared me for these telephone calls,' said Dorothy, putting back the frame on the little table. 'I certainly got into a pickle yesterday. I kept referring to the caller as Mr Thomas until he told me that wasn't his name, so I said, well, shall I call you John? He wasn't very pleased. You're so much more a woman of the world.'

'I wasn't always. When I look back, I can't believe how innocent I used to be.'

'These days innocence seems to vanish overnight.'

'That's often how it happens, love.'

'Oh, you know what I mean.'

Joan picked up her knitting but had barely started when she put it down again.

'I can remember the first time I ever saw an erection,' she said.

'I'm not sure I want to hear this.'

'I'll tell you the story.'

'That's what I was afraid of.'

'It was only a month or so after I had started work as a student nurse. There was a good-looking patient, not much older than me. On this particular afternoon he was asleep. I had to change his dressing, so I closed the curtains and quietly carried on. Suddenly, there it was . . . staring at me! I wanted to scream.'

'Did you?'

'No, I thought there was something wrong with him so rushed off to fetch the sister.'

'Oh no!'

'I was too embarrassed to explain the problem, so she came back to see what it was all about.'

'I'm embarrassed just thinking about it,' said Dorothy, although a few moments later she leant over as if part of a conspiracy. 'What happened then?'

'God, I can't believe it. I pointed and said, "I told you there was something wrong with it. Shall I get the doctor?"'

Neither woman could speak for several moments. Mr Adams, walking slowly along the corridor outside, shook his head in bemusement at how often laughter could be heard coming from that particular bedroom.

'The sister was very kind and fortunately the lad was still asleep. She told me to cover him up, then took me back to her office to explain the facts of life. I can't believe I was ever so naive.

'After Willie died I never considered being with someone else. I just didn't want to. What was it like, being married to more than one man?'

Joan sighed as she reflected upon her life. It wasn't something she generally did, believing much more in living for the moment.

'They were all very different. Looking back, I think that maybe I found each one at the time in my life when I needed that sort of person. Don't misunderstand me. I loved them greatly and was devastated when they died. I don't know, maybe it was all just fate.'

They both resumed their knitting. A tiny *meow* announced the arrival of Tiddles, who had pushed open the door enough to squeeze through the gap. The cat jumped up onto its favourite lap and purred contentedly.

'Joan ... this cousin that Miss Ross has started seeing recently ... you don't think there's something odd about it, do you?'

213

'In what way, love?'

'Well, it's only that you would expect her to be pleased to meet him, yet she always appears subdued beforehand and stays in her room when she gets back.'

The other woman put down her knitting to consider what had just been said.

'Now that you mention it, she does seem out of sorts on those days.'

'I don't think she's been herself for a while.'

'Have you spoken to her about it?'

'No, I don't feel it's my business. There's just something that makes me uneasy. I might be completely mistaken. She's not one to talk about feelings. Please don't say anything. I wouldn't hurt her for the world.'

'I won't. She's one of the old school in every sense. It's good of her to handle all the money side of our little telephone business.'

'Yes, I seem to make exactly the extra I need every week.'

'Fate playing its hand again?'

'Perhaps the Lord has forgiven me for laughing at the minister on all those occasions,' said Dorothy smiling.

'I bet that cockerel never forgave the minister – what cockerel would?'

Forty-Two

The calls to the sex line had increased to the point where Joan and Dorothy were each taking about six per day, but whereas the former appeared generally to find the conversations amusing, the latter normally had no idea what was being discussed and always tried to steer the topic away from anything to do with sex.

Her simple innocence had such an extraordinary power about it that many men ended up apologising for being rude before going on to discuss their personal problems. In these conversations she revealed a deep understanding of human nature and callers quickly discovered here was someone they could talk to frankly without being judged, while obtaining sound advice. She covered the Wednesday morning shifts and had been on a call now for nearly half an hour.

'Even big, grown men can experience domestic abuse, Alan,' she said with her usual gentleness. 'If you try the things I've suggested, you may find the situation improves.' She listened for a moment before continuing. 'Already forgotten, dear. To be honest, I didn't have much idea of what you were talking about. Although it might be some time before I can bring myself to eat a banana. Mmm . . . yes, goodbye dear. Good luck.'

Dorothy put down the receiver and stroked the cat's ear, much to the pleasure of both.

'Oh, Tiddles, all you care about is finding the most comfortable knee. There are so many problems out there that could be solved with a bit of old-fashioned common sense. Everyone's so keen to rush about I think they've thrown it overboard in order to go faster.'

The cat purred but made no other contribution to the conversation.

'I could do with some guidance from someone I haven't spoken to in quite a while. I hope he's not too busy.'

She put Tiddles on the floor, the cat displaying his displeasure with a loud *meow*. She then lowered herself stiffly to her knees before putting her hands together.

'Dear, Lord. Sorry I've not been in touch for a while. I hope everything is good with you. Oh, for goodness sake, of course everything is good with him! I'm not sure if we're doing the right thing with our little venture and would be grateful if you could please give me a sign of what to do.' There was no audible response; even Tiddles was silent, watching from his hiding place under the bed. 'Well, that was it, really. Amen.'

She unclasped her hands and put one on the little table. However, it quickly became clear that this was not going to provide a way to get up. She shifted her weight, tried another position and attempted it again. No, not that way either. After several more unsuccessful goes, Dorothy put her hands together.

'Lord! If you're still there, I would be ever so grateful if you could please help me get up.' As if in answer to her request, the bedroom door opened.

'Are you all right?' said Miss Ross, seeing her friend in the unusual position.

'Ah, you were listening.'

'What's that?'

'Oh, not you, dear. I asked God if he could help me get up and here you are . . . a little miracle.'

'I've been called a few things in my time but never that. Here, let's get you into a position that has a little more decorum.'

Miss Ross had only just taken hold of the other woman's arm when the telephone rang.

'Do you want to answer it, dear?'

'No,' said Miss Ross, letting go.

'But it'll be one of our customers.'

'I answered it once . . . I won't do it again,' she said, walking over to the window.

Dorothy knew that her friend didn't want to speak to the sex line callers, but, even so, just this once could hardly hurt. Now on all fours, she reached over and took hold of the receiver, accidently dragging the telephone onto the floor.

'Hello! Hello, big boy.' Dorothy listened for a few moments. 'A headmistress?'

Miss Ross swung around.

'No! Tell him to leave me alone!'

'What?'

'Put the receiver down!'

'But I think it's for you.'

Her friend strode across the room, grabbed the telephone and put it back on the table.

'Whatever is the matter? Oh, help me get up, dear. I can't talk to you from down here.'

Miss Ross manhandled her into the armchair and

while doing so knocked over the table.

'Damn that thing!' she said, close to tears. 'It's a curse.' She picked up the telephone again and put the table back on its feet. 'I can't do it any more!'

'Do what? I don't understand.'

Dorothy had never seen her in such a state, pacing around in what little space there was.

'That's the problem! You don't understand! You never do! These telephone calls don't make enough to cover your extra fees.'

'But every week you give me the exact money I need.'

'It doesn't all come from the calls!'

'Where is it coming from, then?'

Miss Ross put both hands to her face, as if to hide behind them, as if to bury her shame. She was so close to revealing her awful secret, but once spoken it could never be one again.

'My . . . cousin . . .'

'Your cousin? He's continued to give you money for me?'

She couldn't answer, couldn't reveal the depths of depravity to which she had been dragged.

'Who is this man?' asked Dorothy, sitting forward in her chair as if to give her question more force. But there was only desperation and silence in reply. 'He's not your cousin, is he? Oh Lord, what have you been doing? Tell me what you've done!'

The distraught woman removed her hands. The surroundings were a blur, just the same as everything she had stood for and believed in for so many years. It felt as though her life had been built on sand and the foundations were dissolving in the rising waters of despair, leaving nothing firm to hang on to.

'I can't tell you,' she cried. 'I can't tell anyone.'

With this, the teacher who had inspired generations of children, who had gained the respect and admiration of all those who knew her, rushed out of the room sobbing uncontrollably. Dorothy slumped back into her chair, terribly worried and upset. She tried to make sense of it. Somehow this was all linked to these calls.

What had they done? Deirdre had talked about evil walking the streets and how they had invited it to sit with them at mealtimes. Well, that was nonsense in the case of Julie. But hadn't they given evil a direct line into her bedroom? How many times had she sat in her armchair while strangers had tried to fill her head with images – disgusting, confusing scenes that she didn't understand? Her tiny sanctuary had been fouled.

'These calls have got to stop, regardless of the consequences to me,' she said aloud. As if to mock her, the room was suddenly filled with ringing. 'Go away! Leave me alone.'

Now it felt as though the telephone itself was evil, as if the plastic had been moulded by the devil, who was watching, making it ring and willing her to answer. The sound seemed to echo around the room, becoming louder and more threatening until Dorothy was frightened of it. The devil smiled.

'Lord, help me. Tell me what to do,' she cried.

Ring-ring . . . ring-ring . . . RING-RING.

'What do you want!' she shouted into the receiver.

There was silence at the other end of the line. Not the heavy breathing or menacing silence that she was often subjected to; this was different altogether, as if the shock felt by the other person was so great that it was somehow transmitted physically down the line. Her

219

heart was racing and she was on the verge on putting down the receiver when the caller spoke.

Dorothy uttered one word, put a hand to her mouth and crashed to the floor in a faint.

Forty-Three

It was all very confusing. Dorothy knew she was in bed, but everything seemed wrong. There were strange sounds and smells, and the light wasn't like it usually was in her room. Even the mattress didn't feel right. Then she became aware that there was a figure sitting on a chair nearby. The person got up, walked over and uttered something she didn't catch. Dorothy couldn't distinguish any features. The mist fogging her brain made her afraid.

Oh no. Is this how dementia begins? I can't work out anything.

'Who are you?' she asked in a small, fearful voice.

Then the man, for she at least knew it was a man's voice, spoke again.

'For goodness sake, Mum, put your glasses on.'

He slipped something onto her nose and everything became instantly clear.

'Andrew!'

'Hello,' he said, sitting down and taking one of her hands. 'You gave us all quite a scare.'

'Where am I?'

'Hospital. You fell and knocked yourself out. But you've been checked over and you're all right apart from a wee bang on the head.'

Dorothy gingerly reached up and discovered that she had a bandage on her brow.

'I don't remember.'

'It's best not to bother trying. The important thing is that you're all right. Matron called me after you had been taken away in the ambulance, so I came straight here.'

'It's nice to see you, dear. How was Malta?'

Andrew laughed, but there was something about his manner that betrayed a contrasting emotion, one that wasn't concern about his mother's health. He was attempting to hide something. Dorothy was still too dazed to make anything of it, but there was a hazy memory at the back of her mind that made her uncomfortable.

'It was great, Mum. We all had a fantastic time. It's just been so busy at work since we got back. I'm sorry I haven't visited or been in touch.'

'Well, you're here now, dear, and that's what matters. How are Susan and Olivia?'

'They're good, thanks. Olivia's a handful.'

'It would be nice to see her. She won't know who her old granny is.'

'Less of the old. And we will bring her around, I promise, just as soon as you're back on your feet.'

Dorothy studied her son. He squeezed her hand and smiled, but it was unnatural. She had brought him up from baby to boy to man. What had happened? Miss Ross had been terribly upset, angry with her . . . she had decided that the calls must end . . . then the telephone had rung and she didn't want to answer it . . . but then she did . . . and there was . . .

Her expression suddenly changed from confusion to comprehension.

'You!'

'What, Mum?' he said, trying to sound nonchalant.

'It was you on the other end of the line!'

Forty-Four

Walter leant against the railings that ran along the harbour and watched the waves crashing against the rocks below. The tide was high and the sea was rough, in complete contrast to the beautiful day it had turned out to be. He thought it was strange how independent they could be of each other.

The idea of independence made him smile. His daughter had been delighted when he told her he was intending to move out and buy something near the family. She had been contacting estate agents and posting him details of potential properties ever since.

A little bungalow had particularly caught his eye and the previous month he had caught the train to Aberdeen. Becky had picked him up at the station and they had viewed it together. The owner had recently died and her son wanted a quick sale. The place needed quite a bit of work, but it was all possible with the money he still had.

He hadn't said anything about grooming or the fears he had for his granddaughters. These concerns could be broached later on, once he was settled. Walter became aware of someone standing nearby.

'Julie!' he said, taking her into his arms.

'Sorry to keep you waiting. My bus was late.'

'That's all right, love. I've been admiring the view. Come on, let's go for a walk.'

He told her excitedly about his news, providing as many details about the property as possible. He was used to her quick, agile mind and she fired so many questions at him that he started laughing.

'I should have taken you with me! You would probably have beaten the poor man down to a lower selling price.'

They stopped to look at some cormorants drying themselves on a rock nearby. For a while they were silent, enjoying the moment and each other's company. There was one piece of information he hadn't mentioned.

'The bungalow . . . it has two bedrooms.'

They turned to look at each other. He loved this girl like a daughter and, whatever else had taken place between them, now he felt only protective. He was also so grateful. Without her his life would probably be mapped out before him, just as Smiler had implied on the day of the march.

'I have some news of my own,' she said. 'I met Matron.'

'Did you? When?'

'I rang her and she invited me to dinner at her home.'

'Goodness, I've not heard of that before. What happened?'

'Let's walk,' she said, so they carried on, leaving the birds to their sunshine. 'I told her everything. She was extremely kind. I lost count of the number of times I broke down. When I had finished, we talked at length about what I wanted to do if I had the opportunity.'

'And do you know? You've never told me.'

'I hardly knew myself,' said Julie. 'It was only as we were discussing some of the potential openings that it became so obvious.'

'The suspense is killing me!'

'I want to be a carer. I love elderly people. They seem to like me and . . . well, I'm not squeamish about anything physical.'

'Now you say it, yes, you would be brilliant,' said Walter.

'That was her view as well. She has a sister who manages a home in Edinburgh and called while I was still at the house. I had given permission for my background to be revealed.'

'Go on.'

'Everything happened so quickly, a bit like your bungalow. I went down the next day to meet Amanda, the sister. There's an extension being built at the home and she's offered me a job as a care assistant when it's finished. I probably can't start until November, but I can see hope in the future for the first time in years.'

They stopped walking. Walter looked at her in amazement, then swept her into his arms laughing.

'That's marvellous! I'm so happy.'

'But I won't be with you in your new home.'

'Oh, don't worry about that. You can visit any time. The spare room will always be ready. I'll even decorate it in your favourite colours.'

They held each other in silence for a long time. They both knew that however much they might wish to keep the relationship as it was, there would be an unavoidable change. Julie's new life would gradually give her the confidence to leave behind that frightened girl who so desperately needed comfort. He would be involved with his family and not be a resident in a care home. This would alter him in more subtle ways. But neither of them referred to these fears and reluctantly they finally pulled apart.

'If Amanda is anything like her sister, then you can be

confident of her full support and discretion. I have a great deal of respect for our Matron. In a funny way, I think I'll miss her when I've gone.'

'You'll miss Angus, and he'll be lost.'

He thought about his old friend. They had built their bridges again, after all those decades of anger, hurt and shame. The two men had never referred to their conversation about whether Angus could still perform sexually and Walter hadn't spoken to Julie about it. The weeks had gone by and somehow other events had taken on more importance.

'What are you thinking?' she asked.

'I was wondering if we could give my mate a really good laugh . . . at Deirdre's expense.'

Forty-Five

Thursday, 25th August

I am weak and cannot endure the sordid horror any longer. Dorothy has said nothing of my outburst since returning from hospital and has been vague about her fainting spell. There is more to this than she has revealed. I will not ask her, just as I know she will not ask me what I have been doing to make money. Does she suspect why I have done it? I am making a mess of everything.

Forty-Six

'Yes, I know you're shocked I answered the telephone! I'm shocked that you called such a number!'

It was more than a week since Dorothy had ended up in hospital and she hadn't spoken to Andrew other than to arrange the meeting that morning. After collecting her, he had driven to the local park, where they found a bench in a quiet spot. The weather was pleasant, but it was rare for Dorothy to sit outside these days, so she had brought a blanket and laid this across her legs. He had been subdued since they met and was now on the verge of tears.

'Oh, don't upset yourself, love. I understand you've never done anything like this before. But what possessed you this time?' Her son remained silent, staring at his feet. 'You wouldn't believe the things I've heard over the last few months. I doubt there is anything you can say that will shock me.'

When there was still no response, she tried to shift the conversation to less confrontational ground. 'The home has significantly increased its fees. I had to do something to raise money. The idea for the sex line came from Joan. She's rather more worldly-wise than Miss Ross or me. It wasn't meant to do any harm. If we hadn't done something, I would have been forced to move and leave all my friends.'

'Why didn't you tell me?' he said, looking at her for the first time.

'I didn't want to worry you with my problems and you don't have that sort of spare cash. I know how you fret about things.' She paused for a moment. 'You haven't answered my question, about why you've called such a number.'

A couple of pigeons bobbed their heads nearby, hoping they might be thrown some food. She could remember the time when her father caught pigeons which her mother would turn into a very tasty pie.

'Most of the men who ring do so because they're having problems in the bedroom department. I usually end up chatting to them about their lives and families. Some men aren't very nice but most of them are just . . . well, they're not monsters. I know it's embarrassing, but if you can't talk to your mother then who can you talk to?'

Dorothy stopped. It was up to him to speak, if he was going to. She had opened the way as much as possible.

'Susan and I . . . we haven't made love since Olivia was born. Not once.'

'That's nearly two years.'

She put a hand over one of his and nodded, although he didn't see the gesture. She thought for a while about what he had just revealed before replying.

'I remember what a terrible time Susan had during her pregnancy and the birth. It may be that making love is simply too painful for her and she's frightened of even trying.'

'After all this time?'

'These things happen.'

'She would have told me, wouldn't she?'

'We all keep secrets for our own reasons, dear. Have you spoken to her?'

'No, I've just become more frustrated and . . . angry, I think.'

'They're not good feelings to harbour. Why don't you talk about it? Such situations are best discussed and brought into the open rather than being left to fester.'

They talked for a while until she suggested that they had a cup of tea in the park's little café, where they also had facilities. So they continued their conversation over scones and, despite the initial reason for getting together, neither of them could remember when they had had such an enjoyable time.

Forty-Seven

Dorothy was sitting quietly in her bedroom, thinking about the conversation with Andrew in the park. They had realised that day how much they both missed spending time together, just the two of them. She smiled, remembering how he had teased her, wanting to hear about the most entertaining telephone calls! She had told him not to be so naughty and pour another cup of tea.

Andrew had promised to speak to Susan and then visit to let her know the outcome. That was a week ago and now she wondered if he had sat down with his wife and discussed their delicate issue. Her thoughts were interrupted by the arrival of Miss Ross, who had been going around town collecting the adverts that had been put up to promote the sex line.

'Mission accomplished?'

'Oh my feet,' said her friend, taking off her coat and hanging it on the peg next to the red hat, before walking over and flopping into her chair. 'It's a good job I made a list of the places where they had been put up.'

'You managed to remove them all?'

'Every single one,' she said, taking out from an

old-fashioned leather satchel a pile of small, now rather grubby cards and throwing them into the wastepaper basket. 'And I hope I never have to go into one of those terrible public houses ever again.'

'Did you manage to put up the replacement leaflets?'

'Yes,' said her friend, taking off her shoes and wiggling her feet, 'in the library, the tea shop, the charity shop and everywhere else we agreed, all except the newsagent's. I couldn't face seeing Nigel Ridley and his leer.'

Dorothy had insisted that the sex line should be discontinued and a new non-profit-making venture started. She had decided to call it the 'Pearls of Wisdom' advice line. Her two friends had agreed to be involved in helping answer calls to the new number, which would be at the standard rate.

Miss Ross had suggested that they also changed the telephone. In any physical sense, it made no difference at all, but getting rid of the object that had allowed so much heartache to enter their lives had been a sensible suggestion. They could put the receiver to an ear, knowing that it had no connection or history with disgusting conversations, memories and images.

'This worries me so much,' said Miss Ross. 'I'm full of admiration for your social conscience and what you intend to do . . .'

'It's what we've all agreed to do.'

'Yes, but you're the one who needs to earn money in order to remain in the home. This won't make you anything.' She paused for a moment, then added quietly, 'There'll be nothing more from . . . my cousin.'

The two women had never discussed, or even referred to, that terrible day when the caller asked for the headmistress. Miss Ross had screamed that she 'can't do it any

233

more' and Dorothy had assumed that whatever had been going on did indeed stop, which meant there would be no more cash from this person, whoever he was.

'I can't express in words how much I have appreciated your help. However, it's time I stood on my own feet and had more faith that providence will provide, although I don't think it will provide tea unless I make it,' she said, going over to the dresser in the corner and switching on the electric kettle.

'It is loose leaf?'

Dorothy looked at the packet of tea bags, which was all she had. She didn't want to cause any disappointment but neither could she lie. Her eye was drawn to a small pair of scissors nearby. Picking them up, she quickly cut the corners off two bags and tipped the contents into a spare cup.

'Yes, dear,' she confirmed.

'I've never been a great believer in providence. I've always been more of a Prudential sort of person. You have a great number of very commendable characteristics, but when it comes to money you're a walking disaster.'

'I'm sure you're right. Trusting to the Lord can hardly make the situation any worse.'

'Well, as they say, it's your call, if you'll excuse the pun.'

Dorothy, pouring boiling water into the teapot, hoped that her deception wasn't really such a great sin.

'Here are the spare flyers,' said Miss Ross, pulling out leaflets from her satchel. 'The printer did a good job. They were ready for me when I called, as he had promised.'

'They look so much better than our handwritten cards,' said Dorothy, taking one and sitting down to examine it in more detail. *Pearls of Wisdom. Elderly ladies available for advice. If you have a problem, are feeling lonely or you just want to talk ... we're here to listen. We're not professionals, but we've been around a long time.'*

They were both taking their first sips when the telephone started to ring.

'Goodness, that was quick!' said Miss Ross.

'I fear it shows the level of loneliness out there. I'll get it.'

'No, it's all right. We're all in this venture together.' She put down her cup and lifted the receiver. 'Hello, Pearls of Wisdom. How can I help?'

As she listened to the caller, Joan came in. Dorothy indicated for her to help herself to tea. The new arrival went quietly over to the corner and picked up the remaining cup and saucer, discreetly blowing into the former, which appeared to have bits in it. Joan sat down just as Miss Ross began speaking.

'Ah, bullying at school. Do you know, Jonathon, I've had to give advice about this very subject on many occasions. Why don't you tell me exactly what's been happening and then let's you and I work out a plan of action.'

Forty-Eight

The sun was shining, so Walter was sitting on the bench just outside the entrance to the care home, which allowed him to see the taxi when it brought Julie. She hadn't visited since the confrontation with Deirdre and had agreed to come only this one last time. The previous day Walter had dropped a not very subtle hint to Mrs MacDonald that his niece was visiting this morning, knowing the message would reach the intended ears.

Julie waved at him as she emerged from the car and once they had hugged he led her straight up to his bedroom.

'Is Angus coming?' she asked when the door was shut behind them.

'He had his reservations but I did my best to persuade him. I hope he doesn't let us down.'

'I hope he doesn't let himself down,' she said. 'Is the kettle on?'

'Just about,' he said, going over and flicking the switch. 'Well, your very last visit to We Care For You. How do you feel?'

'There's no doubt I'll miss some of the people,' she replied, taking off her jacket and shoes. 'However, it's time for both of us to move on. Thank you for the money to buy some clothes. They're so sensible and practical, you would be astounded.'

'Your new haircut looks good. I like it.'

'I thought my career required a change of image. What's happened will always be a part of me, regardless of my appearance, but I intend to put it behind me as much as possible.'

He smiled and reached over to stroke her cheek. There was a knock at the door and Angus entered.

'I was beginning to give up on you, mate.'

'We're glad you're here,' she said, walking over and hugging him, much to his delight.

'It wasn't easy letting Deirdre suspect where I was heading without giving her the chance to stop me. They were coming up the stairs as I was nipping along the corridor.'

'All nicely going to plan, then,' said Walter. 'I'll make tea.'

'This has got to be the most bizarre thing I've ever considered doing in my entire life and standing around drinking tea makes it seem even crazier.'

Julie went quietly over to the door and put her ear against a panel on the other side of which Deirdre had hers.

'What can you hear?' whispered Mrs MacDonald loudly. 'Is he there?'

'I'm not sure.'

'What?'

'Shhh.'

'I can hear whispering,' said Julie, joining the others.

'Here you are,' said Walter, handing out mugs. 'Mrs MacDonald gives herself away every time.'

'Well, what now?' asked Angus.

'The floor is yours, my old friend.'

'I don't know that I can do this, not convincingly. Why don't you two just do it as normal and I'll watch?'

'You have to let yourself go,' said Julie, putting a hand on his arm.

'Maybe I've forgotten how to.'

She took both men by surprise by suddenly speaking out in a loud voice.

'Angus! I'm amazed at what you can do with your rook. You've quite taken my breath away with that move.'

'Wait until you see what I can do with my bishop,' said Walter. 'You'll not have ever seen a mitre like it!'

'Go on,' she whispered, 'say something.'

'What?'

'Anything. You'll be surprised at how easily you get into the swing of it,' she said. 'You'll never get another chance like this.'

Angus looked at them despairingly.

'I hope that you're not going to compare my bishop to Walter's,' he said.

'That's it, but give it some welly.'

'That was welly,' said Julie, 'not willy.'

'Oh, Julie,' he said loudly. 'Yes! *En passant.*'

'That's brilliant,' she said.

'Yes, but get some passion into it,' urged Walter.

Angus let out a loud moan of pleasure.

'*En passant . . . en passant.*'

In the corridor, Deirdre was horrified.

'Oh my goodness.'

'What is it?' asked Mrs MacDonald.

'This is exactly what I feared. They have got him in there! They're having a threesome!'

'A threesome? What's one of them?'

'The corruption is spreading. Our home is no longer

safe. This is exactly what I tried to warn everyone of. We've got to save him.'

Deirdre started banging on the door with her hand. If she had thought to try it, she would have found that it was unlocked.

'Angus! Don't be tainted. Save yourself. Get out while there's still time!'

In the bedroom, her cries could be heard clearly. The three culprits looked at each other in surprise at how well the plan had gone. Walter was the first to crack. He bent over laughing, spilling his tea onto the carpet.

'I don't believe it,' he said. 'You've proven to be better than either of us. Well done, mate.'

None of them could speak for several moments as the increasingly frantic shouts filtered into the room.

'What now?' said Angus. 'I'm worried I might have peaked too early!'

'Don't,' said Julie, hanging onto his arm for support. 'I think I'm going to explode.'

'Let's go out with a bang,' said Walter.

'What, another one?' quipped Angus.

With a great deal of effort, Walter managed to regain control of his laughter. In a loud voice, he called out as if in a moment of ecstasy, '*En passant!*' They looked at each other with tears running down their cheeks. Deirdre's cries had now been joined by those of Mrs MacDonald. There was only one course of action. The three of them called out together.

'*En passant! En passant!*'

Forty-Nine

'Sex what?' said Miss Ross. 'I had hoped we had left this sort of topic behind.'

The knitting on their laps had been ignored since the three friends had gathered after supper in Dorothy's bedroom and she had begun recounting a conversation from that afternoon.

'That's what I couldn't understand.'

'Don't upset yourself, love,' said Joan.

'But I was so useless! This poor girl was crying and crying, while I hadn't a clue what she was trying to explain to me. In the end I wrote it down,' she said, picking up the notepad on her bed and reading out slowly what she had written: 'S-e-x-t-i-n-g'.

'Sexting? What does that mean?'

'It's something to do with sending images via a phone,' said Joan.

'A telephone?' queried Dorothy, looking with a baffled expression at the landline on the little table.

'Mobile phones. I know it's something to do with photographs. I've heard my grandson Matthew talk about cyber-bullying, but to be honest I was rather lost as to what he was going on about.'

'We can't help these young people if we're so ignorant about the problems they face,' said Dorothy.

'I fear it's a case of modern technology making communication between different generations more difficult. I never had this sort of issue when I was headmistress. Bullying at school was a lot simpler to solve.'

'What are we going to do? If the Pearls of Wisdom advice line is going to help, then we have to understand what it is youngsters are experiencing. This girl seemed quite terrified at what some boy was threatening. About the only information I got out of her that I did understand was that she was called Emily and was only fifteen. I asked if I could ring her back once I had thought more about it.'

'Did she actually give you her number?' asked Miss Ross.

'Yes, it's in my notepad, but what good does that do us, or her?'

They sat in silence. The animosity that Miss Ross had felt towards Joan when she first arrived had long gone and the three women were now bound closely by their common circumstances, aims and friendship.

'How old is your Matthew?' she asked.

'Fifteen. Why?'

'He's the same age as this girl. Perhaps we old fogies need his help so that we are able to advise others.'

Joan called her grandson the following day and explained the situation. As she was so fond of saying, he was a bright lad and a very mature one. He said to leave it with him for a few days. When Matthew called back, she was surprised at his suggestion but promised to speak to the others, which was why the three women now found themselves sitting in the office.

'Let me get this right,' said Matron. 'Your grandson, along with other students and one of the teachers, wants to come here and act out a drama to explain what sexting is about?'

'That about sums it up. Matthew is heavily involved in the school drama group and they're always keen to have an audience.'

'I know that it's really only us who want to understand because of Pearls of Wisdom,' said Miss Ross, 'but if they're willing to devise and learn a drama, then it would be good to at least provide them with people to perform in front of.'

Matron had come across a lot of things in her life, yet residents setting up an advice line for youngsters . . . well, it had to be admired.

'Obviously,' continued the retired headmistress, 'this couldn't involve anyone like Mr Forsyth or Albert.'

There had been no further incidents between the two men since they had fought in the corridor. However, Mr Forsyth and Beatrice had appeared hand in hand only the previous week and announced that they were getting married. Following the morning, when the two had been found in bed together, Matron had been forced to inform their respective families, which had resulted in some rather heated meetings.

'Well, I think it's very enterprising and that in itself should be encouraged,' said Matron thoughtfully. 'We'll be treading some new ground with this – potentially rocky ground. Then again, maybe it's time that we all saw some different scenery.'

* * *

The lounge was packed the following Tuesday when a dozen students arrived with a teacher and set themselves up at one end of the room. Their rather sparse set consisted mainly of a large screen and a projector with a laptop. Most of the youngsters sat on the floor to watch, several residents moving their legs so that some of them could lean against the front of the chairs.

Mrs MacDonald patted a boy on the head as though he was one of the 'pat dogs' that were sometimes brought around. Rather startled, he looked behind him. Seeing the elderly woman made him think of his grandmother who had dementia and was in a care home not far away. The lad smiled kindly and turned back to face the action.

The drama centred on Matthew and a girl called Hannah. Their relationship went well until he started to pressure her into taking a nude photograph and sending it to him.

'No one else will see it, honestly,' he said. 'It's just so that I have something of you when we're apart. Everyone does it. I'll send you one.'

The play was cleverly devised so that the audience could understand what was happening but were never exposed to anything offensive. Matthew went behind the screen and a pre-recording of him was projected on to the side people could see. The image showed a naked young male, with certain parts blurred. Hannah, studying her mobile, suddenly looked uncomfortable. The screen went blank and Matthew appeared from around the back, dressed as before.

'There,' he said. 'You've got one of me, so I need to have one of you. It's only fair.'

'I don't want to.'

The storyline covered a period of a week during which he continued to press her.

'If you love me, you would do it,' he said in scene five. 'It's not as if I'm forcing you into having sex or anything, is it? I'm the only one at school who doesn't have a picture of his girlfriend. People will think you're frigid. Are you really going to spoil our relationship just for that?'

Almost all of the residents were present, as well as many staff, and they were absolutely spellbound. Matron, standing near the door, had never seen everyone so silent and still. No one fidgeted, whispered to a neighbour or even coughed. It was, she thought, quite an extraordinary response.

People sat forward in their seats, willing Hannah to resist but suspecting she was about to cave in. The girl walked behind the screen and a similar process occurred, where the audience could see a projection of a recording, only this time it was her. The boy, looking at his mobile phone, was suddenly animated, staring with delight at an image that he had just received. Hannah walked back into view.

'You promise it will never be shown to anyone else?' she pleaded.

'Of course,' he said, taking her into her arms. 'I'm not going to show this to anyone. Don't worry. It's only for me.'

They walked away to indicate another scene change and the passage of time. As the play progressed Matthew sent the image to one of his friends, swearing him to secrecy beforehand. He in turn sent it to someone else and soon a large number of students had the photograph.

When Hannah discovered the betrayal, she was distraught, breaking off with Matthew, who then posted the image on his Facebook site in revenge. At this point many of the other pupils stood up and became involved in the drama, pretending to post the image on even more sites.

The play ended with Hannah refusing to attend school and contemplating suicide.

The room was silent. A couple of the women had taken out handkerchiefs and were wiping their eyes. It was only when the actors took their bows that people broke into enthusiastic rounds of applause. The teacher thanked them for the invitation. Matron in turn expressed her praise for the excellent performance and invited everyone to stay for afternoon tea.

'That was marvellous,' said Dorothy to the girl who had taken part. Several students were standing in small groups, although some had remained on the floor, chatting to the residents in their chairs. 'Is your name really Hannah?'

'Yes,' replied the girl, who was standing with Matthew and a couple of other teenagers.

'I'm Dorothy. Thank you so much for coming here to explain all this. I was quite frightened at one point. We were all willing you not to give in, dear.'

'Lots of people take nude pictures and send them to boyfriends or girlfriends,' she said.

'Do they? Well, it was a terrible thing for him to show it to someone else and then to put it on Facebrook.'

'Facebook,' said Matthew.

'Whatever it's called, it was wicked.'

'It's natural,' said a boy who looked about fourteen. 'Like, when two people split up, they're bound to want to get revenge.'

'Are they?' said Dorothy. 'What on earth for? Can't people simply part company if they're not suited? Why do they have to hurt each other? We never did that in my day.'

'Well,' said the youth, not certain of the answer, 'they just do, like.'

'I don't see the sense in that. And why did you give in,

245

Hannah? Isn't it down to you what you do with your body? Why give control of it to someone else?'

'He would have left me,' said the girl. 'He said if I loved him I would do it.'

'Oh, men have been trying that game since time began,' said Dorothy, becoming unusually angry. 'If you love me, you will sleep with me! Now they're doing another version of it using this modern technology. Well, that's not love. If you care for a person, you do your best to make them happy and ensure they're safe and kept from harm.

'Bullying someone like this is just a way of gaining control over them. There's nothing clever or grown-up or honourable about that sort of behaviour. It's outright abuse and young people need to understand that they don't have to put up with it.

'If anyone ever tries to own your body like that in real life, Hannah, you tell them to take a run and jump! And if they don't stop their nonsense, you come and get me!'

A small group of students, along with the teacher, had gathered to listen to this gentle little old lady speaking with such passion. When she finished, they all burst into applause. Dorothy looked around in surprise and then appeared rather flustered.

'Goodness . . . if you'll all excuse me, I must pay a visit. I would recommend the pastries. You need to get in there quick or they'll all be gone. Matthew, make sure you say hello to your grandmother.'

The teenagers stayed throughout the afternoon. They all wanted to see around the building and left the lounge in small groups accompanied by various residents who were delighted to act as tour guides. When Dorothy returned and sat down in an armchair, the teacher came over and sat next to her.

'I'm sorry, I don't know your surname,' he said.

'Oh, call me Dorothy. Everyone does.'

'I was very impressed by your speech.'

'It was hardly that.'

'I don't mind telling you, I would be pleased to get students hanging on to my every word the way they did with you.'

'I think you're just trying to flatter an old woman.'

'I'm not, and to prove it I was wondering if you would be willing to come to the school and give a talk?'

'Me? What could I possibly talk about that would be of interest to anyone?' said Dorothy, taken aback at the mere suggestion. 'It's Miss Ross you need to speak to. She used to be a headmistress, you know.'

'But you're the person who inspired the pupils. You're the one I want them to hear.'

Fifty

The lounge that evening was buzzing with excited chatter. The visit by the youngsters, the moving drama and then showing them around the home had delighted everyone. Joan, Miss Ross and Dorothy had decided to forgo retiring to their usual knitting venue and were sitting in one corner, the latter having just explained the unexpected offer to speak.

'I think you would be excellent,' said Joan.

'I told him to contact Miss Ross. She's the expert.'

'The whole point is he doesn't want a trained teacher,' said Miss Ross. 'I'm sure he has plenty of them already. He wants someone who has experience of life and can pass on some everyday common sense, if you like, some old-fashioned wisdom.'

'Well, you could do that.'

'No, I couldn't. Education is such a part of me that I would always be just another teacher to those students, and these days I'm an ancient one who's completely out of date. You're different.'

'I'm a simple old granny, that's what I am.'

'Why have we set up Pearls of Wisdom if we're not trying to help the young?' said Joan. 'You're brilliant over the

248

telephone. Your problem is you lack the confidence to do it face to face, but it's not that much different, is it?'

Their conversation was brought to a temporary halt when Joyce appeared carrying one of the lighter wooden chairs. She put in down near to them and was about to sit when Joan stood up.

'Here, have my armchair. I'll sit on that, love.'

'Eh, that's good of you,' she said, accepting the offer. 'Sorry to interrupt, but I can't get this helpline of yours out of my mind. I would like to be involved.'

'Part of Pearls of Wisdom?' asked Miss Ross.

'Yes. I've learnt a few things during my time that might be useful when giving advice. Seeing that play today and speaking to some of the students afterwards, it got me thinking that I would like to do something to help. After all, what else am I doing with my life? I haven't any family or anyone who visits and I don't believe I'm so past it that the brain doesn't work,' said Joyce, looking at all three of them.

They, in turn, were wondering how they could possibly fit her into the bedroom.

'I've only got one telephone,' said Dorothy, 'but you would be welcome to share some of the shifts if you want.'

'I was wondering if we could get an extension to my room so that if your line is busy and someone else calls, then it automatically comes through to me. It's not a perfect solution. I'm not about to sit there twenty-four hours a day waiting for calls. But it would be a little better than the present situation, wouldn't it?'

'I think it's an excellent idea, and a very generous offer,' said Joan.

'Hear! Hear!' added Miss Ross. 'Good for you.'

Dorothy reached over and took hold of one of Joyce's tubby hands.

'Welcome aboard the Pearls of Wisdom advice line. Shall we celebrate with a cup of tea?'

In reply to which they all burst out laughing.

* * *

Matron sensed a change in the home over the following days. There was a new vibrancy about the place that she hadn't known before. Joyce had spoken to her about installing a line and she had agreed to sort this out as soon as possible.

Several of the students had said they would return at the weekend and although Matron was sceptical about this, and secretly concerned that people were going to be disappointed, on the Saturday morning eight teenagers appeared, including a couple of new faces who had been brought along by friends.

Walter was reading in the conservatory when Anna came over and said there was someone to see him. He almost said 'For me?' but that would have been a pointless reply, so he put down his book and went to investigate. He could hardly believe his eyes as he entered reception; when his visitor smiled, his entire face was so transformed that the nickname finally made sense.

'Smiler!' he said, striding over to shake the offered hand.

'Hello, I thought you might like this.'

'My walking stick!' said Walter with delight. 'Thank you very much. I'm extremely grateful to you, lad.'

'They were all gathered up after the march but the person who kept them didn't know who they belonged to and it took me a while to track him down. I've already given the others to the carer. Your blackthorn is a beauty. I tried it out a few times myself. Sometimes the weight of the shaft in relation to the handle spoils the overall balance.'

'You know something about them?'

'My grandfather was a keen maker and I liked to watch him when I was little. When he died, all his tools came to me, but I had never been old enough for him to show me how to use them.'

'I see,' said Walter, an idea forming at the back of his mind. 'Come on, I'll stand you a cup of tea. There should hopefully be a decent slice of cake on the go as well.'

The lounge was busy when they entered. Smiler acknowledged several of the teenagers.

'I heard about the play,' he said when they had found a couple of spare chairs. 'The visit by the drama group has created a lot of interest at school.'

'It's good to see some of the students back again,' said Walter. 'We don't get many young people.' Spotting the person he was looking for, he called over. 'Come and meet a friend of mine.'

Angus joined them and was duly introduced. He no longer appeared so gaunt and unkempt, now that he wore Dorothy's jumper. However, he did seem a bit wary of the ear, nose and lip piercings staring back at him.

'I can tell you that as a young man Angus was an extremely accomplished walking stick maker.'

'You're having me on.'

'I'm not. He made this as a wedding present for me and my Moira. I've treasured it ever since, as a sample of craftsmanship and a gift of friendship. I never asked if you continued in later life?'

'Yes, I kept it up until about five years ago. I couldn't easily get into the woods any more and had lost the strength to do some of the more demanding tasks.'

'I'm impressed,' said Smiler, which both men took to be quite a compliment.

'I was thinking . . .'

'Always a dangerous sign,' said Angus, smiling.

'I don't reckon Hamish really needs the whole of that large shed, not if we showed him how to put away his garden equipment more effectively. At the moment it's left all over the place.'

'Go on.'

'Well, Smiler was just explaining that his grandfather was a keen maker and left all his tools, but the lad needs someone to show him how to use them.'

A light came on in Angus's eyes and suddenly the rings and studs didn't matter any more. As the three explored the potential of their new venture, a variety of other crafts were being discussed around them. Joan was teaching two girls and a boy how to knit, while in another corner Meg and Peg were showing some of the jewellery they had created.

However, the passing on of knowledge was not all in the same direction and one youngster, who had brought his laptop, was showing a small group how to access the Internet. People sat around shaking their heads at the vast amount of information so readily available.

'When I was a girl, it used to take me more than half an hour to walk to the nearest library, which was quite small,' said Mrs Weaver. 'When I got there, I would have to show my hands to the person behind the counter to prove that they were clean. Then I could spend ages trying to find out what I wanted and quite often I didn't succeed.'

Mr Adams gave the name of the vessel he served on whilst in the Royal Navy and a few moments later an image appeared on the screen.

'That's my ship!' he said, astonished. 'I don't believe it. I haven't seen a photograph of that in decades. All of mine were lost.'

The student carried on searching and found several pictures of the crew, which he enlarged so that the old man could see the faces more clearly. After a few moments of studying them he became increasingly animated.

'I remember that sailor! And him. He was a good mate. It's easy to lose touch as the years go by. That's me!' he said, pointing excitedly at a young man.

'You were quite good-looking,' said Mrs Weaver, leaning forward in her seat next to him.

'You mean I'm not now?'

'I'm sure it's only that my glasses need a clean,' she quipped.

The student promised to print off as many relevant photographs as he could find and bring them back the following week.

'That's good of you, son. I really appreciate it,' said Mr Adams, wiping away several tears. 'Oh, now I've gone and got something in my eye.'

'There's more,' said the student. 'Some of the ex-crew have set up a Facebook site. There appears to be eight of them on it.'

'What does that mean?' asked Mrs Butterworth, who was also in the small group.

'These people are spread around the UK,' said the teenager, reading the information in front of him. 'There are two in Scotland. They're using Facebook to keep in contact with each other. If you want, Mr Adams, I can help you get in touch with some of your old shipmates.'

This time the ex-sailor couldn't pretend that he wasn't crying.

Fifty-One

The quarterly delivery of incontinence pads was generally an event of biblical proportions. Pads, in every conceivable size for men and women, were available in two-piece, all-in-one and belted options, as well as day and night versions. There was a large variety of pants, some discreet and others less so, offering a multitude of comfort, shape, absorbency, stretch and flexibility. Those with the greatest need could resort to a model that had been nicknamed the 'super pooper'.

By the time the two men had completed unloading the van almost half of the reception area was covered in cardboard boxes. Their arrival coincided with the departure of Deirdre, which rather took away any dignity or decorum that she might have wished the occasion to have.

She had kept her move a secret until the previous week and since then had announced loudly to everyone how her marvellous, caring son, the one no one had ever met, had organised for her to move to a lovely care home much nearer to him in Edinburgh.

Few believed this was the whole truth, yet they all played

along, saying how pleasant it would be to see her family more often. The reality was that she could no longer pay the extra fees and there was a great deal of sympathy for her. People suspected that the alternative would compare poorly against We Care For You and nobody wished such a fate on anyone.

The stacks of boxes at least made the reception seem less empty when she appeared for her final farewell. Matron was there of course, as well as the Escape Committee. Although now disbanded, the members felt that after everything they had been through they should show solidarity to someone who had, in fairness, played her part. They lined up as if greeting the Queen and Deirdre walked along slowly, trying to maintain the facade, as much for her own benefit as anyone else's.

'I shall miss you, Meg,' she said to the first person.

'I'm Peg,' said the woman.

'Oh well, I'll miss you both.'

Dorothy felt the significance of the departure keenly. Her savings were reducing at an alarming rate. In secret she had identified a couple of homes that were less expensive and had decided to contact them in the New Year. She wanted to at least have one more Christmas with her dear friends.

By the time Deirdre came level with Angus, she seemed on the verge of losing control.

'You take care of yourself,' she said with tears glistening in her eyes. 'Don't let yourself be led astray.'

She bristled when facing the next person. If everyone was honest, this was the meeting no one wanted to miss.

'We have never got on and it would be more than hypocritical to pretend otherwise,' said Walter. 'However, I certainly don't wish you any harm and hope that you find happiness in your new home. We may not be able to part as friends, but life's too short for us to part as enemies.'

With that he gallantly stepped forward and hugged his adversary, patting and rubbing her back quite tenderly when he realised she was now openly crying. It was Julie who had made him think again about the real person behind the stern mask of morality. Walter reckoned if she could forgive, then so could he. When Deirdre pulled back, she briefly laid a hand on his arm. No one had ever witnessed such a gushing display of affection.

Matron and Mrs MacDonald walked with her to the minibus, which was waiting outside. Hamish would make sure she got on the correct train at the station. A local removal firm was due later that morning to collect the few pieces of furniture and personal items that were stacked neatly in the bedroom.

The others stood in the doorway, watching the final act of the drama but no longer able to hear what was being said.

'That was unexpectedly moving,' said Angus.

'Yes,' agreed Walter.

'Well, many of us have lived together for several years,' said Dorothy.

'For better or worse,' said Joan.

'At least she isn't leaving with Mr Dunn,' said Walter.

'You would have thought her son could have driven up and taken her back in his car,' said Joan, a sentiment that was widely felt. 'It's a terrible thing to have to leave your home, but to have to travel away by yourself seems unnecessarily cruel.'

'The place won't be the same without her,' said Miss Ross.

'Nor will Mrs MacDonald,' added Dorothy. 'She'll be ever so lost.'

By late morning the boxes had been moved to the storeroom, the removal van had been and gone and the person from the local supermarket had arrived with the latest batch of flowers, which were distributed to various rooms.

The care home operated with a firm sense of structure and routine, but within these parameters there was no such a thing as a 'normal' day. As Ben and Matron were talking in the corridor, Beatrice, demonstrating an impressive turn of speed, rushed past, pursued by the district nurse, who had unsuccessfully tried to give her an injection. A few moments later a hand appeared from behind Matron and squeezed one of her breasts.

'You know you're not meant to do that, Mr Forsyth,' she said without showing any reaction or even turning around. Ben gently removed the offending limb and took the man away to try and find something else to occupy his mind . . . and his hands.

Most people were involved in activities of one form or another around the building. Joyce was in her bedroom fixing a stocking with a strip of white elastic that was really meant for holding catheter bags in place. She wasn't the only female in the home to do this, which was easier than using traditional garters.

As this was the day during which the weekly craft sessions were held, there were a variety of hobbies taking place. In the conservatory Meg and Peg were designing jewellery, Mrs Weaver was making cards and Mrs Butterworth was producing bookmarks. A great deal of what they made was available to purchase in reception and visitors regularly bought items, the money going towards the cost of trips out.

Angus had persevered with his knitting and under the guidance of Joan and Dorothy had begun to enjoy the pastime. However, many of his creations were still open to interpretation and none had yet found their way anywhere near the 'for sale' area.

Fifty-Two

Matron, rarely surprised by much these days, sat in stunned silence as she listened to the visitor. He was a strikingly handsome man and although he appeared about forty she suspected he could be older. He was certainly very well-dressed and spoken, with a confident, calm manner that would no doubt suit his job, which he had explained was a consultant anaesthetist.

'And you're staying nearby?' she said when he had finally told his story.

'I've taken a week's holiday, but would like to spend a few days with my family back in London before beginning work again. Once it starts it's rather a demanding role.'

'Yes, I'm sure. Goodness. As you can imagine, I'm quite taken aback.'

'I've thought a great deal about this. How best to proceed and, indeed, if I should take things any further. However, in the end . . . here I am. Sometimes we have to take risks. I decided to at least speak to you first. She is in good health? You don't think my presence will be too great a shock?'

'No, no I don't think that. Well . . . would you please wait here?'

She left the man and went to find the resident, bringing her back without giving any explanation other than that she had a visitor. After all, it wasn't her place to say anything. Matron couldn't even make an introduction. How could she? Instead, she let the woman into the office and quietly closed the door, leaving both to their fate.

The man was standing and did not speak until Joyce had settled herself into one of the chairs. Only then did he sit down beside her and remove from his jacket pocket a small black and white photograph . . . showing Joyce and Jimmy and a tiny baby.

'Hello. I'm George.'

Joyce screamed and burst into tears before reaching across and pulling the stranger into her arms. But he wasn't a stranger. She had carried this person within her, had given birth to him and had cared for him during the first few months of his life. Her heart had been broken when she had given him up so that he could have a better life.

'My baby, my baby,' she cried, crushing the man's head against her breasts while rocking backwards and forwards. He let himself be held until she had recovered sufficiently to release him so that she could examine his face and he could breathe. 'They kept your name. They kept your name.'

George, now even more appealing because he was a little crumpled, nodded. Having thought so much about what he should say at this moment, he simply sat in silence and smiled, tears rolling gently down his suntanned, finely chiselled face.

'I've hoped . . . hoped so much over the years for this to happen, but I never believed it would,' she said, reaching forward again to hold him. He took a quick breath.

'Are you well?' asked Joyce when they had pulled apart

once more. 'You're not ill or anything? That's not why you're here?'

'No, nothing like that. I'm sorry I've given you such a fright. The adoption agency wanted to write to you first and I know that would have been the proper thing to do . . .'

'No, the proper thing was for you to come and see your mother. There's so much I want to ask that I don't know where to start. Why now? What made you find me now? Have you known for a while and didn't want to come? Were your adopted parents good to you? Were they kind? Did you know you were adopted?'

'I'm staying nearby for the next five days, so we can meet and talk as much as you want during that time.' He had put the photograph on the desk so that they could hold hands. 'My parents – I'm sorry, I can't call them anything else – were extremely good to me. They made sure I had as many opportunities as possible. I'm very close to my three sisters, although now I know we're not related by blood.'

'Do they know?'

'Only my wife.'

'You're married?'

'Yes, with two beautiful daughters.'

'I'm a granny!' said Joyce, starting to cry again.

'I didn't know I was adopted until my father died a few months ago. My mother . . . sorry.'

'That's all right, love.'

'She died last year. When we were clearing out the house, I found an envelope addressed to me. Inside was a letter asking for my forgiveness for the fact they had never told me. It also gave as much information as they had, includ-ing the details of the agency. When I contacted them, they were able to pass on the envelope you had left. With that and the Internet, I was able to track you down here.'

261

Joyce was silent. She took out her handkerchief and blew her nose. He waited for her to respond.

'So, if you have my letter, then you know how I used to earn my living.' He nodded. 'It was only fair to explain everything – about your father dying, why I had to give you up, what I did. I felt that if you knew and still wanted to find me one day, well, that was all right. I've agonised every single day since if I had been foolish and whether my honesty would kill any hope of you ever wanting to meet.'

'Working at the hospital and in some war zones over the years, I've seen the results of wickedness and evil. What you did wasn't anything like that. You lived as best you could.'

They fell silent, so much yet to say but so much imparted in those first few minutes that they both needed time to reflect.

'No one here knows what I did,' she said. 'Not even Matron, and she's privy to most secrets.'

'She seems a good person. I explained to her who I was. I didn't want to give you too much of a shock, if your heart or health wasn't up to it.'

'She probably told you I needed to lose weight,' said Joyce, trying to lighten the mood.

'Matron said nothing of the sort. Here,' he said, taking out another photograph, this one showing his wife and daughters.

'My goodness, they're a good-looking family,' she said, studying the image closely. 'What are their names?'

'I'll tell you. I'll explain as much as I can, but perhaps we should give Matron her office back,' he said.

'Let's go to my room. That'll set the tongues wagging!'

So they walked to her bedroom, the overweight comedian and the handsome consultant, and began to catch up on the previous forty-five years.

Fifty-Three

Saturday, 8th October

Our lives have been thrown into yet more turmoil with the extraordinary news about Joyce's son. His sudden arrival seems to have affected the entire home, giving people a new sense of hope. Perhaps there are other residents with children they have never seen, abandoned because of circumstances beyond their control. Everyone is pleased for her.

I feel an unexpected contentment settling upon me and I don't know if it is somehow because of this event, as if the return of Joyce's son is a sign that everything will be all right in the end. Although I do not believe in God or even in fate, I increasingly feel that all will be well.

Fifty-Four

George and Joyce took every chance they had to spend time together. He hired a car and they drove around the Highlands, stopping to admire scenery and enjoy having a coffee or lunch at quiet cafés where they could talk privately.

It was an extraordinary experience for them both. There was a large period of her life that neither of them wanted to discuss, so he kept his questions focused on the early or later years. She, on the other hand, wanted an almost monthly account since his adoption.

They agreed that he would use her first name and she was happy with this. The woman who had brought him up seemed to have loved him as her own and Joyce felt only gratitude. Her son had certainly benefitted from far greater opportunities than she could ever have provided. Joyce wasn't bitter. You can only play the hand you're dealt.

'You don't get views like this down south,' she said.

They were sitting in the car, which was parked overlooking Loch Shin. It was his last day before returning to London.

'You don't get the peace either,' he said.

'I expect not.'

They were in a reflective mood. During the past few days she had examined hundreds of family photographs on his iPad, had watched numerous video clips of his daughters taken at different ages and had even had a conversation via Skype with his wife, Amy, to whom she warmed immediately. Now Joyce felt saturated with information, emotion and the sheer wonder at the miracle of his arrival.

'There's something I want you to consider and I don't expect an answer quickly,' he said. 'We've had so many years apart that I would like you to think about moving to a home near us. I understand it would be a big step, but I can help with the financial side if that's an issue.'

Joyce didn't answer straight away, partly because she was trying not to burst into tears.

'Whatever happens in the future, I can't tell you how much I appreciate that suggestion,' she said, then began crying. 'Now look at me! I was trying so hard not to do this. Silly old woman.'

'Do you think I haven't cried? I've done it every single time I've been alone after dropping you off. Sometimes I haven't even made it out of the car park.'

'And I've only just made it to my bedroom. There have been a couple of occasions when I nearly didn't get to the dining room for supper, which shows how serious it's been.'

He laughed and she dried her eyes on a tissue.

'We need to start back or you'll miss your supper because we're too late.'

'Oh, don't worry about that. I eat too much as it is.'

'But we do need to set off before we lose all the light.'

He sensed she had something to say, so held back from starting the engine.

'I did want to ask one more thing,' she said.

'Anything.'

'Does Amy know how I used to make my living?'

'No, Mum. It's not because I'm ashamed or anything like that, but it wasn't my secret to tell and revealing such details would have served no purpose.'

But Joyce was crying again, because without even realising it George had just called her 'Mum'.

Fifty-Five

Dorothy and Joyce sat at the front of the lecture room, staring at the banks of empty seats facing them. The drama teacher, who had brought them along from the school's reception desk, had explained that there would be three classes attending, making about eighty pupils.

'Please don't be put off if we have to eject a few early on,' he said cheerfully, as if keeping the number to a handful was a great achievement. 'We have some students who won't be able to sit for more than about five minutes.'

'What's wrong with them?' asked Joyce, baffled at such a statement.

'Why, nothing of course. It's just how they are. There'll be plenty of staff. We'll be watching them, rather than you, and will get individuals out of the hall with as little disruption as possible. Just don't let it put you off. You'll have forty-five minutes, so if you could keep going until the bell rings that would be appreciated.'

'What happens if we finish early?' asked Dorothy.

'Ah, yes . . . in that situation they can get a bit riotous. Don't worry, I'm sure you'll be fine,' he said, before leaving to organise some tea to go with the plate of biscuits that was already on the table.

'What have we done?' said Dorothy, now quite horrified at the prospect of what lay before them. Joyce was there to help answer questions, not give the talk. 'I thought it would be a dozen or so at most. I can't do this.'

'It's too late to back out now.'

'I don't want any of these,' said Dorothy, moving the plate past the microphone and further along the table. 'I'm feeling more than a little queasy as it is.'

'I'll not have any, thanks,' said Joyce, pushing it to the far end. She didn't miss the surprised look. 'The truth of it is, I have something to live for now, so I'm going to take better care of myself. I want to at least be around to see my granddaughters grow into young women. You know, George asked me to consider moving to a care home near to him and his family ... mine now, I guess. I still can't believe it.'

'Will you?' asked Dorothy, fearing the loss of someone whose company she enjoyed so much.

'It's very appealing, but I don't think so. All my friends are at We Care For You. It's probably best if he comes to Scotland for holidays and we all get to know each other gradually, over time. Then perhaps we'll see.'

At that moment the door opened and a stream of students filed into the hall. The two women watched with increasing awe as row upon row of seats were filled with fifteen- and sixteen-year-olds, more than one looking as if they were from another planet.

'This is a bit scary,' said Joyce.

'Oh no.'

'What?'

'I want to use the facilities.'

'You'll have to hang on. It's all in your mind.'

'No, that's not where it is.'

When the hall was full, the teacher introduced the visitors and instructed everyone to show their appreciation and then to pay attention. The rather reluctant applause died down quickly and Dorothy stared as if mesmerised by the faces. The notes that Miss Ross and she had prepared so carefully over the previous four evenings lay untouched on the table. The silence dragged on and a few boys started to fidget.

'Say something,' whispered Joyce.

'I can't read the notes.'

'Once you get going you'll be fine.'

'No, I won't. I've brought the wrong glasses!'

The disturbance grew, one boy saying something that had those around him laughing. A teacher indicated for them to be quiet.

'I want . . .'

'Use the microphone,' said Joyce, pushing it closer.

'I want . . . to tell you a story,' started Dorothy again. 'About the Reverend McBain's cockerel . . .'

Fifty-Six

Snow began to fall during the first week of November and by the third day there was a deep covering outside. While many people wanted to remain indoors, where the precisely controlled temperature was always on the warm side, a surprisingly large number informed Ben over breakfast that they would like to go into the garden and build a snowman!

Dorothy and Miss Ross sat at their usual table in the dining room, the former still making little soldiers out of her toast, although she had long since given up trying to make any impression with them on her boiled eggs.

'I gather Walter will be away for another couple of days sorting out his bungalow,' she said, digging out a spoonful of solid yoke. 'He'll really be missed when he eventually goes.'

'Yes, but it's marvellous that he's recovered so much to be able to live independently again,' replied Miss Ross. 'I don't imagine that happens often.'

'None of us knows what's around the corner, not even here where you tend to expect life to revolve around a routine. At least, I used to feel that.'

'I don't think any of us can say our lives are routine

these days. There's another group of students due later on. Perhaps they'll help build the snowman.'

'And I've received a letter this morning asking me to speak at another school in a couple of weeks' time,' said Dorothy. 'I can't believe so many people want to hear anything I have to say.'

'It's your fault for doing so well the first time.'

'Oh, don't. I still have nightmares about turning up with the wrong glasses and all of the work we have done together being wasted.'

'Perhaps not entirely. Anyway, I gather you bewitched the entire audience within minutes. In all my years of teaching, I've never experienced a standing ovation from a group of fifteen- and sixteen-year-olds. It sounds to me as though you have a new career.'

'I don't think I had one in the first place.'

The students arrived at ten, just as people were putting on their coats, hats and gloves. Several residents had sat down in the conservatory to watch the activities through the large windows. As if to mark the occasion the snow had stopped falling and the sun shone brilliantly.

* * *

Mrs O'Reilly was lying in bed, staring at the ceiling, when someone knocked softly at the door. Moments later the priest walked in.

'Oh, hello Father Connelly,' she said weakly.

'Hello, Mrs O'Reilly. How are you today?' he said, walking over to stand by the bed.

'Not too good. What's all that noise outside? You would think people might have more respect when someone's at the end of their life.'

271

'Anna was telling me downstairs that the teenagers have organised the residents into two teams. They're going to have a race to see who can build a snowman the fastest.'

'A race? In the garden?'

'Apparently.'

'Help me up!' she said, tugging at the bedclothes.

'Oh,' said the priest, suddenly uncomfortable and already backing away. 'I'll find a carer.'

'There's no time. We'll miss the start.'

'But . . .'

'Don't worry, Father,' she said, wriggling her legs towards the edge of the bed and trying to sit up. 'I don't think the sight of my body in a nightdress will send you to the wrong place! It's only a sin if you enjoy it.'

The old woman was suddenly gripped by such a fit of laughing that the top set of her false teeth shot out. The priest, although middle-aged, had been a very keen rugby player in his youth and without any conscious thought he caught them in mid-air. She shrieked at the sight and fell back onto the mattress, her frail arms beating the duvet in delight.

'You'll be the downfall of me yet, Mrs O'Reilly,' he said, looking at the warm, moist object in his hand and wishing he hadn't reacted so automatically. 'Perhaps you would like these back?'

It took quite a bit of pulling and pushing to manoeuvre the old woman into a position where he could put a dressing gown around her, although actually getting her into it proved too difficult.

'Don't worry about that. Get me over to that chair by the window. A race!' she said excitedly, as he manhandled her across the room. 'Are they taking bets? Which team is your money on?'

'I'm sure they're not gambling on the outcome. It's just a bit of fun.'

'So is betting!'

Once she was deposited in the chair, he brought over a blanket and put it around her.

'There you are, Father. I'm warm and you're safe from temptation!' She quickly assessed the people below. 'Ten pounds on the right-hand team.'

'Mrs O'Reilly! I couldn't possibly gamble with you for money. I'm surprised that you're even suggesting such a wicked thing.'

'How about a bottle of gin, then?'

'A full bottle of Gordon's?'

'Of course.'

'You're on,' he said, sitting in the chair beside her.

* * *

'Isn't it beautiful?' said Joyce, admiring how the thick snow had formed intricate shapes over the various objects it covered. She was on Dorothy's side, each team having been allocated its own section of garden.

'It is lovely, though I wish we could get moving,' said Dorothy, rubbing her hands together.

'Right!' shouted Ben, as if he had heard her. 'I want a good clean race with no cheating, stealing or hindering of the opposite team. Anyone found in breach of these rules will not get a piece of the excellent carrot cake that I spotted earlier in the kitchen. Three . . . two . . . one.'

When he blew his whistle, the students were instantly a whirlwind of activity. However, if the residents couldn't match them for speed they were equally as focused. While the teenagers in Miss Ross's team started rolling an increasingly large ball of snow to create the body, Meg and Peg began making the head, handing over to others as soon as they tired. Those in Dorothy's team were rapidly building a mound, wildly throwing shovelfuls of snow, which the older members were patting and moulding with their hands.

In the conservatory the audience were as caught up as those outside and there was plenty of cheering and shouts of encouragement. Mr Forsyth and Beatrice, hand in hand on the settee, cried out as enthusiastically as anyone.

With so many involved, the snowmen quickly grew in size, although their different constructions made them appear completely unalike. The mound took shape faster and soon reached the stage where Angus could push in a couple of walking sticks to create arms. Mrs Butterworth fitted woollen mittens on the ends and when the head was added Joyce took out a brown wig from her coat pocket and placed it on top.

'I recognise that,' said Dorothy.

'Shh, don't say anything. I'll return it to Beatrice before she knows.'

Angus had brought a bishop from the chess set in the lounge as a nose. As he was trying to fit this – the flat base making the task more difficult than he had expected – an assortment of other items were added and the snowman was rapidly adorned with a large red scarf, a flat cap, a knitting bag and a pair of spectacles over two dark-blue coat button eyes.

Although they couldn't hear her through the double glazing, Mrs O'Reilly, now on the verge of hysteria, was shouting for all she was worth. The priest was not far behind her in this. Anna, a short way down the corridor, had to lean against a wall for support because she was laughing so much at the noises coming from the old woman's bedroom.

Across the garden Miss Ross was urging on her team as if she was once again a teacher overseeing the school's sports day. Joan was bent over, about to roll their snowman's head just a few more times before it was lifted into place, when a snowball hit her squarely on the bottom.

'Hoy! Who did that that?' she shouted, turning around and glaring at the opposing team. Everyone seemed busy and no one paid her any attention. She had just bent down again when another missile hit her in exactly the same spot. Mrs O'Reilly, seeing everything clearly from her vantage point, clapped her hands in glee. Joan swung around and her eye was immediately drawn to Joyce, who was bent over double.

'You! I'll . . .'

Joan didn't finish her sentence. Instead she quickly made a snowball and hurled it. Despite the size of the target, it hit Angus full on the chest. He stepped back in surprise, searching for the source.

'We're under attack!' he cried.

The audience in the conservatory was making so much noise shouting and banging whatever they could grab that Matron came along from her office to investigate.

'Give them a broadside,' cried Mr Adams. 'Give them a broadside.'

'This is even better than milking cows,' said Mr Forsyth, smiling fondly at Beatrice.

Everyone in Dorothy's team stopped what they were doing and made a snowball.

'On my command,' shouted Angus. 'Take aim . . .'

Only Joan and Miss Ross had spotted the immediate danger and both turned their backs just as the order was given.

'Fire!'

The other group were so engrossed in the race that they were completely unprepared for the attack. Angus, now totally swept up in the moment and perhaps having read a few too many novels about British Redcoats during the eighteenth century, called out again. 'Reload!'

Miss Ross's team were now desperately fighting back, but their efforts were piecemeal and, as the enemies of the British army had discovered so long ago, this was ineffective against coordinated volley fire.

'Take aim! Fire!'

Ben started blowing his whistle.

'Stop. Stop!' he shouted. 'Penalty to Dorothy's side. No more throwing.'

Everyone was now armed, old and young alike grinning and panting, their rapid breaths condensing immediately in the frosty air. They paused to look at the carer. He saw their expressions change as the same idea swept through them all and each person turned to face him.

'No! That's not fair!' he shouted, just managing to add, 'There'll be no cake for anyone,' before he was hit by around two dozen snowballs.

Fifty-Seven

The snowmen, although a little grubby, were still standing at the end of the following week (Beatrice's wig having long since been returned safely). The conversations that Saturday were nearly all related to the impending 'Storm Tegan' which was expected to hit Scotland during the night.

Although such events were hardly unusual in the Highlands, this was being portrayed as potentially dangerous and after supper most people gathered in front of the television to hear the latest news updates. When the coverage had finished, Angus turned down the sound.

'When I was young, nobody gave names to a bit of wind,' said Mrs Butterworth, sounding unusually indignant.

'I suppose it's progress,' said Mrs MacDonald.

'It's meant to help people prepare,' said Miss Ross.

'But how does calling a storm something do that?' asked Mrs Butterworth. 'It's not going to blow any less.'

'Couldn't we choose something,' said Dorothy, 'then send it to the appropriate person? I'm sure Matron would know who.'

'It always seems to be a first name,' pointed out Joyce.

'That's no reason why we can't set a new trend,' said Joan. 'We could have . . . Storm Miss Ross!'

This caused considerable laughter, including from the retired headmistress. She was not against being teased, up to a point anyway.

'Or we could have Storm Joyce,' said Mr Adams, who then pretended to be a news reader. 'A big front is moving from the west, heading along the corridor and expected to arrive in the lounge at any moment!'

'You wouldn't dare say that if you were sitting nearer,' said the large woman, shaking her fist. However, she had seen far too much in her life to be offended by a bit of leg-pulling and laughed as much as anyone.

'It's a sort of health-and-safety issue,' said Miss Ross, unable to resist the urge to pass on knowledge.

'Not more health and safety,' said Dorothy.

'By identifying impending storms with a title, the Met Office hopes to make the public more aware of potential dangers. The names have already been chosen for several months ahead.'

Storm Tegan hit shortly after three o'clock in the morning and few residents got much sleep after that. The nightshift was kept busy reassuring those who were frightened by the noise and ferocity. In the morning most people got out of bed later than usual, only to find there was no power. Matron arrived early, suspecting that there might be some extra work to do but having no idea of just how much.

* * *

'Right,' she said, once all the staff had squeezed into her office. 'I've spoken to the electricity board and they say it's unlikely we will be reconnected until the end of the day. This means we have a major incident.

'We've only got a handful of portable gas heaters and no way of making hot food or drinks or even filling hot water bottles. The lift, stairlift and several of the hoists will be out of action, as are the landlines. In addition, none of the alarms will work, so we won't be alerted if someone wanders out of the building. Even the pressure pads under the doormats won't work.'

Those who had never experienced such a situation at the home glanced around anxiously at their colleagues.

'So, it's all hands on deck to get everyone up, dressed in warm clothing and safely into the lounge, where they'll have to stay until we've sorted out a generator. They can have anything they want to eat that doesn't need cooking, so cereal, bread, fruit, cheese. I'll leave it to the kitchen staff to decide what's feasible.'

Storm Tegan left a wake of destruction in its path. There were large areas without power, roads blocked because of fallen trees and widespread damage to buildings. However, inside We Care For You there was almost a carnival atmosphere. Some residents loved to help out and Mrs Butterworth put on an apron and happily went about as if she was employed there. Mrs O'Reilly particularly enjoyed being carried down the stairs.

'Help! I'm being kidnapped,' she shouted as Ben reached the last few steps. 'Don't tell Father Connelly.'

'I reckon he's after your body, Mrs O'Reilly,' said Joyce, who happened to be passing. 'You be careful. Tell him that you're a respectable woman.'

'Bugger respectable. Don't put me down.' This last comment was directed to the carer, who was about to deposit his bundle into the wheelchair he had left for this very purpose. 'I haven't had this much fun in ages.'

Ben knew he wasn't going to win any arguments and straightened up again, as if her weight was meaningless to him.

'That's lovely hair you've got,' she said, stroking his head as he set off along the corridor. 'Why don't we go around the block first? There's no hurry to catch up with the others.'

'You're incorrigible,' said Ben.

'Hey, there's no need for friggin' bad language!'

Her laughter seemed to set the mood for the first hour or so of their forced captivity. However, the temperature outside had dropped drastically and by mid-morning a few of the frailer residents were beginning to feel cold.

Matron was worried. The promised generator was stuck on a blocked road, while the usual emergency help she might have called on, such as the local Women's Institute and church, were all in the same situation. No one had power to do anything.

It was just as she was finishing another fruitless call from her mobile that she saw an unfamiliar van pull into the car park, followed by two cars and then the school minibus.

More than a dozen students emerged from the vehicles and she recognised the headmaster and the drama teacher. They began collecting boxes and cases from the van and then made their way towards the entrance. She left the office and went to meet them.

'Smiler! What on earth is going on?' she asked the teenager in reception.

'Hello, Matron. Angus rang me to see if I was all right and he explained the problem here. There's no power at the school either, but the kitchen has several large urns that use gas. I got in touch with one of the teachers and everything seemed to take off.'

As he was explaining this, a stream of people walked past and headed for the lounge. A couple of men she didn't know were carrying in gas heaters.

'But what's in all the boxes?' she said.

'Hot water bottles. I sent a text to the others to get to school with as many as they could bring. As we were filling what we had, an increasing number of strangers turned up and dropped off more!'

'How many do you have?'

'Almost two hundred. Do you think it's enough?'

'I think half a dozen per person should do the trick!' she said laughing, feeling relief washing over her.

'We've also filled more than twenty flasks. The water might not be boiling now but it should still be good enough to make tea and coffee. Some of the dads have helped. That's them bringing in the heaters.'

When Matron walked into the lounge, the place was alive with excited chatter and noise, with residents being fussed over and tucked up with more hot water bottles than they knew where to put. Anna and the headmaster set up the growing number of flasks on a table and the production of hot drinks was soon underway. Ben went to fetch more cups while one of the kitchen staff left to collect more supplies of cakes and treats. It wasn't long before everyone was sitting around chatting. Smiler pulled up a stool next to Angus.

'That's a tremendous thing you've done, lad,' said Angus. 'I'm proud to call you my friend.'

'Ah, it was nothing,' said the lad, but it was obvious he was pleased.

Matron was allowing herself a few minutes' rest near the door when one of the students came up to her. It was Hannah, who had performed so well in the drama.

'Do you still have no way of cooking food?'

'No, I was just thinking about that.'

'My father is the manager at the pizza restaurant. They use wood-fired ovens and he says if you telephone him with all the orders during the next hour he'll get them delivered for lunchtime. I've brought a pile of menus.'

When the generator, having finally arrived, started working during the afternoon and the power come back on there was almost a feeling of disappointment. The students packed up the flasks and hot water bottles, said their farewells and set off in the minibus and cars. The building quickly warmed up and people drifted back to their rooms and routine.

Storm Tegan was over.

Fifty-Eight

The day before Mrs O'Reilly's one hundredth birthday she sent a message to the kitchen outlining what she wanted for breakfast. Afterwards, Anna relayed the story to Matron, making a fair impersonation of an Irish accent.

'I want two boiled eggs and lots of toast and the yoke is to be runny. If it's not, I'll come down and cook them myself. I've survived one hundred years on this planet and I'm not going to keel over because I've eaten a bloody hen's egg! And if the new owners are so worried, I'll sign a piece of paper saying that I won't sue them for damages if I die.'

'That sounds like her,' said Matron laughing.

'She doesn't seem to realise that she won't be around to sue anyone.'

'Don't be so certain. Mrs Reilly has a mind as sharp as her tongue.'

The following morning Anna arrived with the requested breakfast and was surprised to see someone else in the bedroom.

'Dorothy has kindly offered to help,' said Mrs O'Reilly.

'Oh, that's very good of you,' said the carer, putting down the tray on the bed. 'If you're sure?'

'Yes, dear,' said Dorothy, who was making a pot of tea in the corner.

As soon as the young woman left, the two conspirators set about their secret plan. Dorothy quickly cut the toast, then retrieved a tray hidden beside the wardrobe, along with a spare plate and cutlery. Having made sure her friend was all right to eat, she took one of the eggs and a pile of little soldiers before sitting down in the chair by the bed. They looked at each other in triumph.

'Happy birthday, Mrs O'Reilly.'

'Enjoy your treat. Aren't things so much more fun when they're forbidden!'

* * *

By coffee time the home was alive with anticipation. The home's only centenarian, dressed in a new outfit, sat in the lounge surrounded by four further generations, including a baby that was laid carefully in her lap, the mother tactfully holding on to prevent the latest addition being dropped on the floor. A photographer and reporter from the local newspaper took shots and carried out interviews.

Bunches of flowers, cards and presents had been arriving since early on and this included a specially made cake donated by the local bakery. These had been joined by the Lord Lieutenant for the area and a piper from the nearby estate. Unfortunately, the event clashed with a wedding and a funeral being conducted by Father Connelly, who would arrive when he could later in the day.

The residents had also put on their smartest clothes and they gathered together, along with staff and well-wishers, to hear the card from the Queen being read out by Matron. This was followed by several speeches, anecdotes and stories. Mrs O'Reilly's seventy-nine-year-old son had put together a huge scrapbook charting the life of his mother and the contents caused a great deal of interest and entertainment. There was no mention of the Windmill Theatre.

Later on, the piper led everyone into the dining room for lunch. Mrs O'Reilly sat at an extended table with family members and beamed with pleasure throughout the meal. It seemed that there was no end of people giving her a hug. Joyce was particularly careful to be gentle and when she bent down to put her arms around her, the guest of honour whispered in her ear, 'Thank God that man has stopped squeezing that friggin' dead sheep!'

By the evening the various guests had long gone, people had changed back into their ordinary clothes and the 'birthday girl' was tucked up in bed. When her one remaining visitor arrived, she had been lying quietly for an hour or so, replaying the recent events in her mind.

'I'm sorry I missed all the celebrations,' said the priest, sitting down by the bed. 'You're probably awash with presents you don't know what to do with, but I've brought you something as well.' From a small bag he produced a bottle of gin. 'It can't be said that I don't honour my bets!'

She looked at the gift and smiled.

'You've been a dependable friend all these years,' she said.

'And for a long while yet, I hope. Shall we have a wee nip?'

'Not for me, thank you, Father. You help yourself, though.'

'Don't tell me you're turning over a new leaf?'

'My leaves have all blown away. I've no more to turn.'

They sat looking at each other in silence. He put the bottle on the floor and took hold of one of her hands.

'What is it, Mrs O'Reilly?'

'They keep going on in this place about having a good death, but I think it's better to have had a good life beforehand.' He nodded, but didn't reply. 'I've had that. I've been blessed in so many ways. Today has been one of the best ever. Now I've reached the grand age of one hundred. I think that's enough, don't you, Father?'

'That's not for me to say.'

'You can do one thing for me.'

'Name it.'

'Take that gin away and when you're having a nip you think of me and the many laughs we've had.'

'We've certainly had a few. Goodness, I've lost count of the evenings we've spent sitting around your fire putting the world to rights. I'll toast you with joy in my heart for having known your friendship,' he said, giving her hand a tiny squeeze. 'Can I get you anything? Do you want me to fetch one of the carers?'

'They'll be busy and there's nothing they can do.'

'Shall I sit and pray with you?'

'You're a kind man, Father. I don't think you'll have long to wait.'

And he didn't.

* * *

Everyone stood in reception the next morning when Mr Dunn and his assistant brought the coffin down in the lift and then slowly along the corridor. Even Mr Forsyth and Beatrice stood respectfully in the background. They appeared to have made a connection with the reality of the event and Matron had decided it was easier to let them stay.

Mrs O'Reilly had left precise instructions for every aspect of her funeral, from the shroud that she was to be dressed in and the music to be played as her body was taken away, to the details of the church service.

'Mrs O'Reilly was thrilled by yesterday's events,' said Matron to the assembled group. 'She reached the tremendous age of one hundred, saw all her family and friends again, and loved the party immensely, as she was keen to point out to me several times later on.

'She was a great person and will be hugely missed. She requested that we should gather around and enjoy one of her favourite songs before she leaves We Care For You for the last journey.'

People shuffled forward and a few put their hands on the coffin as a last gesture of closeness and friendship. In the corner Ben started a CD.

'I don't believe it,' whispered Walter.

'You can't escape that tune around here,' replied Angus.

There was a brief moment of surprise and then a general release of tension as people laughed at the sound of 'Mairi's Wedding'. It was exactly what she would have wanted.

Fifty-Nine

Walter didn't want to say his goodbyes walking along a line of people, so during the three days before his departure he spoke to everyone. He wanted to ensure he thanked staff who might not be on duty that last day and also have the opportunity for a proper conversation with people on a quiet, one-to-one basis.

The work on his bungalow had been completed a few weeks earlier but he didn't want to leave the area until Julie was going. His Aberdeen train left early that afternoon, only about half an hour before hers left for Edinburgh. It meant that he had the morning free before meeting her for lunch.

Angus came up to his room after breakfast to offer help with any final packing, but it was all in hand apart from a few personal items.

'Shall I put your chess pieces in their box?' he asked, seeing the board still set up on the table.

'Thanks, you can put them away, but I'm not taking them. They're for you.'

'Me?' said Angus, taken aback. He knew his friend

loved the figures and the beautiful handmade board.

'It would give me great pleasure if you would accept them as a small gift.'

'That's not small,' said Angus, 'and I've nothing for you in return.'

'I've got your friendship. That's the best present I could possibly have. I shall miss you, mate. I'm glad that after all those decades fate threw us together again.'

'So am I.'

The two men, who had been separated by almost half a century of hurt, anger and resentment, looked at each other with a mixture of sadness, happiness and regret. Walter glanced at his watch.

'Come on, Smiler should be arriving soon. Let's go downstairs and meet him.'

They waited in reception, watching the rain beating down outside in the car park. Angus had become fond of the teenager, who now visited every week for a lesson in making walking sticks. When it had been explained to Hamish why they would like to use the shed, he had willingly cleared an area so there was plenty of space for two people to use the workbench.

'It's funny,' said Walter. 'Although I'm really excited about moving into the bungalow and starting my new life, being near to Becky and the girls again, I'll miss the companionship and banter. The home provides a family of sorts.'

'Yes, I suppose it does.'

'You're not too sad here, are you?'

His friend thought about the answer for a while before replying. 'No, I'm not sad. I've reached the stage where I can't live by myself and if I've got to be somewhere this is a good place to be. With everything that's happened, We

289

Care For You is hardly recognisable compared to what it was when I arrived.'

'The place does have a different feel about it!' said Walter. 'Crikey, there's hardly a day goes by when we don't have youngsters here doing one thing or another. The sense of purpose everyone's gained has transformed them.'

'Ben was saying how much quicker he gets around with the drug trolley these days. Even the alcohol consumption has gone down.'

They talked amicably for a while, then stopped when they heard music playing softly.

'Where's that coming from?' asked Walter.

'It's not a recording. Let's have a look.'

They set off and quickly tracked down the source. In the conservatory Albert and a lad who they knew was one of the regular visitors from the local school were sitting on the settee, each of them holding a mouth organ. The two men hung back near the door, where they couldn't be seen.

'Well, I'll be damned,' whispered Angus.

Albert was very precisely explaining how the instrument worked before skilfully playing a few scales and then listening while the youngster, clearly following carefully what was being said, tried himself. They laughed at something and then Albert began to play 'Mairi's Wedding'.

'Do you know,' said Walter quietly, 'that's not such a bad tune after all.'

★ ★ ★

Walter waited in the little café unaware that he was in the seat in which Mr Forsyth had sat while enjoying his tea and scone, naked, apart from a strategically placed tea towel

290

and a tablecloth. It had been a strange morning. Some residents had gathered in reception to see him off, even though he had tried not to make a fuss of his departure.

He was surprised at the sadness he felt at parting from the people he had come to know so well. In reality, there were only a handful that he was close to, but many of them had been very kind to him when he had arrived two years earlier and he was fond of them all.

Walter could barely recognise himself in that desperate figure who'd been unable to boil an egg. He knew he was lucky in making such a recovery and that Julie had been an important part of the reason. She hadn't visited the home again after that time in his bedroom when Angus had joined them.

After they had reached their finale, with Deirdre and Mrs MacDonald shouting and banging frantically, the three of them hadn't been able to speak for about ten minutes. Laughter is a great tonic, an enormous healer of so many ills. If only one could make the world laugh . . .

The tinkle of the bell above the door caught his attention and he rose when Julie entered, wheeling two suitcases. He put them out of the way and then hugged her for a long time before sitting down. The café was quiet and few of the other customers paid them much attention. He ordered tea.

'I've eaten so much cake in the home that I've rather gone off it,' he admitted when the waitress had gone. 'They do tend to force it on you at times.'

'You'll be cooking for yourself soon, no more meals brought on a plate. In fact, you'll have to get used to doing your own shopping, cleaning, ironing . . . everything. There'll be no one running around after you.'

'Hell, I hadn't thought of all that! My furniture is still in

291

the room. Perhaps I should rush back and pretend it was all an elaborate joke.'

'How was it this morning?'

'Surprisingly sad. I've lost touch with the friends I used to know years ago and only have the people I've met in the home. Now, in one fell swoop, I've left them behind as well.' She reached over and took hold of one of his hands. 'Oh, it was all right, love. People were kind and it's been rather nice over the last few days having a quiet chat with everyone.'

'But time to move on,' she said.

'Yes. And look at you! I see what you mean about your clothes. Talk about practical.'

'They are a bit different.'

'New clothes and hairdo . . . new adventure.'

The waitress arrived at their table, so their conversation was interrupted while she set out the cups and teapot. He had often visited and knew that this was the owner.

'You must be leaving shortly?' she said.

'Yes, actually today. My train leaves in just over an hour.'

'Well, I wish you all the best. You've always been a very welcome customer.'

'Thank you,' he said, standing up and shaking the woman's hand.

'This is on the house. I wish everyone was as courteous and polite as your grandfather,' she said, before walking away, leaving Walter at a loss as to what to say and Julie grinning mischievously.

'Shall I pour tea, Grandfather?' said Julie loudly, picking up the teapot. 'And have you remembered to take your tablets today? You know what the doctor advised. We don't want you having one of your funny turns again, do we?'

'I'll have less of your cheek, young lady.'

'Well, you've obviously made an impression here,' she replied, lowering her voice. 'Maybe the women of Aberdeen need to be warned.'

'Just pour and I'll have some milk while you're about it.'

Their last time together went too quickly and while they waited on the platform they held hands tightly. Each had been such a crucial support for the other. Although they were both strong enough to have no concerns about the future, they both feared this parting.

'It was good of Amanda to sort out some nearby accommodation for you,' said Walter, repeating a topic they had spoken of earlier but needing to say something to try to ease the tension.

'Yes.'

'You'll write and ring often?'

'Of course. And you as well.'

'A letter a day.'

'You won't have time for that.'

'I'll always have time for you,' he said.

She buried her head in his chest and wrapped her arms around him. He held her close.

'Thank you for everything,' he said. 'Without you I wouldn't be getting on this train.'

'Well, you can come down from Aberdeen in two and a half hours,' she said, pulling back to look up at him.

'To Edinburgh?'

'I checked it out.'

'So you could come up in the same time.'

'Yes,' she said smiling.

'That's not so bad, then. Perhaps sometimes we could meet halfway, if we just wanted lunch or something. Then we could each get home again that day.'

'Home . . . I haven't had one of those for a long time.'

'Don't forget what I said, about contacting your parents. Maybe once you're settled and . . .'

'Respectable.'

'You've always been respectable, Julie. Always. Don't ever forget that.'

An announcement over the loudspeaker system prevented any further conversation and it continued until his train had arrived.

'Time to go,' she said.

Walter only had a small suitcase with him, containing enough items for the few days he would spend with his daughter. His possessions at We Care For You would arrive at his bungalow the next morning. Most of the other furniture he needed had already been bought, delivered and subsequently unpacked by Becky and the family.

'There's no need for tears,' she said, reaching up to wipe them off his cheek. 'We'll still see each other.'

'Of course we will,' he said, gently wiping away the tears falling down her cheeks.

Then he was in his seat. She looked so tiny and frail standing by herself with only the suitcases for company. A sudden gust of wind blew. Julie smiled, hugging her coat to indicate the cold. He felt such an urge to rush out and take her in his arms, but then there was a slight jolt and the carriage started to move. Walter pressed his head close to the window to keep her in view for as long as possible.

Julie waved. He raised a hand. Then she was gone.

Sixty

'Hello, dear,' said Dorothy to Miss Ross, who had just walked into her bedroom. 'You have had a long day. I thought you would be back for supper.'

Her friend had just returned from seeing one of her ex-pupils but had been delayed on the return journey. She sat down wearily in her chair.

'So did I. It doesn't matter. I had a big lunch with Donald.'

'Did you enjoy yourself?'

'Yes, it was lovely. He is a very good minister. I always knew he would be. But my goodness he can talk. It's a wonder his parishioners get a word in edgeways and I should imagine poor God has to make an appointment!'

'You look exhausted. Sit there and I'll make some tea,' said Dorothy, putting down her knitting and going over to switch on the electric kettle. 'Matron had some exciting news. The manager at the garden centre has been in touch and offered to cover the costs of the line rentals for all of the telephones we use for Pearls of Wisdom.'

'That's very generous of him. Word about our advice line certainly seems to be spreading. It's a good job we're getting other residents to help answer calls.'

'This afternoon I gave some more training to Meg and Peg. Heavens, listen to me . . . giving training. Speaking of calls, Ben took one from Walter saying that he got safely to his daughter's house yesterday and that his things arrived at his new bungalow at lunchtime. He was able to make sure that the delivery men put everything where he wanted.'

'I think he'll be very happy. However, the home won't be the same without him. We have too few men as it is.'

'Yes. Angus has been wandering around a bit like a lost soul. It's amazing how they rekindled such a friendship after all those years apart. I don't think even Deirdre ever found out what had happened between them when they were young men.'

Miss Ross was about to make a comment about secrets. She didn't. Instead she took off her shoes and massaged her feet until Dorothy came over with two cups of tea.

'Here you are, dear.'

'Thank you. When I came in, I spotted Joan in the conservatory with son number two. That'll be her tied up for the rest of the evening.'

'I expect so. There aren't many of us who can rival our Joan for family visits, although I had my Andrew on the phone and he's bringing Susan and Olivia over on Sunday. They're getting on much better and I'm being taken out for lunch. No cost to be spared apparently, although I think that's a bit tongue-in-cheek, as there isn't anywhere nearby that's expensive.'

'That's excellent. I'm so pleased for you. There's been a lot going on while I've been out.'

'Oh, there's no hanging around these days. Even my knitting has taken rather a back seat.'

They sat in amicable silence for a while, drinking tea and feeling totally at ease in each other's company.

'People are already getting excited about this year's pantomime,' said Dorothy, relaying items of news as they came back to her, which meant that the topics had no logical progression. 'The rumour is that Mr Dunn is going to play one of the ugly sisters.'

'There are some things that you really don't want to imagine and the undertaker in drag is definitely one of them.'

'Smiler, I still can't get used to that name, is coming tomorrow, so that will cheer up Angus. It's odd, isn't it, the friendships that people form?'

Friendships . . . it's hardly the right word.

'It is. No one can dictate or predict how or when they're going to meet someone and discover emotions that they've never known before, that they didn't know were possible to experience. It can turn everything you've understood on its head, so that you're left reeling under the implications.

'I never believed such things could happen and certainly not in such a way. For it to occur near the end of a life could so easily be felt as tragically sad. All you can do is wonder how you might have lived if you had only realised earlier. However, it's best not to think like that. Better to be grateful that you have had such a relationship.'

Miss Ross realised that weariness was making her almost ramble and so she suddenly stopped speaking. But when, after a while, there was no reply, she looked over and discovered that Dorothy had fallen asleep.

Where have the years gone? Where has the love come from?

How many times had she asked herself those questions over the last twelve months? Some secrets have to be kept because revealing them would benefit no one.

Quietly, she put down her cup and saucer, stood up, then carefully removed Dorothy's cup from her lap. With no more pressure than if her hand was a butterfly, she stroked the sleeping woman's hair. It was such a simple thing, yet she had wanted to do this for so long. She watched Dorothy for several moments. As silently as possible she knelt down on the floor and gently laid her head against one of Dorothy's legs.

Just for a moment.

It would only be long enough to have the memory, something that could be cherished.

Another secret.

Miss Ross put a hand up to her face, resting it on Dorothy's knee. She closed her eyes and inhaled the scent of lavender soap, which made her smile. On her cheek she could feel the warmth of Dorothy's skin coming through the material of her skirt.

The building was unusually quiet, as if everyone in it was holding their breath, everyone except Dorothy. Miss Ross listened to the soothing sound, which seemed to ease the tension in her body, enveloping her in a sense of peace and tranquillity. She had never known such happiness.

Just for a moment.

* * *

It normally took a while for Dorothy to wake up sufficiently to take in what was going on around her. She gradually became aware that Tiddles was in his favourite place and was already reaching to stroke him before even opening her eyes. But it wasn't the cat, and when she looked Dorothy was surprised to see Miss Ross resting against her leg.

Her friend had been working far too hard and had appeared terribly tired recently. Dorothy had meant to speak about it. She gently stroked the hair, tied up in its formidable bun, unaware that this very gesture had recently been done to her.

Here was a good woman, a decent, honest person whom you could trust to do the right thing. Dorothy didn't mind in the slightest that her friend had fallen asleep against her leg, but she had been sitting in the chair for too long and needed to move. She called out quietly.

'Miss Ross. Miss Ross.'

When there was no sign of stirring, she spoke more loudly. Then she did it again and shook a shoulder with increasing force. When nothing resulted in a response, Dorothy put a hand to her mouth, a single tear trickling down her cheek.

'Oh dear . . . oh dear.'

Sixty-One

The church was so well attended for the funeral of Edith Ross that many people had to stand at the back. The minibus had also been full, and such had been the demand to attend the service that Matron had to organise for several cars to make the hour-long journey as well.

No one at We Care For You had appreciated just how highly regarded the retired headmistress had been during her long career. There were some families in the congregation where all three generations had been taught by her.

When the occupants of the minibus entered, they had been surprised to see Deirdre, although they knew Mrs MacDonald had written to pass on the sad news. Dorothy indicated for her to join them and after a bit of persuasion she left her seat. There were so few relatives that the residents took up most of the space in the front pews, as they considered themselves to be as close as anyone to the deceased.

It had been a heart attack, according to Matron. The simple coffin near the altar had a small spray of red roses on top. Dorothy stared at the wood, still finding it difficult to believe that her friend was lying inside, that the person who had provided so much help and guidance was no more. They would never again sit chatting and knitting in her bedroom or walk around the garden in fine weather. They would never share a breakfast, laughing about the runniness of the boiled egg.

The minister, a round-faced cheery man in his sixties, greeted people as they arrived, and when it appeared that everyone was present he went to the pulpit.

'We have gathered to say farewell to someone who has touched the lives of so many of us, from grandparents to grandchildren. Edith Ross wrote to me several months ago, to put in place the arrangements for her funeral. As ever the practical person, having reached a certain age she wanted to make sure that everything was in hand. As it happened, we met for lunch on the very day that she passed away.

'I wouldn't be standing here before you at all if it wasn't for the extraordinary skill Miss Ross had in seeing the real person behind the tiny part that any of us reveals on a day-to-day basis. I had been taught by her for several years when, at the age of fifteen, I became rather rebellious!'

This admission resulted in some laughter from the congregation who knew him and there was a general easing of the tension that had settled upon them while waiting for the service to start.

'I know it's difficult to believe. I had been brought up in a very religious family. It was a caring, fun and interesting family. I think the only thing I could find to rebel against was religion and I did it with passion, turning against the teachings of the church that I had been brought up with. My poor parents didn't know what to do with me.

'That was when Miss Ross became involved. She spent a great deal of time with me over several months, listening to my teenage complaints, gently steering me, opening my eyes to what she could see but which I refused to.'

The minster paused to look at the coffin for a moment in reflection and silence.

'I have never forgotten that young woman who put me on the right path and I will be grateful to her for the rest of my life. I travelled a great deal after my ordination but we kept in touch via letters. Miss Ross was an avid letter-writer and was always interested to know where ex-pupils had gone and what they were doing. Now I'm back in the area where I grew up. Life often comes full circle in so many ways.

'We continued to correspond once she was in the home and one particular friend that she made was mentioned more often than others. Dorothy, that friend, is going to tell you about her recollections.'

The minister came down from the pulpit, while Dorothy got herself out of the pew. He gently took her arm to ensure she made it safely up the two steep steps and over to the lectern. She didn't have any notes, but the lectern had a small microphone and he adjusted this to the correct height before sitting down to one side. The mass of faces looked so different to the audiences she had encountered in the schools.

'The Reverend McBain . . . goodness, I'm reminded of a story about another minister by that name who I knew when I was a child. He kept lots of hens . . . yes, well, that isn't something for today. The Reverend McBain has very movingly and eloquently told us about Miss Ross as a young woman and the huge influence she had upon him. I would like to tell you about the person I knew in later life.

'All of us at We Care For You have been around a while and by that very fact we've encountered a great number

302

of people during our long lives. Occasionally you meet someone and immediately know that you're going to get on. Miss Ross and I were like that, becoming close even though we were opposite in so many ways. For instance, she was a highly educated woman who loved learning and passing on knowledge, a skill at which she excelled.

'Although she loved to laugh and had a very sharp wit, I imagine that some people thought she was slightly frosty and reserved. She was certainly not one to go around hugging others or showing physical affection. Miss Ross liked things done properly and could be a bit fussy. If I say she insisted on loose tea, you get the idea.'

This caused a murmur of laughter and a few nodding heads.

'Underneath that apparently stern surface was the most loyal, steadfast and trustworthy person I have ever met, someone who would endure huge personal sacrifice to help a friend . . . as indeed she did for me.'

Dorothy stopped for a moment to take out her handkerchief and blow her nose. The church was silent and the congregation spellbound, hanging on to every word she said.

'As we have heard from the minister, Miss Ross was a great inspiration to others. I could not possibly have believed a few months ago that I would visit schools and talk to students as I have been doing. It is even more unbelievable that they would want to hear me! Much of this "new career" of mine is because of my dear friend.

'She played a vital role in the formation of Pearls of Wisdom, a telephone advice line for young people which has been set up at the care home. Indeed, I chose the name as a tribute to Miss Ross, who took a very active part in the service once it was up and running.

'Recently, for a while, we had a regular visitor to We Care For You. She was a beautiful, lively young woman who had a gift of being able to connect with people from all walks of life and had a strong desire to help them if she could. Not long ago, Julie went to work in a care home in Edinburgh and once there she told the other staff about the advice line we had set up in the Highlands.

'Our Matron,' said Dorothy nodding to Matron in the second row, 'said to me a few days ago that this care home is now in the process of establishing a similar helpline. They had been in touch, asking for advice and wanting to know if they can call it Pearls of Wisdom.

'We old folk . . . we have a lot of knowledge to impart to the young, but we in turn have so much to learn from them. I can think of no better monument to Miss Ross than that Pearls of Wisdom is expanding and, who knows, perhaps one day there might be branches throughout Scotland.'

Dorothy had spoken quietly but clearly and confidently, even without any prompts. She now stopped and was silent as she examined the faces staring back. Beyond the front two rows she didn't know anyone, yet because they knew or were connected with Miss Ross everyone in the church felt like a friend.

'Well . . . that was what I wanted to say. Thank you for listening. It was very kind of you.'

The minister moved quickly over as she stepped away from the lectern.

'That was extremely well done,' he whispered as he took her arm. 'The other Reverend McBain you referred to, if he was in this area he would have been my grandfather.'

'Oh!' said Dorothy, slightly alarmed.

'He kept lots of hens . . . and there was a funny story that came down through the family about a cockerel,' he said, helping her back to the pew.

'Really? A cockerel . . . how intriguing. You must tell me that tale sometime.'

★ ★ ★

Miss Ross could not have faulted the delicious spread in the church hall afterwards. Some of the women making the tea had very fond memories of the old teacher and in respect they ensured that only loose leaf was used in the large metal teapots. Dorothy was chatting to a local family when she became aware that someone was standing nearby.

'Walter!'

'Hello,' he said, giving her a hug.

'I didn't know you were here.'

'Angus wrote to me. I simply had to come, but my train was delayed so I only just made it in time. Someone gave up their seat for me at the back. It's only now we're in the hall that I can see who's here from We Care For You. And did I spot Deirdre?'

'Yes, up from Edinburgh. How are you?'

'Well, thank you. I see a great deal of my family and I love it. And you?'

'Oh, our days are so full. We've got several residents involved in Pearls of Wisdom, including Angus. He offered to do some shifts so that callers had the option to speak to a man if they wanted. I've heard him on the telephone and, do you know, he's a natural at it.'

'That makes me so pleased. I must hunt him out.'

'Of course, the place isn't the same without Miss Ross.'

'Your eulogy was very moving. She would have been proud.'

The church hall was full, as most of the congregation had stayed on for a tea, sandwich and blether. Standing near a plate of millionaire's shortbread, Angus and Mrs MacDonald were listening to Deirdre talking about her new home. He sensed a change in her that was difficult to define.

'To be honest,' she said, 'it's not We Care For You. I didn't appreciate how lucky I was. There are more residents at the new place with dementia than without it, while the carers . . . I never knew they could be so different to Ben and Anna.'

Angus and Mrs MacDonald were almost at a loss as to what to say. It was as though the recent experiences had made the moral crusader realise something about herself and she was resigned to being lonely.

'It was good of you to come all this way,' said Mrs MacDonald, searching for conversation before the three of them fell silent again. There was no avoiding the degree to which the relationship between the two women had changed.

'I miss my friends,' admitted Deirdre. 'So often you don't appreciate the value of what you have until you don't have it any more.'

'You see your son now, though,' said Angus, trying to think of something positive.

Deirdre gave a little nod, although it wasn't convincing. However, just then Walter and Dorothy appeared beside them and there was a bout of hugging and handshaking, followed by enquiries about health.

'And how are you doing, Deirdre?' asked Walter.

'I'll survive, thank you for asking. But what's more important . . . how is Julie?'

Sixty-Two

By the end of the afternoon everyone had returned safely from the funeral service and they were once again spread around the home. Sometimes the death of a popular resident could affect the atmosphere quite dramatically and the staff would have to work extra hard to reassure people and try to keep everything on an even keel.

It was, of course, natural to grieve at the loss of a friend. Matron herself felt a great sorrow, although as she collapsed into her chair early that evening the most overwhelming sensation was weariness. It had been a long day at the end of an unusually busy week.

All of Miss Ross's furniture and clothes had been taken to the local charity shop. Her smaller personal effects, including jewellery, letters and other correspondence, had been carefully placed into a cardboard box, which had been put on a chair in the office.

The bedroom was empty, stripped back to the impersonal basics, ready for the next occupant. No matter how brightly they were painted or how well fitted out, the rooms always conveyed a sense of sadness in these situations. The mattress was bare because the previous user would never again sleep there.

Matron didn't think she had the energy to go through the box at that point, but she picked up the black book on the top and idly flicked through a few pages. It was a diary. Her eyes were tired enough without more reading. After a few minutes she put down the book and left the office. She returned a short while later with a coffee. With the diary open at the beginning, Matron began again.

It was after ten o'clock when she finished the last page, an entry made by Miss Ross only days before her death. With great respect, she closed the book and laid it gently on the desk. Matron was many things – a listener to those who needed to confess, a peacekeeper, and a strict enforcer of rules when necessary. She was also a keeper of secrets.

The diary was, in part at least, a confession of something that the ex-headmistress could tell to no one. It was only in the act of writing down her feelings that she was able to display the part of her that nobody even suspected existed. The diary provided a means of trying to understand these new emotions that had come upon her with such surprise.

To live a life and never fall in love until old age, by which time passions and desires are dust ... What had Miss Ross written? Some secrets had to be kept because revealing them would benefit no one. Matron was certain that Dorothy had no idea. And what good would it do to tell her? With a heavy sigh, she put on her coat, picked up the book and left.

It was time to go home.

Sixty-Three

Dorothy settled herself into a chair in the office. She had been brought there by Anna, who had found her knitting in the conservatory. The other person in the room was a smartly dressed man in his fifties, a stranger as far as she was aware. Anna left the room, closing the door behind her.

'Good morning, Mrs Cameron,' said the man politely. 'Thank you for making the time to see me. My name is Anderson and I am the solicitor handling the estate of Miss Edith Ross.'

'Oh,' said Dorothy in surprise, wondering what the man could want with her.

'Miss Ross, as was her nature,' he said with a little smile, 'gave me very precise instructions as to what was to happen to her estate upon her death. She had sold her property prior to entering the care home, so her estate consists of cash plus stocks, bonds and shares, some of which have had to be converted following her death.

'As you probably know, there were only a few distant relatives. Originally her estate was to be split between various charities. However, a little over a year ago she made a new will and has left everything to you.'

'My goodness,' said Dorothy, putting a hand to her mouth. 'What does that mean?'

'Well, it's not a huge amount, but neither is it insubstantial. I'm aware of the fees here and this should, if it's not indelicate of me to put it this way, certainly be sufficient to see you financially comfortable at We Care For You for the rest of your life.'

Dorothy felt tears welling up in her eyes and she couldn't speak for several moments. The solicitor sat quietly while she composed herself.

'I have all of the relevant paperwork with me and these clearly show the various figures and valuations. There are also some documents for you to sign.'

'Mr Anderson, would it be possible to see if Matron could join us? I'm afraid I will quickly become terribly confused by this sort of thing.'

'I think that is an excellent idea and I happen to know that she is available. However, before I seek her out, I have something that I must pass on to you in private.' With this, he retrieved a small pale blue envelope from his bag.

'What is it?'

'I believe it to be a letter, although I've never seen the contents. Miss Ross came to see me a short while before she sadly passed away. Her instructions were very specific. If she was to die first, then I had to personally hand this to you and to no one else. If this was for some reason not possible or it was felt that you were by this stage not in charge of your full mental abilities, then I was to destroy the envelope and contents unread.'

Dorothy took hold of the envelope, displaying her name and address in the familiar copperplate handwriting. She put her finger on the 'D' and slowly traced out the letters.

The solicitor watched silently for a moment, then put down his folder and stood up.

'Let me go and fetch Matron,' he said.

He left the room. Dorothy realised she was going to have to really concentrate on what was to come, so she put the envelope into the pocket of her cardigan.

★ ★ ★

Her head was spinning when she finally entered her bedroom. Without Matron's help, Dorothy didn't know what she would have done. Mr Anderson had proved to be a kind man and had patiently gone over the figures several times. The stocks and shares were rather baffling, but the gist of everything was that she could stay in the home.

Dorothy lifted the cat off her chair, sat down and put him on her lap. Tiddles purred contentedly while she absentmindedly stroked his ear. Her emotions were such a whirlwind of confusion that she didn't know what to think or feel. To learn that she would never again have any money problems and could remain in the home should have had her running down the corridor excitedly, telling everyone her tremendous news. Instead, she felt reflective, almost sad.

'Oh, Tiddles. You don't know how lucky you are.'

Was it really only nine months ago when they received that awful letter informing them about the rise in fees? It seemed as though that day belonged to another era. Dorothy was amazed when she thought about all that had happened since then: the formation of the Escape Committee, the march, barricading themselves into the lounge. Had they really done that? Then there was the decision to set up a sex line. What madness had possessed them?

There had been so many changes. Joan and Angus's arrival had been followed by other new faces after the deaths of Mrs Campbell and Mrs O'Reilly, plus the departure of Walter and Deirdre. Beatrice had been moved by her family and no one appeared to know where to. When they took her away, Mr Forsyth had been inconsolable for almost the remainder of the morning, until announcing over lunch that he was going to marry Mrs Winchester-Fowler.

Now Miss Ross was gone.

'How has so much changed in such a short space of time?' she said to the cat. 'You and Matron are two of the few things that have remained the same, aren't you?' Tiddles moved a paw and rested it over the pocket that contained the letter. 'Yes, you want to know what's in there as well.'

Dorothy took out the envelope and studied the writing again. She was just about to open it when the telephone rang. With a little sigh, she picked up the receiver.

'Hello, Pearls of Wisdom. How can I help?' For a few moments, there was silence and then there was the sound of a girl crying. 'Oh, whatever's wrong, dear?'

'Can I talk to you?'

'Of course you can. That's what I'm here for.'

'I just want someone to talk to.'

'You sound so young.'

'I'm ... I'm sixteen.'

'Ah, you're just a child, dear. My name's Dorothy. What's yours?'

'Samantha.'

'That's lovely. Aren't your parents around to talk to?'

'They're always so busy. I'm left alone.'

'That's often the way. You know, Samantha, loneliness ... it's a bit like love. It doesn't understand the concept of age.

312

You can be lonely at sixteen and ninety-six. There's no shame in it.'

'I don't fit in, not at school or the local clubs, not anywhere. I'm just not right for anything.'

'Maybe it's that they're not right for you.'

'But there's nothing else! My life is so empty and without purpose and no one even notices.'

Samantha, who had gradually been gaining control, burst into another fit of crying. So many youngsters felt lost these days, their large numbers of virtual friends always seeming to disappear when needed. Dorothy wanted to give the girl a big hug, although of course you aren't supposed to do that sort of thing now. However, she didn't believe in being bound by every regulation.

'Let's see if we can't find that purpose. Where did you see the advert, dear?'

'In the library.'

'Are you there now?'

'I'm standing outside.'

'Well, you're very nearby. Could you easily get to the little teashop down the road?'

'Yes, but why?'

'How about we meet there in twenty minutes?'

'Could we?'

'Out for tea with a lovely, interesting young lady . . . just you try and stop me!'

'How will I recognise you?'

Dorothy thought for a moment, looking for inspiration around her room. She couldn't very well take Tiddles and say look out for an elderly woman carrying a slightly overweight cat. Cat!

'I'll wear my red hat . . . and I'll look out for a girl with red eyes.'

'*Thank you*,' said Samantha, managing to laugh.

'There. Life's already looking a little brighter, isn't it?'

'*It's so cold standing here.*'

Dorothy's eye fell on the large green scarf she had almost finished. She picked it up with her free hand.

'I've got the very thing to keep you warm. I just need to cast off. Bye for now, dear.' She had been so engrossed that she hadn't realised the envelope was lying on top of the cat's head. 'Sorry, Tiddles,' she said, picking it up. 'Are you all right under there?'

The resulting *meow* confirmed that he was, indeed, perfectly well. She held the unopened envelope in her hand for a moment, then laid it gently against the framed photograph.

'Can you look after that for me, Willie?' she said to the image. Willie smiled back at her, as he had always done.

Dorothy stood up and put Tiddles back on the seat. It would save time if she took the knitting with her and finished it in the teashop. Perhaps Samantha might become interested in the hobby. Having put the scarf, along with spare wool and needles, safely in her bag, she walked over to the door and retrieved her hat and coat.

'You be a good boy.'

The cat looked back fondly at the old woman. Then she was gone. Tiddles rested his head on a paw and closed his eyes. He would wait there until Dorothy returned.